DEAD POLITICIAN SOCIETY

DEAD POLITICIAN SOCIETY

A CLARE VENGEL UNDERCOVER NOVEL

ROBIN SPANO

ECW PRESS

Published by ECW Press
2120 Queen Street East, Suite 200, Toronto, Ontario, Canada M4E 1E2
416.694.3348 / info@ecwpress.com

LIBRARY AND ARCHIVES CANADA CATALOGUING IN PUBLICATION

Spano, Robin
Dead politician society : a Clare Vengel undercover novel / Robin
Spano.

ISBN 978-1-55022-942-4 (BOUND). – ISBN 978-1-55022-983-7 (PBK.)

I. TITLE.

PS8637.P35D42 2010   C813'.6   C2010-901254-2

Cover and Text Design: Cyanotype
Typesetting: Mary Bowness
Production: Troy Cunningham
Printing: Solisco – Tri-Graphic 1 2 3 4 5

Mixed Sources
Product group from well-managed
forests, controlled sources and
recycled wood or fiber
FSC www.fsc.org Cert no. SW-COC-001352
© 1996 Forest Stewardship Council

The publication of *Dead Politician Society* has been generously supported by the
Canada Council for the Arts which last year invested $20.1 million in writing
and publishing throughout Canada, by the Ontario Arts Council, by the
Government of Ontario through Ontario Book Publishing Tax Credit,
by the OMDC Book Fund, an initiative of the Ontario Media
Development Corporation, and by the Government of Canada through
the Canada Book Fund.

Canada Council   Conseil des Arts   ONTARIO ARTS COUNCIL
for the Arts   du Canada   Canadä   CONSEIL DES ARTS DE L'ONTARIO

PRINTED AND BOUND IN CANADA

ECW PRESS
ecwpress.com

For my aunt, Linda Spano, 1948-2006

TUESDAY / SEPTEMBER 7

ONE
CLARE

Clare Vengel tossed a leg over her Triumph and kicked it into gear. The sun was shining, the mayor was dead, and Cloutier wanted to meet with her. As she sped along Dundas Street, weaving a bit too quickly through traffic, visions of her first undercover assignment played in her head.

At Dundas and Dupont, she found the agreed-upon donut shop. Sergeant Cloutier was already seated with two enormous coffees.

"So." Clare flashed her brightest smile. "Who am I?"

She slid into the cushioned booth, and set her helmet on the seat beside her.

Cloutier opened a bag and pulled out a dutchie. "I'm not pleased to be using you."

"Okay." That was fair. She was as green as they came. Clare determined to please him with results.

"We need someone who looks young. We also need someone with field experience. Apparently in this enlightened age it's the packaging that counts."

Clare sipped her coffee. What was she supposed to say?

Cloutier nodded to some sugar packets in the center of the

table. "You're not gonna use those?"

Clare wrinkled her nose. "No, thanks."

Cloutier took one and added it to his own coffee.

"You're going back to school." He slid a plain white envelope across the table. "You're a third-year political science student."

"Political science?" Clare opened the envelope and discreetly observed a student card, driver's license, and other documents that identified her as Clare Simpson. "Is that more like politics or science?"

Cloutier shook his head irritably. "Politics."

"Oh." Clare would have preferred science.

"You think you can get up to speed fast enough?"

"Of course." She'd stay awake all night if she had to. "Is there a reason I'm only half undercover?"

"You're keeping your first name to make things easier on you."

"Thanks." Clare wasn't sure whether to feel protected or insulted.

"This isn't a permanent transfer." Cloutier broke a piece from his donut. "Screw this case up, and it's back to the beat for a very long time."

"Okay." Again, fair. Most cops had to put in years in uniform before they'd be given an undercover assignment. She'd been on the force for three months. "How did the mayor die?"

"Do you live on this planet?"

Clare eyed Cloutier's dutchie. She wished she had one of her own. Or something greasy, like bacon or sausage, to soak up her mild hangover.

"Hayden Pritchard died at last night's Working Child Benefit. He collapsed in his own vomit. It was all over the news."

"Oh." Clare was supposed to feel ignorant because she didn't spend her evenings glued to the local fucking news? Fine, maybe she felt a little bit ignorant, but she wasn't going to show it.

"Just read this." Cloutier passed a printed email across the stained Formica table.

Hayden Pritchard: July 27, 1954–September 6, 2010

We hereby launch our campaign to create a political utopia for the real world. Hayden Pritchard made a dramatic exit from life last night, facilitated by the poison we slipped him.

Pritchard became mayor thirteen years ago, at which point he began to skillfully destroy the city's economy. He spent piles of money to cultivate all kinds of fringe votes, and when he went over budget, he simply raised taxes to compensate. Small business owners closed up shop or moved to the suburbs in response to punishing tax hikes, and Toronto was ranked the worst place in the western world to do business. We might have been fine with this if that money had been used to save some wildlife or give scholarships to inner city kids, but as far as we can tell, society's problems have remained intact. Pritchard and his staffers are okay with all this; they've received a fifty percent pay raise.

With another election three long years away, we have decided to free taxpayers from Pritchard's socialist nightmare.

You're welcome.

This has been a message from the Society for Political Utopia.

Clare wasn't sure why her fingers trembled as she handed the page back to Cloutier.

"This email was sent to Annabel Davis, the assistant obituary editor at the *Star*."

"Obituaries?" Clare rolled her eyes upward, and saw that the drop ceiling was badly in need of repair. "I guess there isn't a homicidal rants editor. Is the newspaper printing it?"

"Not for now."

"Do we know who sent the email?"

"Yeah. That's why we need the investigation."

Clare wanted to groan, but reminded herself to stay positive.

"The source computer was wireless." Cloutier took one of the unused creamers and added it to his coffee, not bothering to stir it in. "A laptop, or one of those fancy Internet phones. The address was nicknamed 'Utopia Girl.'"

"I presume we know that the mayor actually died from poison."

"You don't need to do any presuming. We have detectives for that. But yes: the medical examiner found massive organ damage consistent with some common poisons. Pritchard's genitals and urinary organs were congested with blood."

"You mean his cock was hard," Clare said, then immediately felt morbid.

Cloutier looked Clare in the eye. "Pritchard's death was painful and miserable."

Of course it was — her comment had been callous and horrible. She tried another tack. "Had he recently started a new medication? Viagra maybe? If he was already on some other drug, for his heart or something, the two could have interacted badly."

"Thanks for your medical opinion."

Clare tried to take a sip of coffee, but ended up dribbling most of it down her chin and onto her favorite T-shirt.

"Your job is basic, Vengel: go in as a student, keep your eyes and ears open, and get in touch when you find something that might help us."

"Okay." Clare stroked her helmet, which sat beside her on the plastic bench. "How about an obvious question: Why do we think this 'Utopia Girl' is the killer? Doesn't every nutcase and his brother pop out of the woodwork when a famous person dies?"

"The inspector obviously thinks there's something to it."

Clare leaned forward. "Which inspector?"

"Detective Inspector Morton hand-picked you for this assignment."

"Cool." Clare liked Morton — and apparently he thought she was worth a chance. He had hardly been exuberant when she'd met him, but he at least hadn't laughed her out of his office when she'd approached him about undercover work. "And — last question, I swear — what's the connection to the university? Is that where the email was sent from?"

"Looks that way." Cloutier ate the last of his donut and stuffed his crumpled napkin into the bag. "Your first class is at eleven a.m. if you can make it, but the course that most interests us is your two o'clock. It meets twice a week. Tuesday afternoons and Thursday mornings. It's called Political Utopia for the Real World."

Clare's eyes scanned the obituary upside down. "Is it a large class?"

"Twenty students, plus you. Now go. You have pencils and notebooks to buy."

"Can I invoice the station for them?"

"Of course. Just don't buy anything fancy."

"Do I look like I'd want something fancy?" Clare picked up her helmet.

"No, you don't." Cloutier smirked. "Have a good day at school."

Clare rode off into the morning.

TWO
MATTHEW

Matthew leapt aside to avoid the tattooed adolescent riding full speed down the footpath. He protectively balanced his full, steaming coffee, and allowed himself a cautious sip once the kamikaze student was three buildings away.

On another day, Matthew might have snarled at the kid, or thrown him a sarcastic comment about being more considerate. But today was his favorite of the year: the first day of school. Students rushed around campus, energizing it with their flurry of self-centered activity. The Gothic buildings were regal in the late summer's light. Matthew himself felt natty and hip in designer blue jeans and his retro tweed jacket. It would take more than a socialist on a bicycle to knock him off his perfect cloud.

Since he'd been a child in Scarborough, he'd always loved the first day of school. The first day held the promise that the coming year would be the great one. He could be voted school president by an overwhelming majority, or win an academic award that had Oxford knocking on his door, or Mariana Livingstone might finally recognize his *je ne sais quoi* and fuck his brains out behind the football field.

Now, Matthew felt like his great year had come, at last and to stay. He arrived at his office building, the concrete and glass block that was home to several other departments in addition to Political Science. He climbed the wide stone staircase, and smiled at a group of teenaged girls who had the doe-eyed look of first-year students. They made up for all the Marianas who never had given him the time of day, behind the bleachers or anywhere else.

"Dr. Easton!" An eager voice accompanied light footsteps running up the staircase behind him.

Matthew turned to see a student from a previous year's introductory course. She was a stunning girl — tall, fair-complexioned, and full of original ideas. "Jessica. How was your summer?"

"Terrible." The girl scowled. "I spent it looking after my sick grandmother in her gloomy old mansion."

"How altruistic."

"How depressing." Jessica shifted the faded leather bag on her shoulder. "I was supposed to go tree-planting out west, which I was totally stoked about. Anyway, her health conveniently cleared up right at the end of the summer."

"Well that's . . . good news?"

"It is." Jessica sighed. "And I'm thrilled to be taking Poli Real World this year. It's great to have one course where we're actually encouraged to have strong opinions."

"I'm delighted to hear it." Matthew reached for the door handle. "I look forward to your contributions in class."

"I'm just so angry sometimes with the whole system. It boils my blood that there are no checks and balances to keep the politicians accountable."

"Frustration keeps the course going," Matthew said. "And it's useful. Last year when we submitted our course conclusions to our local representative, he brought two of our ideas to the table in Parliament."

"Yeah?" Jessica seemed rooted to the steps. "Did it change any policy?"

"Not this time. But we'll get there. Was there anything else?"

"Um, no, I don't think so." Jessica chewed on her lip. "I'll see you around?"

"Brilliant."

Matthew slipped inside the building, opted for climbing two flights of stairs instead of making conversation with his colleagues in the elevator, and let himself into his office for the first time in four months.

The room was ugly and institutional. The cheap metal bookshelf held political texts spanning the twenty years from his high school days until now. All that was missing was a book with Matthew's name on the cover. Although of course he would have preferred sturdy wooden shelves in a musty room in an ivy-covered hall, having his own private corner of this large, prestigious university made him feel like he'd arrived.

He dusted off his swivel chair and a portion of his desk, and pulled a pile of paperwork from his briefcase. He enjoyed one short sip of coffee before a knock at the door interrupted him.

"Come in, Shirley!"

"Is my knock so distinctive?" Dr. Rosenblum poked her head into Matthew's office, and followed with her compact body. "How was your summer?"

"Productive," Matthew said. "I've finished the first draft of my book, and my editor finally seems to understand my vision."

"You relented on the editorial bias, then." Shirley lifted an eyebrow. "Good for you. Have you also considered changing your public outlook on Hayden Pritchard?"

"Public? I don't think Pritchard is anywhere in my book."

"I meant for your students. I know you've circulated at least two summer reading articles bashing Pritchard and his policy."

"I'm flattered that you take such an interest in my courses."

"Oh, stop your preening. I'm serious. I don't want you maligning a man whose corpse isn't even cold."

"What do you take me for? Some kind of lunatic zealot?"

Shirley patted her already immaculate gray curls into place. "It's not the worst description."

"Well you have my word of honor." Matthew took a long sip of coffee before continuing. "I won't bring champagne to class, and I won't expose my real opinion, which is that I think Pritchard self-destructed naturally when his crummy karma came knocking."

"Funny. By the way, you have a new transfer student. Clare Simpson. I know you like to hand-pick the class list, but I took the liberty of adding Clare to Poli Real World."

"You what?"

"I'm sorry. But the Registrar asked as a special favor. I got the impression that Clare's parents are friends with someone important in administration."

"You just got that impression, did you?"

"It was implied that the Chancellor would appreciate the concession."

Matthew shook his head. "This is exactly what's wrong with the system. Don't you see? Privilege breeds privilege."

"I thought it was socialists you hated."

"I hate socialists when they're hypocrites." Matthew couldn't get the coffee into his system fast enough. "Like Hayden Pritchard. May he rot in peace. But a million times worse is some entitled little bitch who gets to bypass all the hurdles that make an accomplishment worth anything. How am I supposed to congratulate my twenty other students on being selected for the course when Clare fucking Simpson comes breezing in with Daddy's gold card?"

"I agree that the world shouldn't work this way," Shirley said. "But it does, and there it is. More power to you and your students when you finally succeed in changing it."

"Fine," Matthew said. "I'm not going to fight you. But no special grades. Clare either holds her own like the rest of the students, or I won't hesitate to fail her."

"That's all I'm asking."

"Shall I cc you in the email when I send the class their revised reading list?" Matthew felt this was a strong enough dismissal, except that when he turned back to his work, his elbow caught his nearly full coffee and launched it into its death spin. He scrambled to save the papers on his desk, which thankfully were minimal after a summer away from the office. He faced Shirley, and noticed the misshapen ceramic mug in her hand, "World's Coolest Grandma" painted inexpertly onto the side.

"Oh, not your look." Shirley grimaced, but her eyes were smiling. "It isn't your gourmet dark roast, and I can't offer you any fancy soy milk, but yes, I have a pot of coffee on in my office."

THREE
LAURA

Laura Pritchard was washing up from breakfast when Penny Craig called from the *Star*. It was a shame, Laura thought, that Hayden wasn't alive to appreciate the drama. He wouldn't care that he was dead — even as a young man, he'd never seemed particularly involved in his own life. But all this press and intrigue? He would have been in Hayden Heaven. Laura closed the dishwasher and gazed out upon her backyard garden.

"Thanks for calling," she told Penny. "I promise, not a word until the story comes out."

"I appreciate it," Penny said. "The police have asked us to hold publication indefinitely."

"Can they make you do that?" Laura pulled a stool out from the marble counter, and sat down.

"They can ask. It helps that the inspector in charge has promised the *Star* an exclusive interview once they've finished their investigation. If that letter isn't a hoax, this is the story of a lifetime."

"I imagine it must be."

"My god. I'm so insensitive. Are you going to be all right? I'm tied up all morning, but I can make time for lunch if you want to chat."

"Thanks, but my head's going to be all over the place." When had she ever met Penny to chat? "Does anyone else know about the email?"

"Only Annabel Davis. The poor woman has been made to fear for her job if the smallest word slips through her lips."

"I can imagine." Laura had witnessed Penny's wrath in high school, thankfully never directed her way. "So why are you telling me?"

"God, Laura, I'm not a piranha. Sure, I want my exclusive, but friends come first. Besides, I trust your discretion."

Friends?

Susannah stomped muddily through the kitchen door, causing Laura to shake her head with mock horror.

"These tomatoes are coming up nicer every year." Susannah plonked three juicy-looking samples onto the counter Laura had just finished scrubbing.

"Listen, Penny. I appreciate the call. Susie's come inside, and it's her first day back at school, so I'd like to see her off."

"How cute. Have you packed her a lunch?"

"Don't be ridiculous. She's thirty-five. She's been getting her own lunch for a year now."

Penny laughed. "You won't say anything about the email, though, right? Not even to Susannah."

"I've promised I won't." Laura turned off the telephone handset.

Susannah helped herself to a mug of the coffee Laura had brewed. Masses of dark curls seemed to fly in all directions. Laura touched a strand of her own carefully blow-dried hair, and wished she could be so unconcerned with her appearance.

She smiled at Susannah. "I swear, you must lie down and make dirt angels when you're back there. I've never seen a filthier gardener."

"I like to feel the earth between my fingers." Susannah pulled up a stool of her own.

"Don't you have class this morning?"

"I'm taking off in a few minutes. The course I'm stoked about isn't 'til this afternoon. Poli Real World. Hey, you think you could get me an interview with your ex-husband on how *not* to create a utopian political climate?" Susannah clapped a hand to her mouth. "God, Laura. I'm sorry. I talk without thinking. I forgot for a second that he . . . you know . . . died."

Laura leaned into the counter, and rested her chin in her hands. "I just got some strange news about Hayden."

"And you were talking to me about dirt angels?"

"The *Star* received an email this morning taking credit for his death."

"The newspaper? Are they taking it seriously?"

"The police are. They don't normally." Laura felt her voice shaking. "Last week, Penny said, they had three separate people claiming to know the whereabouts of Jimmy Hoffa's body."

"Are you all right?" Susannah pushed the fruit bowl aside to reach across the counter for Laura's hand. She held it firmly. "I'll skip my morning class."

Laura squeezed back. "Go to school. I'll be fine."

"Really," Susannah said. "I can miss the opening lecture from Dr. Robertson. That man defined the word *pompous* then expanded the definition to fit himself in."

They sat for several moments before the doorbell broke the silence.

Susannah got up. "I'll grab it."

The ground floor was an open concept, and Laura watched Susannah hop the half-flight of stairs down to the living room, then open the door for two men. They weren't wearing uniforms, but they introduced themselves loudly as Detective Inspector David Morton and Detective Sergeant Raj Kumar.

Laura stood up from her stool, and Susannah led the detectives up to the kitchen at the back of the house.

"Laura Pritchard? We need to ask you some questions."

Morton was slight and anxious-looking. Probably around Laura's age, she thought; maybe a few years younger.

"Am I a suspect?" Laura surprised herself by blurting out the question. "Sorry. What I mean is would you like some coffee? Please sit down."

Kumar pulled a chair from the round kitchen table and made himself comfortable. He was good-looking, somewhere in his thirties, and his warm brown eyes moved constantly. Laura had the sensation that he was memorizing her kitchen, but she didn't find it unsettling.

"No coffee, thank you." Inspector Morton continued to stand. "Pritchard is the right name?"

"It's fine," Laura said. "I've been using my maiden name, Sutton, since Hayden and I separated. But technically, yes, I'm still Pritchard. Would you like anything at all? A glass of water?"

Kumar seemed about to accept, but Morton's reply pre-empted him. "No, thank you, ma'am. You initiated the separation, is that correct?"

Ma'am. When had fifty become over-the-hill? Laura felt like her life was just beginning — apparently the outside world would disagree. She sat down opposite Kumar, who silently made notes.

"Yes," Laura said. "I left Hayden."

"And yet you never agreed to sign the papers for a divorce?"

"What is this?" Susannah was perched on a stool at the counter. "Your perverted version of a bedside manner? Laura has lost someone who meant a lot to her."

"Your name, please?" Morton asked.

"Susannah Steinberg. But you haven't answered my question. What gives you the right to come in here, all highbrow and —"

"Do you live here, Ms. Steinberg? Are you a friend, or a room-mate, of Mrs. Pritchard's?"

"Girlfriend," Susannah said. "As in, I like to see her naked. And caress her. And run my tongue along her inner thigh until I come to — well, you get the point. And yes, I live here too."

Morton smiled thinly. "How long have you been together?"

"Three and a half years." Susannah refilled her coffee mug. "Plus I was after her for a year before that."

"How did you meet?"

"At a homelessness rally, originally." Laura tried to move the tone back to friendly. "Then we worked together on a literacy campaign in Regent Park."

"Then Laura moved here — as in, away from her husband — and I haunted her local pub." Susannah seemed to delight in the detectives' discomfort. "I bought her a glass of fucking expensive Cabernet Sauvignon every Friday for about six months before she agreed to dinner."

"Please. You bought me house wine."

"Not at first."

Kumar coughed into his hand.

Morton glanced at him, then turned back to Laura. "When did you and your late husband separate?"

"Four years ago."

"Susannah was 'after you' while you were married?" Kumar looked up from his notepad.

"Only briefly," Susannah said. "But she didn't know I was flirting until later."

"Now Mrs. Pritchard — Ms. Sutton — I'll need you to account for your whereabouts yesterday. From the morning, please."

Laura ran through a brief account of her more or less typical day.

"You both attended last night's Working Child benefit?" Morton's thin eyebrows lifted.

"The Brighter Day hosted the event. We were volunteering."

"In what capacity?"

"Supervisory, mainly," Laura said. "We'd both been on the planning committee from the get-go. Susannah was in the kitchen, running damage control and making sure the food came out in good time. I was out front, greeting guests, assisting with last-minute seating changes, that kind of thing."

"Why did you choose those roles?" Morton asked. "Or were they selected for you?"

"A bit of each, I suppose." Laura stroked the handle of her coffee mug, a Mother's Day gift from when her daughter had been ten that had somehow survived the years and the move. "Susie has catering experience, and I've entertained a good chunk of the guest list in my home at one point or another."

"In this home?" Morton glanced around the split-level, cottage-style house. The furniture was expensive, and the colors were vibrant and warm, but Laura knew the overall effect hardly suggested impressive guest lists.

"In the home I shared with Hayden."

"When did your husband buy his ticket for the fundraiser?"

"Oh, Hayden didn't buy his own ticket. The political parties always take a table or two at events like this."

"All right. At what point was it known that Mayor Pritchard would be attending the benefit?"

"I don't know." Laura wrinkled her brow. "A few weeks ahead of time, I suppose."

"Who would have had access to the guest list?"

"Well, the Brighter Day, of course. Maybe Elly's Epicure, the caterer, although I doubt that. Susie, do you still have their card?"

Susannah shrugged.

"Did your husband have a will?"

"Estranged husband," Susannah said. "Isn't there such thing as a common-law divorce?"

"No," Morton said. "Mrs. Pritchard, do you know if your late husband had a will?"

"We had wills when we were together. I've since changed mine. I assume he has, too."

"Do you know the approximate value of his investments and real estate holdings?"

"Can you leave us alone now?" Susannah said. "I'm sure violent suspicious death is all in a day's work for the pair of you, but Laura has received an enormous shock. This is information you could get from Hayden's lawyer or accountant or bloody mistress."

Morton eyed Susannah for several moments before speaking. "Have you finished talking?"

Susannah rolled her eyes. "Laura, you want me to stay? I'm thinking I'll take off to class if that's okay with you."

"Where's your class?" Kumar asked, pen poised.

"It's at the school of None of Your Fucking Business," Susannah said. "And after that, I'll be joining friends at the You Can Fuck Yourself Café. Stop in if you're not busy."

FOUR
CLARE

"Is someone alive in there, Simpson?"

It took a second for her name to catch, and when it did, Clare was taken back to high school, caught daydreaming by a teacher who had failed to keep her attention.

"Pardon me?" Clare batted her eyelashes, which solicited stifled giggles from the students.

"Oh god. Not a comedienne." Dr. Easton grabbed at his hair and pulled it. "We were talking about the questionnaires you've been filling out. Or did you want more time to complete yours in light of having just returned to Earth?"

Dr. Easton was younger than Clare would have imagined, not the stodgy old professor type at all. He had a mildly pompous accent, like he thought he was British. And there was that stupid tweed jacket that hung on the back of his chair. But he was cute, in a prep school prefect kind of way.

"I finished the survey," Clare said. "I only zoned out for the last couple of minutes."

"Delightful. Now if everyone's ready, I'd like you to pass the completed *questionnaire* to the person on your left."

The classroom was arranged in a two-tiered rectangle, with

eight students in the front row and thirteen in the back. Clare guessed that the layout was designed to mimic Parliament.

When she had finished decoding her right-hand neighbor's questionnaire, Clare got her own results back from Jessica, the blond on her left.

"B, huh?" Clare said. "I wonder if this secretly predetermines our grade for the course."

"Don't feel too bad." Jessica smirked. "I got a C."

"Who's feeling bad? I'm thrilled with a B."

"Does everyone have their results?" Dr. Easton waited while papers were shuffled and general nods of assent came from the room. "How many As?"

Five hands went up.

"You guys are the Rednecks. How many Bs?"

Ten hands, including Clare's.

"It always starts out this way." Dr. Easton seemed personally offended by the results. "We'll take the same questionnaire at the end of the year and half of you will have converted to something more sensible. You Bs are the Commies.

"The rest of you — that should be six, since we have twenty-one this year —" Dr. Easton paused to glare pointedly at Clare. "— are the Tree-Huggers."

Clare felt like she'd landed on an island where the natives all spoke Zulu. She gathered that the party names were sarcastic, but she didn't get the jokes. Her only hope for survival was to smile through that day, then scour the Internet for political wisdom when she got home.

"The Commies are going to form a minority government. Now it's time to get into groups and choose a leader for each party."

Clare said goodbye to Jessica and joined her group. A woman took charge straightaway. She had messy dark hair and seemed older than most of the class, maybe somewhere in her thirties. "All right. Who wants to run this party?"

"I'll run." A sandy-haired guy in khakis and a dress shirt

puffed out his chest. "I'm Brian Haas. I'm a card-carrying Communist in real life, so clearly Dr. Easton's questionnaire is effective. I have several bills already drafted, but the one I'd like to start with deals with safe, affordable, and integrated public housing. My father used to be president of the federal Communists, and I'd love to follow in his footsteps to lead this party to greatness." He spoke for a minute or so, carefully, as if he'd scripted his speech in front of the mirror before coming to school that morning. He reminded Clare of a very serious child all dressed up to attend an adult party. She wasn't sure why it made her sad.

"Anyone else?" The older woman spoke up again. When Clare and the others shook their heads, she said, "Fine. I'll put myself up. I'm Susannah Steinberg. Damn right I'm a Commie, as insulting as Dr. Easton may think the term is. The biggest challenge we have — in Canada, sure, but I'm thinking globally, too — is equalizing people's opportunities. Why should a kid in Africa have to die of malaria instead of living into his twenties and being here in this classroom with us? Also, I don't think anyone should ever vote party line over their own principles; in my government, all votes will be free votes. I can't stand hypocrisy. I say let's get real and change the world."

The ten group members put their votes onto paper. Susannah won, and named Brian her deputy. Brian's chest deflated, but he congratulated Susannah and kept his smile bright.

Dr. Easton called the class back to order. "Can I have the party leaders come up to the stage?"

Three students arranged themselves on the raised platform by the chalkboard.

"Next we'll hear a short speech from our leaders. The Commies have the most representatives, so Susannah, that makes you World Leader. Go ahead."

Susannah wiped her palms on her jeans and nodded at her classmates. "My government will be dedicated to social causes, redistributing wealth, and creating a world that works. I'm not looking to dominate by numbers; instead, I'd like to incorporate good ideas from across the spectrum. All votes will be free votes. Let's make this country fabulous."

"Sounds benevolent," Matthew said. "How many of you think she would be taking such a generous stance if she had a majority?"

The class tittered, and Clare felt left in the dark.

Next up was Diane Mateo, the leader of the Rednecks. She wore black dress pants and a red polyester top. A large, sparkly cross hung from her neck, and her dark brown hair was pulled back into a bun. "Great theory, Susannah, but show me a minority government that gets anything done. For me, fiscal responsibility is the first premise of responsible governing. And that includes an accountable government. In the private sector, every employee, even a CEO, has to justify their wages or they lose their job. For too long, in government, we haven't made our politicians earn their keep. I plan to seek an alliance with the Tree-Huggers in order to give this 'world' the leadership it deserves. Without a balanced budget, it doesn't matter how wonderful the Commies' ideas are — we won't have the money to make them happen."

"Thanks, Diane. Let's hear from the Tree-Huggers."

Jessica stood up. "The environment is the most neglected and essential issue facing us today. Our party will focus on maintaining and restoring wildlife habitats, reducing carbon and other emissions — duh — and promoting weekly wilderness visits as part of every child's education — gotta get the love for the Earth flowing forward, right?

"Then there's the economy — the other parties have only made a mess of it. Our fiscal policy will be conservative — yes, arts funding will suffer. If you like the opera, either pay to go see it or donate to keep it alive. And yes, social welfare will be revised: instead of giving homeless people shelters they don't want, we'll give birds the sanctuaries they do want.

"Our mandate is conservation — or to use the hot word of today, 'sustainability.' We want the earth and the economy to thrive in tandem."

"Thanks, leaders. You can sit with your parties again." Dr.

Easton smoothed back his short, sandy hair. "I'll be your Speaker of the House, with the odd lecture thrown in for good measure.

"You've all taken language courses that were conducted entirely in French or Spanish. This course will be run almost entirely as a mock parliament. The focus should be global — I want ideas that make the world a better place, not just the microcosm where we live. The culmination of the course is twofold: by the end of the year, you will each hand in an independent package describing your personal utopia. Also, the class will, through debate and voting, determine its collective utopia. No one can cross the floor to join another party, but alliances and coalitions are fair game."

Clare hoped this was all written down somewhere in a class summary, because she was already lost.

"Your assignment for Thursday is to bring one bill to be tabled and voted upon. There is no taboo topic — gay porn, child marriage, it's open season as long as there's no hate — but I insist upon two things: you have to want the bill passed, and you must believe that it could realistically be implemented."

Jonathan, from the Tree-Huggers, spoke up. "What about legalizing marijuana? Is that in the too-unrealistic category?"

"No, that's a good one," Dr. Easton said. "By unrealistic, I mean I'm not interested in debating the merits of having flying cars available for public use.

"Anyway, it's five past four. It was great to meet you all. Now go away."

FIVE
JONATHAN

"Hey, Jessica. Wait up."

Jonathan watched as Jessica stopped walking, turned slightly, and gave a small frown when she saw that it was him.

"What is it?" She brushed a pale strand of hair from her face.

"Well . . ." Of course she was busy, had somewhere to be. What could he say that she might possibly find interesting? "I was thinking we could get together later. Talk over our tree-hugging strategy."

Did she know that he'd copied her answers to the questionnaire, so they'd be in the same group for Poli Real World? Could she tell that he was the lamest guy to ever walk the planet? He didn't think much slipped past her, but he hoped that those two things had.

The sun was in her eyes, and Jessica squinted. "You're not wiped from work last night?"

"Nah." Jonathan was exhausted, not from working, but because he'd been tossing and turning in his bed for hours afterward. "I overheard the other groups making plans to meet. I wouldn't want to fall behind, be less prepared."

"Have you asked our other group members?"

"Right. Them. No. I just thought, since our ideology is so similar, maybe you could use a right-hand man." Shit. Jonathan hoped that only sounded dirty to him.

"I guess it wouldn't hurt to get together for a coffee. Tomorrow afternoon works better for me."

"Tomorrow?" Jonathan scanned his schedule in his head. "I think I'm working."

"Me too. I was thinking before work, maybe around three. Maybe we could invite the other party members."

"Yeah, okay." Jonathan didn't like the addition of the other party members, but he had to start somewhere. "It's a date."

"It's a meeting." Jessica smirked.

"L-O-L. That's what I meant."

"Did you say 'L-O-L' out loud?"

Jonathan laughed. "Shit. How lame is that?"

"It's not so bad." Jessica shrugged. "I said 'B-R-B' to my grandfather the other day. He had absolutely no clue what I was talking about."

"Are you online a lot?" Jonathan relaxed a bit.

"Don't tell anyone." Jessica leaned in closer. "But I'm addicted to this game. It's called *Who's Got the Power?* I spend at least half of my free time playing it."

"For real? You don't look like a computer geek."

"I know. I look like a tree-hugger. Does this shatter your image of me?"

"Are you kidding?" Jon was thrilled. "Which country do you play? Or do you switch it up?"

"The States," Jessica said. "I'm surprised you know the game."

Jonathan decided not to tell her right away that he'd invented *Who's Got the Power?* as a high school independent study. "It's easier to win as China."

"Yeah." Jessica's voice lifted playfully. "If you can suspend your morals and keep your citizens suppressed."

"We should get online together and lock in for a face-off."

"I'll crush you," she said.

"I'll make you weep."

Jessica grinned. "Now that's a date."

SIX

MATTHEW

"This Clare girl," Matthew said, pouring himself a glass of red wine. She isn't like the other students."

"You're just pissed at your boss for telling you what to do." Ethan took a swig of his Corona without shifting his glance from the European football highlights. "Which, in most parts of the world, is what a boss is supposed to do."

Matthew pumped the air out of the wine, and made sure the rubber stopper was firmly in place. "You might be right. But I certainly don't like her."

"Don't like Shirley?"

"Don't like Clare." Matthew sat in the armchair facing the TV. He wasn't big on sports, but he had more patience for soccer than for hockey or American football.

"What do you think her problem is?"

"I don't know. She's smug. She's overprivileged. She's laughing at me because I was forced to accept her into my class. Plus, she looks around at everything, like it's not fucking good enough for her."

"Could she be getting her bearings?" Ethan said. "New class, new people? Taking it all in?"

"Maybe."

"Is she also suspiciously good-looking?" Ethan grabbed a couple of Pringles from the tube on the coffee table. "She might be one of Charlie's Angels."

"No." Matthew glowered. "There's nothing suspicious about her looks. She's a skinny, plain brunette in jeans and sneakers."

"Sounds like a cover."

"She's not a cop." Matthew glared at Ethan's argyle dress socks, which were resting on the glass coffee table. *His* glass coffee table. "And she's certainly no Angel."

A commercial came on, and Ethan turned from the TV to look at Matthew. "Put it out of your mind. You want to order Chinese?"

"Can't. I have to shower and change into someone suspiciously good-looking. I'm meeting Annabel."

Ethan shook his head. "That woman is in serious danger of falling in love with you."

"Why do you say danger?"

"I'll put it this way: If my sister was visiting, and she so much as contemplated dating you, I'd have her on the next plane back to England and I'd ship her suitcase later."

"I treat women well." Matthew found Ethan's assessment unfair. "But until I fall in love, I don't see why I should commit to one."

"What about the women who fall in love with you?"

Matthew contemplated this. The truth was he thought they deserved what they got, but it would sound cold to say it out loud.

"Or those little freshettes? Barely off the plane from the farm they grew up on."

"I'm a good education for them."

"Yeah. Like the Big Bad Wolf was for Red Riding Hood."

Matthew rolled his eyes.

"Do you eat them, like the story says?"

"If they want. But I prefer for them to eat me."

SEVEN
ANNABEL

"'And if you so much as breathe a word of this to anyone...'" Annabel mimicked the smug, throaty voice of her boss. Her eyes scanned the busy bar to make sure no one she worked with was in earshot. "'... your promising little career will take a major nosedive.' I swear to god, that woman is living in the Dark Ages."

Katherine glanced into her empty martini glass, plucked out the oversized olive, and popped it into her mouth. "Why the Dark Ages?"

"When employees would quiver in their boots if their boss threw a dissatisfied glance in their direction."

"I think that's peasants who would quiver and feudal lords who bullied."

"Whatever. Like I should be grateful to be stuck on that nowhere-bound obituary desk." Annabel touched her head, conscious of her new chin-length haircut. She didn't love the way the stylist had blow-dried it, but she felt lighter for having so much less hair.

Katherine frowned. "Thought you liked your job."

"I liked it when I thought it might lead to some real journalism.

But I'm starting to feel like I'm going to be writing about dead people forever."

"Can you transfer to another section of the paper?"

Annabel stroked the stem of her wine glass. "I've tried. I would kill to write fashion. Even news would be better than death. I forwarded Penny my writing portfolio a few months ago — not that much is in it; just some articles from university, which was the last time I wrote about the living."

"You sent your undergrad newspaper articles to the editor-in-chief of the *Star*? Is she even in charge of everyday writing assignments?"

"I don't know. No one else was listening to me."

"So what did she say?"

"Nothing. I don't even think she knew my name with my face until I showed her that death letter this morning."

Katherine motioned to the waiter for another drink. "Why don't you look for a scoop no one else has, and write a juicy fashion story?"

"How would I get an inside scoop on fashion before the paper? They're in the loop. I'm in the lineup at the retail counter."

Katherine laughed. "Have you always been this defeatist?"

"And if she wanted me to keep my mouth shut about the correspondence in *my* inbox, Penny should have asked me for a favor, like any normal person who wants something from someone." Annabel began furiously folding the cocktail napkin she'd been given as a coaster.

"So Penny's a bitch. What's the big deal? She's the one who has to go home with herself at night."

"I want to show her that she can't push me around."

"She's your boss. Of course she can push you around."

"I'm not going to let her." Annabel tore a strip from her napkin, and let it drift down to the hardwood floor below them. It felt good, so she did it again.

"Annabel. Think. What will you accomplish by printing the obituary? You'll get Penny angry, you'll lose your job, and she'll make it impossible for you to get hired by the other Toronto papers."

"I'm not planning to print the rant. Tempting as you make the consequences sound."

"What, then? Your eyes are scaring me. Not to mention your newfound enjoyment of littering."

Annabel rescanned the area around their high-top table. She leaned in and lowered her voice. "I'm going to reply to the email."

Katherine's eyes and mouth fell open all at once. "From Utopia Girl?"

Annabel nodded.

"How singularly stupid. Have you considered that this person might actually be the killer?"

"I hope she's the killer. It makes a much better story than 'The Obituary Writer Who Was Fooled by the Girl Who Pretended She Killed the Mayor.'" Annabel picked up a candied nut, looked at it a moment, then replaced it in its ramekin.

"Gross," Katherine said.

"We share food all the time."

"I meant gross for the next customer who sits down with those nuts."

"Aren't we feeling conscientious?" Annabel muttered. "I'm pretty sure they change the nuts between guests."

"I'm pretty sure they don't." Katherine's second martini arrived, and she eyed it appreciatively. "Be careful, Bella. If anything goes wrong, this nut knows who you are and how to find you."

Annabel spotted Penny coming in the door of the bar.

"Don't look now, but there's my evil boss."

"Where?" Katherine spun around.

"I said don't look now. But since you have, she's the dirty blond at the door. Penny Craig. Red blouse, glasses. Entourage of acolytes."

"Must be nice to have so many manservants."

Annabel snorted. "She had to sell her soul to get them."

"She looks young to be in charge of a paper as big as the *Star*."

"She's fifty. She just happens to look fabulous."

"God, why so negative? You're twenty years younger and you look even more fabulous."

"Thanks." Annabel would have liked the compliment more on a different day. "Penny's on my short list for Utopia Girl."

"Why would Penny kill the mayor?"

"For the story."

"And why do you need a short list? Since when were you a private investigator?"

"Since I decided to take control of my own destiny. I spent my childhood playing with dolls, and my teenage years hanging out in shopping malls."

"I spent mine reading classics in our basement. At least you were out in the world doing something."

"At least you were stimulating your mind," Annabel said. "I've lived all my life doing everything normal. And here I am now. Nowhere."

Katherine put her elbows onto the table, and leaned forward. "When did all this start? Have you been down on yourself for a while?"

"Not too long." Annabel frowned. "I'm just starting to realize that if I stay on this path, this is all there will ever be for me. Maybe one day I'll get married. Maybe one day I'll have kids. But I'll never know what it is to live unless I take this chance right now."

"So take up skydiving. Learn how to sail. Break up with that horrible boyfriend and date someone who makes you feel good about yourself. You don't have to risk your life and your career to open your world."

Annabel watched Penny leave the bar — she must have come in to have a quick word with one of the senior staff members who were crowded into a booth near the entrance. Now she would be off home to some lonely penthouse with a cat she liked to kick.

As Penny left, Matthew entered.

Annabel turned to Katherine. "Here comes Matthew. Don't say anything."

"Not even hello?"

"Funny."

Annabel got up to give her boyfriend a hug.

"Great hair. Love the highlights." Matthew kissed her quickly, then pulled up a stool.

"You like it?" Annabel smiled, stroking a hair back from her face. "I was worried it would be too different."

"Different works for me. It'll be like sleeping with a new woman."

"Whose sister can hear you."

"Sorry," Matthew said pleasantly. "Hi, Kat. How was today in the life of a dazzling crown prosecutor?"

"Don't flatter me. It's Annabel who falls for your crap."

"Ah, right. Then have you heard this new dead lawyer joke? Annabel, what did you do to that napkin?"

EIGHT
CLARE

Clare poked her head out from under the old Honda Civic. "These people are fascinated by the most inane concepts. Remember back home, we just accepted that politicians were crooks, and that voting was a waste of time?"

"Have you never voted?" Roberta was at her workbench, bent over the carburetor she'd removed from the same car.

"Nope," Clare said. "Have you?"

"Uh, yes. Most elections."

"What does your vote accomplish?" Clare switched her wrench end and slid back under the car.

"It gives me the right to complain when the guy who's elected screws up."

"Some comfort," Clare said loudly from under the Civic. She undid the bolts on the part she wanted to work on.

"Don't you want your voice heard?"

"You mean drowned out by millions of other voices? No one's ever won an election by one vote."

"What if everyone thought that way?" Roberta's voice was irritatingly reasonable.

Clare emerged from under the car with the starter motor in

both hands. "Then no one would vote, and maybe my 'voice' would mean something."

"So is it scary going to school with a bunch of axe murderers?"

"They're not axe murderers." Clare sat at the double wide workbench opposite Roberta. "You know you can't repeat anything I'm saying, right?"

"Who would I tell?" Roberta's thick red ponytail fell across her shoulder, and she pushed it back with a frown.

"Promise?" Clare was worried she might say something to Lance.

"Relax, honey," Roberta said. "We're friends. We trust each other."

"About most things." Clare checked the starter's cogs for broken teeth.

"What does that mean?"

Clare shrugged. "You never told me when Lance was cheating on me with half of Orillia."

"I'm sorry." Roberta set down the float she was holding to look at Clare, although Clare was avoiding her eye. "Lance is my son. I wish he was smarter about his choices sometimes, but you can't ask me to break his confidence."

Clare set down her half-disassembled motor and stared at it.

"He's wrong for you, honey. As much as I'd love to call you my daughter-in-law, you need a man who's gonna treat you better."

"It's weird. I thought time had cured me of caring who Lance slept with."

"It will." Roberta picked up the float, assessed it for another moment before setting it in a bin of old but potentially functional parts. "Now will you give me some details about these little axe murderers?"

"They're not axe murderers." Clare stood up and went to the shelf where Roberta kept her solvents and aerosols. "What confuses me is this: If the killer really is in the Political Science Department, why would she lead the investigation to the university?"

"You don't like the detectives' theory?"

"What theory?" Clare said. "They think because I'm twenty-two I have no brain. They certainly don't share ideas with me."

"What if someone saw the murder?" Roberta got up too, plucked the cleaning solvent Clare was looking for from the shelf, and sat back down. "What if a witness wrote the letter?"

"I don't think so." Clare followed her back to the workbench, and began cleaning the starter's coil. "Then there would be two psychopaths: a killer, and a witness who would rather play games than call the police."

"If he or she were afraid to call the police?"

"But not too afraid to write the letter?"

"Hmm," Roberta said. "You said it was a group that took credit for the death?"

"The Society for Political Utopia," Clare said.

"Is that a campus group?"

"Not an official one. But I haven't done much asking around, unofficially. I'm still trying to figure out how to make friends with these weirdos."

"Drink a beer with them. You'll find them awfully similar to other human specimens." Roberta took a new float from her repair kit, and replaced it in the carburetor.

"Yeah yeah, I'm sure they're great. And did I tell you my handler hates me?"

"Your handler doesn't hate you."

"Have you met him? He treats me like I came into his life to piss him off. But fear not. I plan to dazzle him with results and win him over through this case."

"Clarissa the Brave."

Clare rolled her eyes. "No one calls me Clarissa."

"Only your birth certificate and driver's license," Roberta said. "But what do they know? If you want to impress your boss, I'd look into infiltrating this society."

"If it even exists."

Roberta pulled a few washers from the repair kit, and set them at the perimeter of her work space. "Have you seen your dad recently?"

"Where did that come from?"

"I was up north last week to see everyone. You should visit him, Clare. He looks terrible."

Satisfied with her cleaning job, Clare started to put the starter back together.

"I don't know how much longer he has. I can't get a straight answer from your mother, poor thing. But your dad looks like he's half in the grave already."

"Thanks for that moment of uplifting inspiration." Clare grabbed the tool she needed and slid back under the car with the starter motor.

"He misses you. Your mom does, too."

Clare made a loud humming noise, hoping Roberta would get the point. She bolted the starter back under the engine, connected it to the battery lead, and waited a few moments before coming back out.

"You still speaking to me?" Roberta said, once Clare was on her feet.

"If you're not trying to run my life I am."

"Come on, honey." Roberta was cleaning the jets on the carburetor with the same solvent Clare had used. "This is something you could regret forever."

"What will I regret? Not being there for them when my parents insist upon living half a life? Neither of them will call the disease by its name. I go up there, we sit around, and all three of us lie. That's not what I want to remember."

"You can change that dynamic."

"It's not my job."

"Fine." Roberta shook her head. "Did I tell you Lance is getting married next summer?"

"What?" Clare was glad she was already visibly angry, so Roberta wouldn't notice her heart sink through her feet, then through the concrete floor of the garage, then settle somewhere deep beneath the surface of the earth. "Is it anyone I know?"

"Shauna Bartlett," Roberta said. "They've been dating for —"

"I know how long they've been dating." Clare kept her voice light. "But I never thought it would end in marriage. When we were kids, Lance and I used to impersonate Shauna and her gang — 'Ooh, my nail, I think I chipped it. Let's go shopping and feel better.'"

Roberta grinned. "Hey, I'm not marrying her."

"Are you happy about the engagement?" Clare didn't see how she could be.

"Sure." Roberta furrowed her brow as she looked at the carburetor. "They're happy enough with each other. If I get grandkids in the process, even better."

"Wow," Clare said. "Well, congratulate him for me. She's gorgeous."

Roberta laughed. "You're more so. Shauna's just better at using all those fancy gadgets like makeup brushes and blow dryer attachments. You'd look twice as nice if you spent half the time getting ready."

"Don't make me blush." How would Roberta feel if Clare told her she had the raw tools to be a kind woman, if only she'd brush up on her communication skills? "Anyway, I have to go home. Between now and the morning, I have to become a credible political science major."

"I'm glad you came over," Roberta said. "And I appreciate the help. Here, let me give you some money."

"I don't want money." Clare smiled despite herself. "I'm an adult with a job now. I'm here for the company."

"Nah, I can't let you help me for free."

"So consider it a trade. It helps if I can mull over my case with someone."

"All right, honey. This time only. Next time, I'm charging for my mulling services."

"Say hi to Lance."

"Good luck with your acting job."

NINE
LAURA

Laura watched Susannah pick up a book from the chrome-legged shelf. Even her glance was forceful, as she looked at the book, pursed her lips, then tossed it into the giveaway box. Laura wished she had the same strength in her own movements.

Susannah turned to look at her. "You want the books about Hayden, or do they qualify as giveaways?"

"I guess I'll keep them. I can always donate them to the library later." Laura had no idea what she wanted.

Susannah put two books into the keeper box. "Did you like living here? Because I can't see it."

"You can't?" The question surprised Laura. In the twenty-odd years she'd lived in the house, she'd never thought to ask it.

"This place is all sleek lines. Even the art on the walls is cold. I can see it working for Hayden and your kids. But you're so much softer."

Laura studied her old bedroom. She glanced at the darkened doorway to the ensuite bathroom, where at this time of night she would have been getting ready for bed. "I didn't hate it. But you're right that I was never myself here."

"Imagine if you'd stayed. You should send Hayden's mistress a thank-you card."

Laura saw her old desk in the alcove where she'd written dozens of nice, polite thank-you cards. Why hadn't she noticed years before that there was no lightning bolt coming down for her if she failed to say the right thing, or send the right card?

"And spend another of Hayden's hard-earned dollars on that gold-digging tramp?"

"Please." Susannah snorted. "It's the taxpayers who worked hard for Hayden's money."

"That isn't fair." Laura opened the jewelry box on the dresser and wondered if it would be seriously tacky to sell some of the watches. "It's not easy to live in the public spotlight."

"Spare me the hard luck story." Susannah picked up another book, frowned at it, and put it in the giveaway box as well. "I still don't get why this responsibility falls upon you. You left the jerk years ago."

"I don't mind. Who else would go through his things?"

"Hayden's parents, your children, his mistress . . ." Susannah ticked off alternatives on her fingers. "Anyone he didn't cheat on or publicly humiliate."

"I was his wife, Susie. He died alone and unloved. Do I need to spite him past the grave?"

Susannah shrugged.

"Are you all right on your own for a bit?" Laura said. "I'd like to tackle the closet."

"Sure. When I finish with this shelf I'll move on to the books in the study."

Laura grabbed an empty box and immersed herself in the walk-in closet, one of the few features of this skinny house that had ever felt spacious.

She checked Hayden's pockets before packing the clothes. All told, she found forty dollars, several pieces of lint, and a ridiculous number of business cards.

She packed the suits, shirts, and accessories into boxes for the

Brighter Day charity shops, and stacked them in the hallway. It would be a field day for whoever opened the boxes. Hayden's clothes had always been more expensive than Laura was comfortable with. Not that she didn't love shopping at Holt Renfrew, but she had always felt that when you made your money from the public, you should dress like your average constituent could afford to. Especially if — as Hayden had — you called yourself a socialist.

She put the forty dollars in her pocket, and flipped through the business cards.

There were a few cards for jewelers — maybe a ring in the cards for the mistress? More likely a new pair of cufflinks for Hayden's elegant wrists. Several cards were for lawyers — was he suing someone? Being sued? A couple of accountants' cards, and then a bunch of one-offs, including a caterer, a dentist, a birthday party clown (?!), and a house painter. Then there was one that made no sense at all.

It was simple card in black and white. The letters SPU were slightly off-center in a small font, with no name or contact info. Laura doubted the card had been professionally made — it looked like a bad job with some card stock and an inkjet printer. She flipped the card over to find the words — also typed, but in a different, more cursive font — *Your death will be your greatest public service.*

Laura tried to remember which pocket she had pulled the card from. It couldn't have come from the tuxedo Hayden had been wearing at the benefit; that would be with the police. So when did Hayden receive this card, if not the night he died? Had someone mailed it to his office — or, worse, his home? Public figures received threatening messages all the time — was this another empty statement, or did this card actually relate to Hayden's death?

"Hey, Laura, check this out!" Susannah called from the bedroom.

Laura slipped the SPU card into her pocket and went out to join Susannah. "What is it?"

"This fell out of one of the girlie mags." Susannah waved a small sheet of paper in the air.

"Out of one of what?" Laura eyed the July copy of *Penthouse* with surprise.

"It's a prescription for Viagra."

"You're joking." Laura knew she was laughing too loudly. "Just when you think you know a person, you find out they like to have sex."

TEN
ANNABEL

Annabel waited until Matthew's snores were loud and constant, then instead of putting in her earplugs, she slipped noiselessly from her bedroom. She didn't pause to watch him sleeping; the sight could break her heart. So long as Annabel kept her nesting instinct at bay, her relationship was safe. But as soon as she began to demand more than the fragments of himself that Matthew was prepared to give, he would be gone.

So why did she stay with him? That was another day's question.

She turned on her computer and waited for it to boot up. She put the kettle on — stainless steel to match the rest of the kitchen — and prepared her bunny rabbit mug with mint tea.

She loved the city at night. This condo stretched the realistic limits of her budget, but it was worth every passed-up pair of shoes to gaze out the floor-to-ceiling windows upon the old St. James Cathedral, and the St. Lawrence Market beyond.

She wished she could be given some kind of sign to know if her plan to contact Utopia Girl was intelligent or just plain dumb. She willed the city to do something dramatic with its lights and buildings, anything at all, to alert her if she was heading into disaster.

When ten minutes had passed and the Cathedral was still standing, Annabel opened her email software and plunged in.

"Whatever you do, don't respond to the email," that strange little man, Detective Inspector Morton, had told Annabel and Penny when he'd spoken to them together at the *Star*. "This person clearly wants attention. If you feed them, you'll be playing right into their hands."

Annabel felt guilty. She shut down the program. Who was she kidding, contacting a maybe killer, opening some kind of dialogue so she could write a book that probably no one would want to publish anyway? Why did she think she stood a chance in hell of lifting herself out from the rat race?

Then she thought of Penny, and her rage came back in an instant. That woman made her working life hell, and what disgusted Annabel most was her own inability to fight back. It was like Penny shot some kind of stun substance through her eyes that immobilized Annabel — or worse, turned her into a ridiculous pet puppy dog — until the editor was long gone and all of Annabel's pride had vanished with her.

She opened Outlook again. Life wasn't going to happen to her. It had dropped this opportunity at her door, and Annabel wasn't fool enough to think a new chance would be along shortly.

Okay, she typed. *I'm intrigued. Your obituary isn't going to print in the* Star. *The police have officially put a ban on it, until you're caught, so sending it to other papers will only yield the same result.*

Was this too obvious a lie? Would Utopia Girl know that the police couldn't technically ban publication? It was worth a try.

But if you give me a bit more, like your motivation, and some background info, we can turn this into a pretty great book deal. You'll get your story told, I'll get my name in lights.

Respond to this address if you're interested. Or instant message me — my screen name is Death Reporter. Anything you send to my work email will be monitored by my boss and the police.

She clicked Send before she could change her mind, and the message went away into the night.

WEDNESDAY / SEPTEMBER 8

ELEVEN
CLARE

Clare woke up to heavy rain. She heaved her window shut, and mopped the already warped wooden floor with a towel from her dirty laundry pile. No one could say her apartment didn't look like a student's.

She tried to envisage a scenario in which she could ride her bike to school, but in the end she chose to endure the crowds on the public transit. She grabbed her ugly black umbrella, and braced herself for the windy walk to the bus shelter. Clare liked the Junction — it was a hodgepodge neighborhood, originally working class, but now the yuppies were coming.

On the sidewalk, she watched mothers struggle to manage strollers, umbrellas, and wandering toddlers. She was intrigued by the high-tech baby gear that seemed to be the norm nowadays. These superbuggies were a far cry from the plain stroller that Clare got pushed around in as a kid, with the broken wheel that her father kept fixing but never got quite right.

When the bus came, all the seats were taken. Clare stood where she could, and held onto a pole to prevent herself from launching into other passengers. She didn't mind the crowd — the rain outside made it feel almost companionable. But she was glad when the bus stopped at Dundas West subway station, where the crowd dispersed and she made her way down to the trains.

When she changed trains at St. George Station, Clare saw Jessica, her nose stuck into a giant textbook as she rode the escalator up to the southbound platform.

Clare caught up with her when she was standing on the platform. "What are you reading?"

Jessica glanced at Clare with a surprised smile. "Chemistry."

"You seem like you like it."

"I do." Jessica's shoulders relaxed, which made Clare notice that they'd been tensed. "It's so organic and logical."

"How can something be both organic and logical?"

Jessica grinned. "Therein lies the beauty. So which party did you end up in?"

"I'm a Communist. Or Commie. I'm not sure what our official name is."

"Commie. None of the names are real parties." Jessica opened her funky leather shoulder bag and slid the textbook into the main compartment. "Dr. Easton hates you guys."

"How can he hate the whole party?"

"Secretly? I think he's a closet socialist."

The subway arrived, and they stood together near the door of the train.

"Have you taken one of Dr. Easton's classes before?" Clare reached up to grab the metal rail as the train lurched forward.

"Uh-huh. I took his intro class two years ago."

"He's kind of cute."

"You think?" Jessica rode the train's movement without holding anything for support. "He'll date his students, so if you mean that, you should go for him."

"What?!" Clare sputtered. "Is that, like, common knowledge?"

"Fairly common. He slept with Diane Mateo when she was in first year. Totally did a number on her self-esteem, but my guess is she had too much of that to begin with. You're new this year, right?"

"Right."

How tight were the poli sci students with each other? Did Clare, as an outsider, stand any chance of being welcomed as one of their own?

The train stopped at Museum Station.

Clare paused. Her first class was a short walk from the Museum subway entrance, but Jessica was clearly staying on the train. Although it would make her a couple of minutes late, Clare opted to stay and talk. "Isn't that Diane over there?"

"Yeah," Jessica said. "Speak of the devil, huh?"

"Hi, guys." Diane had soon bustled her well-groomed self through the subway car. "Having a little cross-party meeting?"

"Hi. I'm Clare."

"I know," Diane said. "Clare Simpson, Commie. I had my party secretary note the names and affiliations of everyone in the class."

"Your party secretary?" Jessica smirked. "Did she attach photos?"

"No photos, no. Now what I'd really like to know, and I'm prepared to trade information here, is what kind of confidence treaty you two have been negotiating."

Clare was about to tell Diane that they'd met up coincidentally when Jessica spoke instead. "You first."

"All right." Diane nodded. "I have it on good authority that Dr. Easton is a Libertarian in real life, and the highest marks go to students whose assignments reflect his values."

Jessica put a finger to her chin, and appeared to assess the information before forming her response. "Since I already knew that about his politics, but I think he grades fairly, I don't see how that merits us giving you details about our alliance."

"Aha!" The train stopped, and Diane continued talking as the three of them got off and headed to the station's exit. "So there *is* an alliance."

"Maybe yes, maybe no." Jessica's long legs took the stairs two at a time, leaving Clare and Diane scrambling to keep up.

Diane pouted. "Fine. What kind of information are you after?"

Jessica reached the top of the stairs. "I don't know. You curious about anything, Clare?"

"Of course I am." Clare got to the top a few seconds later, with Diane. "But I don't want to trade information without first okaying it with my party. Sorry, Diane."

"You guys think you're funny." Diane briskly searched her purse until she pulled out a tiny umbrella.

"No, we think you are." Jessica made a shooing motion. "Now be off. Clare and I have grown-up business to discuss."

Diane looked questioningly at Clare to see if she was actually on Jessica's side, but Clare kept her face blank, and Diane, perhaps to save some dignity, turned and walked away. Clare felt a little bit mean, but Diane seemed plenty strong enough to get over a childish snub.

TWELVE
JONATHAN

Diane was coming straight at him, in her shiny black rain slicker. She reminded Jonathan of an important little missile with a moving target in its sights. But her mission was moot, because Jonathan ducked into the library, and headed straight for the men's room.

His phone beeped — a text message.

Jessica: *Diane thinks Tree-Huggers have alliance with Commies. Will probably rope you into conversation.*

Jonathan leaned against the window sill to type his response. His original plan had been to hide inside a stall, but the glass was frosted over — no chance Diane could see inside.

Jonathan: LOL. *Ducked into bathroom to avoid her.*

Jessica: *Good move. Totally raging from what Clare and I told her.*

Jonathan: *Clare?*

Jessica: *From Poli Real World. She's funny. I like her.*

Jonathan, stupidly, felt jealous.

Jonathan: *You busy now?*

Jessica: *Biochem lab in an hour. Plan to grab coffee and look over text.*

Jonathan: *Want to meet in library instead? Rescue me from*

Diane's evil clutches?

He tapped his foot against the painted brick wall as he waited for her next message. What felt like ages was probably under a minute.

Jessica: *You're fine. Diane will be long gone by now. Scenting out new prey. Want rematch, by the way.*

Jonathan: *Told you I could make you weep.*

Jessica: *Hardly wept. But impressed. You had tricky maneuvers I haven't seen used before.*

Jonathan wished he had some real life maneuvers. Instead of pining after Jessica, he should have spent the past two years gathering experience, so he'd be ready for her. He hoped he didn't choke when the moment came. If it came.

Jonathan: *Because I rock that game. Who's Got the Power?*

Jessica: LOL. *Know what game you mean.*

Jonathan: *I mean say it. Who's got the power?*

Jessica: OMG. *Fine, you've got the power. Oh wise mighty Jonathan, with slippery moves only malevolent dictator would make.*

She was feistier one-on-one than he'd imagined. Instead of taking his time undressing her, as he'd always presumed she would want, maybe she'd prefer that he aggressively rip off her clothes.

Jonathan: *Can beat you playing any country.*

Jessica: *Finland?*

Jonathan: *Tricky, but you're on. Probably right handicap given relative skill levels.*

Jessica: OMFG. *No wonder you don't have a girlfriend.*

Jonathan: *This mean you won't change coffee plans to rescue me?*

Jessica: *That, and get ready to weep, Finland.*

THIRTEEN
ANNABEL

Annabel took a sip of tea from the Styrofoam cup on her desk. She hated the way it crunched in her teeth; chewy bits of foam did nothing to enhance the taste of peppermint. She'd had a terrible night's sleep. Every time Matthew twitched, she jolted awake. She'd lain there for hours, petrified that the email she'd sent to Utopia Girl would either land her in jail or in the morgue.

But now it was morning — almost lunchtime — and in the light of day, or the rainy gray that passed for light, terror had been replaced by anticipation. She glanced around at the neighboring cubicles and the big open work desk in the center of the room. If all went well, Utopia Girl would be her ticket out of this crummy place.

Ugh. Here came Penny. Annabel had been feeling attractive today, despite her fatigue. But watching Penny glide along in her perfectly cut pantsuit made Annabel feel about as polished as if she'd been climbing trees and making mud pies.

To Annabel's shock, Penny made eye contact as she approached her desk.

"Hello, Annabel."

"Hi, Penny. Um, Ms. Craig."

"Penny's fine. I like your hair. Where did you have it done?"

Annabel combed her fingers through her new, chin-length haircut. "I, uh, use the Aveda Institute on King Street."

"Hmm. Well, it's a great cut. Makes you look sassy."

"Thanks." Annabel liked sassy. "I really like your suit."

Penny smoothed down an already flush pocket. "Have you heard anything more from your electronic pen pal?"

"Utopia Girl?" Did Penny know she'd sent the message the night before? It hardly seemed possible.

Penny nodded, putting a finger to her lips as if Annabel didn't know enough to be discreet.

"No." Annabel heard her phone beep inside her purse. "Just the one email."

"Right. Well, contact me immediately if something more comes in." Penny reached onto Annabel's desk and wrote a number on a sticky yellow memo pad. "My cell, in case I'm out of the office. Use it anytime, day or night."

"Absolutely."

Penny scurried off to wherever she was going, and Annabel grabbed her phone. Her heart started thumping when she saw that the new message was from Utopia Girl.

Had Penny done that deliberately? Stopped by right when she knew the instant message would be coming through?

Annabel turned her BlackBerry screen so no one else could see it.

Utopia Girl: *So you told cops about the obituary. Why should I trust you with anything else?*

Annabel stared at the tiny screen. She typed out a response.

Death Reporter: *Police don't want me talking to you, so it's against my interest to mention it. You also have my word, which I'm hoping you'll come to find means something.*

I'd like to work with you. Think that together, we can send the world an original message and make good money in process. Haven't figured out how you'll get paid . . . thinking anonymous bank account, or cash in post office box.

A few minutes later, her phone beeped again.

Utopia Girl: *Have two offers. Want you both to audition. Send portfolio with writing samples.*

Who was the other offer from? Penny? Annabel shouldn't be surprised. At least that meant Penny was less likely to *be* Utopia Girl. Still, this plan was about taking control. Annabel wasn't about to let some crazy criminal dominate her, even electronically.

Death Reporter: *Not going to audition for this deal. You either want it or don't, and I'm not interested in entering into a relation-ship where I'm bullied. If your other offer comes from who I think it does, then we both work for the newspaper. You can get writing sam-ples by Googling both our names.*

Shit. That was the wrong thing to say. Penny's career was filled with brilliant interviews and editorials. Annabel's was limited to the obituary desk and her campus review.

Clearly Utopia Girl knew this, because the response came back almost instantly.

Utopia Girl: *Yes, your publications to date are impressive. Particularly enjoyed "In Loving Memory of John Doe."*

Going with you, though. The other person has more to lose, thus more likely to stab me in back if things don't go her way.

Like that you try to stick up for yourself. You're wrong, of course. I will retain absolute control over you. But maybe it will make you famous.

So congratulations. I reserve the right to change my mind.

"Motherfucker," Annabel said under her breath. The scoop was hers.

FOURTEEN
CLARE

"You sure we can get the Tree-Huggers to support us?" Susannah bit off a chunk of her carrot stick and began to chew it slowly.

"I think so." Clare told the nine other Commies about running into Diane and Jessica on the subway. "I felt mean afterwards. Diane looked crushed when Jessica shooed her away."

"She wasn't crushed." Brian set down his homemade chicken sandwich. "Diane has an agenda of her own. She doesn't care if people like her."

"She must care a little."

"Really?" Brian said. "So how come in our freshman year — Dr. Easton's second year at the school — Diane went out of her way to get him fired, even though the rest of us found him totally inspiring?"

Susannah snorted. "Maybe something to do with them sleeping together." She turned to Clare. "Dr. Easton is a pig. Yes, he's an inspired professor. Yes, I'm glad to be taking his class. But as a man, he's despicable."

"Is sleeping with a student so horrible? Presumably Diane was a willing participant."

Susannah narrowed her eyes in Clare's direction. "It's an abuse of power."

"Not really." Brian shook his head. "It's true that Dr. Easton kind of . . . well . . . discarded Diane after a few months. But everyone knows he wouldn't screw her over for grades. He gave her all As for the rest of the term, even though some of her assignments weren't that well thought-out."

"Grades?" Susannah slammed a hand down on the cafeteria table. "You think grades can make up for taking a naive freshman and giving her every reason to hate herself?"

"Come on, that's extreme," Clare said. "Is it worse to get dumped by a professor than by another student?"

"It's wrong." Susannah had calmed down a bit. "He played with her head for the sake of his penis. Dr. Easton's a good prof, and I want to take his courses. But Diane wasn't wrong to plead her case with Admin."

"So . . . what happened with Diane's mission to get him fired? It obviously failed."

"It more than failed. It backfired." Brian grinned broadly. "The rest of us rallied around Dr. Easton, wrote letters saying how much he inspired us."

Clare looked to Susannah for confirmation.

"It's true." Susannah shrugged. "Though we didn't *all* write letters. Dr. Easton denied the affair, and came out looking like a concerned professor. He helped Diane get counseling that she, needless to say, did not want, and his two-year contract got extended to a tenure track position. He got tenure last year."

"Diane must be livid."

"She hates his guts."

"So why is she in his class?"

No one spoke for a moment, then Brian broke the silence. "We're not really sure about that either."

"Keep up the good intelligence work." Susannah met Clare's eye. "Maybe if you could, find out for sure if we can count on the Tree-Huggers if we need them."

"How should I do that?" Clare asked. "I'm no good at subterfuge or espionage."

Susannah smiled thinly. "I meant keep the line of communication open. You know, maybe ask Jessica directly. Now down to business." Susannah addressed the group. "I want to hear about everyone's proposed legislation for tomorrow."

There was general hemming and hawing. Clare guessed that most of her fellow Commies were at about the same stage as she was with the assignment — not even close to beginning.

Thankfully, Brian spoke up. "I have two ideas ready."

"Of course you do." Susannah groaned good-naturedly. "Okay, Brian, let's hear them. You mentioned a housing bill already. What's the other one?"

"Redistribution of wealth. I think anyone who has a net worth of more than a million dollars should be forced to donate the rest to charity."

Susannah rested her chin in her hand. "What about someone whose house is worth more than that?"

"A family can pool its quota." Brian's answer came fast. "So a family of four can own up to four million dollars in assets and investments."

Clare had never known anyone whose net worth was more than a million dollars. Still, she thought this was a terrible idea. "How would you promote a work ethic?"

"You mean, why would anyone keep working when the rest of their income would go to charity?"

Clare nodded.

"People would, paradoxically, work harder." Brian's eyes were almost shiny. "They could choose their own charities and oversee as much or as little of the spending as they liked. How empowered would you feel if you had helped ten inner city kids get through college, when the statistics said they were more likely to end up as drug dealers?"

"I'd feel great," Clare acknowledged.

"Better or worse than if you bought a yacht and spent your

summers cruising up and down the Mediterranean?"

"Better." Clare shrugged. "But forcing it seems so . . ."

"Communist." Susannah put her napkin in her yogurt cup and stood up. "But that's okay. All votes are free votes, so bring it in, Brian — at the very least, it's creative — and the rest of you can vote on it how you like."

FIFTEEN
LAURA

"Thanks for making time for this." Penny sipped her sparkling water, and several thin gold bands clattered gently on her arm.

"Time, I have plenty of." Laura speared a piece of avocado with her fork. "What I'm quite sure I don't have is something to contribute to your story."

"You'd be surprised what people are interested in."

"No," Laura said. "I would not be. When I was married to Hayden, our housekeeper took the garbage to the curb when she heard the truck coming down the street. If we put it out the night before, reporters didn't feel it was too uninteresting to rummage through our trash to find out what we'd thrown away."

"I hope they weren't *my* staff." Penny's smile hadn't changed since kindergarten. Laura wondered if it had been phony even then.

Laura put her fork back down. Why did people call lunch meetings if they intended to talk the whole time and never let you eat? "I'm sure some were yours. But don't think it worries me. I know privacy isn't part of public life. What is it you think I can I help you with?"

"Well ... I heard a rumor that you found a business card ..."

"A rumor about a business card?" Laura sipped her wine, hoped her laugh seemed natural. "That sounds so cloak and dagger."

"I agree." Penny raised her ultra-thin eyebrows. If Laura hadn't known Penny to be an extremely hard worker, she would think her days were spent being pampered and perfected in the spa. "But is it true?"

How could Penny have found out so quickly? Laura had only turned the card in that morning. "Not that I recall. What sort of business card?"

"Come on, Laura. You can tell me. We're friends before anything."

That might have worked when they were seven, when the promise of friendship with someone more charismatic had still held a certain allure. "I think your source must be winding you up. This wine is lovely, by the way. Is it expensive?"

"Yes."

Laura took another sip. "French?"

"Laura, you can stop playing games. I know you found a card. I don't know what it says or why it might be significant. If you're not going to talk to me, then fine. I understand. But you can at least level with me. I'm leveling with you."

"Fine. Here's the truth." Laura leaned into the table and met Penny's eye. "I promised the police I wouldn't tell anyone. Especially not the press."

"The press?" Penny hooted.

A man at the next table glanced at the women briefly, then returned to his companion.

"You do still work for the *Star*," Laura said.

"Work for them? You make me sound like a common reporter." Penny prepared a bite of Caesar salad on her fork, then set it down before eating it. "The police think you made the card yourself, to deflect the investigation away from yourself."

"They what? How do you . . . ?"

Penny poured more white wine into Laura's glass, then topped up her own.

"But why would I be a suspect?"

"Please. The estranged wife? The divorce not even finalized? Political pensions heading your way annually until you die? Compound that with Hayden leaving you for a younger, sexier woman. Caught by the *press*, no less. Hell, I'd be tempted in your position."

"But I wasn't tempted." Laura reached for her water and took a long sip. "What a stupid thing to say."

Penny pursed her lips. "Well, I believe you, of course. Nice little Laura Sutton. You couldn't hurt a fly. It's the police who aren't as sure."

"How do you know?"

"The same source that told me about the business card."

Laura threw her hands in the air. "So what do you want from me, Penny?"

"Collaboration. Let's prove your innocence and figure out who the real murderer is."

"Penny."

"You mean, what's in it for me?"

"Mmm. That's just what I mean."

"Look at us, Laura. We've known each other since we were children playing hopscotch, and now here we are, two women of the world."

Laura wondered if Penny had grown up expecting to be a woman of Pluto.

"To think we took classes in high school that were all about being a perfect wife."

"I *was* the perfect wife. For twenty-five years."

"But look at you now. You're a lesbian!"

The man at the next table glanced over again. He met Laura's eye and cracked a smile.

"Penny, what are you getting at?"

Penny lowered her voice. "I'm saying why should we sit around and let the good policemen do their work? We are two intelligent women, and between us I'm guessing we have access to a few more contacts than the local police force."

"You want to use our political connections to become a crime fighting team?" Laura was more than a little bit skeptical.

"Why not?" Penny's smile was broad. "Well, crime solving, at any rate. I'm not suggesting we slip on our danger suits and try to take down the bad guys by force."

"How would we do that?" Laura guessed that Penny already had a detailed plan.

"First, we pore over archives. You can come to my office, and we'll scour the *Star* resources for possible motives. Find out who might have wanted Hayden dead."

"And then?"

"Once we've gathered information, we meet with people. Other politicians — maybe someone else has received a similar card. Activist groups — we let them think we're giving them a turn in the spotlight, but really our interview questions are designed to draw out the truth about the murder."

"Okay. And then?"

"We present the police with our conclusion. Wrapped up neatly, ready for an arrest."

"You don't think we should include the police every step of the way?"

"Certainly not." Penny looked appalled at the idea. "They'd want to control our investigation as well as their own. It would impede our progress, and complicate theirs."

Laura took a bite of prawn and chewed it carefully.

"What are you thinking?" Penny asked.

"I'm thinking that at our age, we're supposed to be more sensible than this."

"What do you mean?"

"I mean no. I have so much to do already. With Susie, the Brighter Day . . . I'm sure this investigation can be left to the police. To whom, incidentally, I did give my word about that card."

"Just like that?" Penny's eyes grew dark. She moved her white napkin from her lap to the table. "After I went out on a limb to tell you all I knew about Hayden's death?"

"I'm sorry."

SIXTEEN
MATTHEW

The rain had not let up. Matthew wondered how much water a cloud could hold. Was it even the same cloud, dropping rain for hours on end, or did a new cloud roll in every time an old one had used up its supply?

His tweed jacket was soaked through. It would begin to smell as it dried, but that was later. He wished he owned an umbrella, but every time he saw one he liked, it wasn't raining, and it seemed like a waste of money for the two times a year he might want one.

"Dr. Easton! Wait up!"

Matthew sighed. Waited.

From behind, Brian approached him, panting. He wore old man's overshoes that made a squishing sound as he ran. "I'm glad I caught you. I was, um, wondering if you could help me out with something."

Though Matthew cringed to admit it even silently, Brian reminded him of himself as an undergrad. Minus the galoshes.

"What can I do for you?"

"It's the SPU." Brian extended his oversized plaid umbrella to cover them both as they walked. "I'd do anything to join it."

"sᴘᴜ?" Matthew gave a slight shake of his head, and noticed Clare following close behind. He nodded at her — couldn't be rude for no reason — but she was rifling through her knapsack while trying to keep her own umbrella in place, and she appeared not to notice him. "What does that stand for? Do you want me to write a recommendation letter?"

"Please?" Brian's eyes grew wide. "It's the Society for Political Utopia. I know you're involved."

"The Society for a what? I love it. How come I'm not a member?"

"But I thought . . . well, all the members are your students . . . and it was founded the year you started teaching here."

Matthew glanced behind at Clare, who had her knapsack back in place, and was now toying with her cell phone with her non-umbrella hand.

"I'm flattered if I inspired a club of any kind. But I don't understand. If the members are your classmates, why don't you ask them if you can join their group?"

"Because they deny it exists."

"Ah. You mean it's a *secret* utopia society?"

"They make their own utopia." Brian looked at Matthew intently. "And they don't mind breaking the law to achieve it. Remember a few years back, when seven cancer patients were found dead in their beds at Mount Sinai Hospital?"

"Of course I remember." Matthew glanced at his watch, and hoped the kid would get the point.

"The society was behind those murders."

How did Brian know this? As far as Matthew knew, even the police were unaware of the connection.

"I don't see how that's possible," Matthew said. "Elise Marchand was behind the murders."

"I know. She was a student of yours, and she volunteered at the hospital." Brian's knapsack strap was slipping down his shoulder. He shrugged it back up, shaking the umbrella a bit, splashing them both with drops of rainwater. "But the part that never made the papers is this: Elise left an SPU business card at each of the victims' bedsides."

How did Brian know this?

"The society has business cards, but they don't print the members' names on them. Just the initials of the group. They leave the cards in places when they've committed a Utopian act."

Matthew's stomach was churning; he was glad he hadn't eaten lunch. "Do they always leave a card?"

"That's the idea. On the back of the cards, Elise wrote *You're Welcome* in her own handwriting. She used her left hand, but the analysts still matched the writing to hers. When they caught her, she admitted to everything freely."

"I remember the confession." Inside his jacket pocket, Matthew clenched his right hand into a fist. He reminded himself that the kid was innocent; it was Matthew alone who was guilty. "She said her mandate was complete."

"Well, by her mandate," Brian said, "she meant the club's mandate."

Matthew raised his eyebrows, shifted his briefcase once more so that he could glance back at Clare inconspicuously. Still there, and still ostensibly oblivious. Not that it mattered; he wasn't telling Brian anything he wouldn't tell an outsider.

"No wonder they keep themselves a secret. Do you know who the members are?"

"Not the students. They change from year to year, and the alumni have their own club they keep active. But — are you sure you're not involved? My dad says that's the one thing he does know."

"Your dad?"

"It's his idea for me to join."

"Why on earth would your father ask you to join a club that condones murder?" Matthew didn't have to feign confusion this time.

"He's impressed by how the society gets things done. And he thinks the members are the movers and the shakers of the incoming political generation. So the motivation is twofold: I can begin to make some changes that we'd like to see made in the world, plus he thinks the society is the right place to begin networking. For when I go into politics."

"Are you planning to run for office one day?"

"That's the plan." Brian was glum.

"Well, cheer up. It's not the worst job you could apply for."

"You really can't help me?"

"I really can't."

Matthew watched Brian fall back into step with Clare. They had probably been walking together before Brian had run ahead to bug Matthew. He must be getting paranoid as he aged — he could have sworn Clare had been hanging about to eavesdrop.

Why didn't he trust her? By all external signs, Clare was an unspectacular student who had probably chosen the wrong major — in other words, as normal as a person her age could be. But his real concern was Brian. He hadn't mentioned a particular cause he wanted to champion, but there must be a reason Brian's father wanted him to join the SPU. What terrible pressure to put on your son. What terrible overshoes to send him off to school in.

SEVENTEEN
CLARE

"Promise you won't be insulted." Jessica Dunne caught up with Clare after their U.S. Politics class. Her blond hair flopped messily around her shoulders.

"Insulted?" Clare glanced down the long, immaculate corridor. Their classmates had all left for the day, and their words seemed to echo in the emptiness. "Why would I be?"

"Just promise." Jessica hooked a thumb into the belt loop of her expensive-looking ripped jeans.

"Fine," Clare said. "I promise."

"So every year my grandpa gets me these tickets for my birthday. Sometimes it's an art opening, sometimes it's the opera. This year it's an environmental fundraiser at the St. Lawrence Hall."

"Environmental fundraiser?" Clare tried to picture such an event.

"It's mainly corporations who sponsor it. You know, oil companies trying to appear green. Definitely not the save-a-tree-by-living-in-it crowd, but it should be interesting. The finance minister is opening the event, and the prime minister is the keynote speaker."

"That's cool." Clare was waiting for the insult.

"Yeah, it's cool. Except we have this family tradition. It's so condescending, and I totally hate it, but in principle I don't think it's that horrible."

"Okay." Clare took out her smokes. If she couldn't light one indoors, at least she could feel the pack in her hand.

"So this tradition started when I was a kid, and my grandma always made us invite poor kids on family outings."

"Poor kids?" Was Clare's humble origin so obvious?

"Yeah. Well, not exactly poor, I guess." Jessica shifted her weight from one foot to the other, then back again. "We went to the neighborhood public school, but it was a pretty affluent part of town. Still, we had to make an effort to find someone whose parents couldn't or wouldn't expose them to things that Rory — my brother — and I had access to on a regular basis."

"That sounds noble." Clare was impatient for her cigarette. "Where does the mean part come in?"

"In the form of my brother. He started calling the tradition Educate a Fool, and despite my grandmother's wildest protests, the name kind of stuck with the rest of us."

Clare started walking in the direction of the exit, and was pleased when Jessica followed suit.

"Anyway, I wouldn't call it by that name, except that my brother isn't subtle, and he thinks it's really funny to refer to invites as 'fools' in front of them. I figure it's less insulting if I give you the context beforehand."

Clare opened the heavy door leading to the stairwell.

"Am I your fool?"

"Um, if you want to be. I'm not saying I think you're poor, incidentally." Jessica adjusted her shoulder bag. "Just, you seem like you're new to politics. It's a cross-party event, but half of the speakers are politicians, and the rest are environmental lobby-ists."

Politicians and lobbyists sharing the spotlight? "Sounds like a disaster waiting to happen."

"They stay civilized." Jessica grinned. "Both sides want to look like the heroes. Since poli sci is your major now, I thought you might enjoy coming out and listening to some speeches."

"I'd love to." They arrived at the bottom of the stairs, and Clare pushed open the door to outside. "And by the way, I grew up in a trailer. Tell your grandma the opportunity isn't wasted."

Shit. Clare wasn't supposed to be herself. At least she hadn't said which trailer park.

"Seriously?" Jessica's eyes grew wide. "What was that like?"

"Like anything else when it's all you know." Clare lit her smoke and stood in the shelter by the doorway. Rain was pouring all around them. "I'd take a loving family over a wealthy one any day of the week."

"So would I." Jessica stood with Clare.

"Oh god! I'm sorry. I didn't mean to imply that your family isn't loving."

Jessica laughed. "It's okay. They are what they are. They grew up in a world that gave them a certain outlook. But I don't think it's their fault. They push their own boundaries, in a way. And in other ways they don't."

"Like the rest of us," Clare said.

"I guess." Jessica frowned. "Hey, can I try a cigarette?"

"Have you ever smoked?" Clare reached into her pocket for her pack, and held it open, amused.

"At camp one year, this one girl had them. I snuck off with her a few times. It was fun."

Clare lit Jessica's cigarette for her. Surprisingly, she didn't cough at all, but inhaled it like a natural.

"Yeah," Jessica said, after exhaling her first drag. "I like this. Thanks."

"Which day is this prime minister thing again?"

"Saturday."

"Saturday. Groovy." Clare preferred to reserve Saturdays for drunken debauchery, but she supposed she could sacrifice this one for the cause.

EIGHTEEN
ANNABEL

Annabel was getting sick. She was cold in her bones, her nose was running, and — here was the real sign — she didn't crave alcohol as soon as she walked in her front door. She poured herself a glass of juice, popped a cold prevention pill — did those things actually work? — and changed into her fuzziest pair of sweatpants.

She called Matthew. No response, which generally meant he was with someone. Probably eating dinner. Somewhere nice, if she was new. Chinese takeout, if they'd been at it for awhile. Annabel remembered when she'd been new. Matthew had taken her to Lewiston for dinner and a play. Ha ha, he'd even paid.

She couldn't bother Kat. Her sister was off living her own life, cooking dinner for her daughter, exchanging loving banter with her husband, who adored Katherine and would never be off eating Chinese food with someone he was fucking on the side.

Maybe Utopia Girl would talk to her. Annabel pulled out her BlackBerry and toyed with the dial on the side. She could type more easily on her computer, but tonight she preferred to recline on the couch with sitcoms on TV.

Hey, Utopia Girl, she typed. *Tell me something about your childhood.*

The response came in a few minutes, an instant message instead of an email.

Utopia Girl: *My childhood? Are you my shrink?*

Death Reporter: *I want a sense of who you are, what you come from.*

Utopia Girl: *If I said that I came from a happy loving home?*

Annabel laughed, although she wasn't sure what she found funny. Maybe it was *Two and a Half Men*. Maybe it was the medication kicking in.

Death Reporter: *I'd ask how old you were when all that changed.*

Utopia Girl: *When all that changed. Did you take Psych 101 when you were my age but decide to pursue journalism when you figured out you sucked at analysis?*

Her age? Annabel tossed her blanket aside and got up off the couch. She found a notebook with some empty pages and jotted *Utopia Girl — university age?*

Death Reporter: *Sorry if I upset you. You don't expect a killer to come from a happy home.*

Utopia Girl: *I'll give you some details. But understand that this is the background picture I choose to give you. It may bear little resemblance to my actual childhood.*

Death Reporter: *So let's start with the broad strokes. Did you grow up in Canada?*

Utopia Girl: *Yes.*

Death Reporter: *Small town or big city?*

Utopia Girl: *No comment.*

Death Reporter: *Are your parents Canadian? Did they grow up here, too?*

Utopia Girl: *No offense, but these questions are boring even to me.*

Why did people only say "no offense" right before they insulted you?

Death Reporter: *Did your childhood bore you?*

Utopia Girl: *If only it had.*

Death Reporter: *Was the environment abusive? Did one of your parents drink?*

Utopia Girl: *No abuse, no drinking. We all got along, you know, loved each other.*

Death Reporter: LOL. *So how old were you when all that changed?*

Utopia Girl: LOL *right back to you. Glad you find my tragedy so comedic.*

Death Reporter: *I was laughing at myself, too.*

Utopia Girl: *Now we share jokes?*

Death Reporter: *What's wrong with being light and pleasant?*

Utopia Girl: *Think Hayden Pritchard's family is feeling light and pleasant?*

A killer who was also sanctimonious?

Death Reporter: *Do you feel badly for having killed him?*

Utopia Girl: *If that's how you write English, I can see why you haven't advanced as a reporter.*

Death Reporter: *What?*

Utopia Girl: *You just asked if killing Hayden Pritchard had diminished my ability to feel. Which I suppose is an interesting question in its own right, but not what you meant.*

Annabel scanned her last couple of sent messages.

Death Reporter: *Fine. Do you feel* bad *for having killed Pritchard?*

Utopia Girl: *Feel bad for his family. Think the world's a better place without him.*

Death Reporter: *Can you talk about your motivation?*

Utopia Girl: *I can talk about whatever I like.*

Death Reporter: *Will* you *talk about your motivation?*

Utopia Girl: *In time. For now, though, know that I am trying to right a wrong.*

Death Reporter: *A personal wrong? Or do you have the common good at heart?*

Utopia Girl: *Exactly. One or the other.*

Death Reporter: *But there will be more deaths, right? In your letter, you said Pritchard was your first step.*

Utopia Girl: *You sound almost hopeful. On that note, I'm out.*

Annabel set down her phone, feeling no better than when she'd arrived home. Score one point for cold prevention pills being a fraud.

NINETEEN
JONATHAN

Finland: *Who's got the power?*
USA: *You do, but it's temporary.*

Jonathan looked around his bedroom. It was time to update the décor, if he planned to entertain Jessica here anytime soon. He still had *Star Wars* posters on the wall. He still had wizards on his bedsheets.

Finland: *Temporary? Really? I've taken over your oil interests worldwide, and you can't afford to arm your men. And — oh, look — I've secured China as an ally.*

USA: *Well if I sell all my women to Russia as mail-order brides ... like so ... that gives me enough money to train my soldiers and fully arm my military.*

Jonathan took a gulp of iced tea. Maybe Jessica liked *Star Wars*.

Finland: *Mail-order brides don't go to Russia.*

USA: *They just did. Now if I distract China by sending over some domestic trouble ... like, say, poisoning all the rice fields ... then their troops are occupied at home, and I can launch a full-on attack of Finland.*

Poisoning the rice fields. That was clever. Jonathan considered how to fend off Jessica's American soldiers. Well, since she'd sent all their women to Russia . . .

Finland: *But look . . . your men are here trying to invade me, and they're so starved for love that all they want to do is Finnish women. A little attack of gonorrhea and — presto! — the American soldiers are toast. No money, no army. You're done. Good game. Again?*

USA: *You are so not funny.*

Finland: *No, but I won as Finland. So now can we have that date?*

USA: *That was the deal.*

Finland: *Don't sound so thrilled.*

USA: *Sorry. I'm looking forward to tomorrow.*

Finland: *If I can win as Tanzania will you be nice on the date?*

USA: *I'm always nice. I just don't lose gracefully. Will I see you at work tonight?*

Finland: *You're working tonight too? I'll polish my bow tie extra nice.*

Jonathan got up from his computer desk and found that he was shaking. Things were going well, right? Okay, so nothing physical had happened yet, but that would come.

He went back to his desk and pressed Play on his iTunes. "The Neverending Story" started playing, and he smiled. The setting was on random, so the song had chosen itself. It was a good sign. He'd played this for Jessica, in his head, so many times before. Could she hear it, on some level? And when she heard the song, did she know it was from him?

TWENTY
CLARE

Clare cleared a space on her desk for her coffee mug. Maybe one day she would be neater, but she wasn't waiting anxiously. She watched her laptop go through its grueling opening routine, and wondered when she would justify the expense and buy a speedier desktop model.

She was waiting to hear back from Sergeant Cloutier. Clare was dying to tell her handler about the conversation she'd overheard between Brian Haas and Dr. Easton. Surely even miserable Cloutier would have to acknowledge that she'd done good work. If the Society for Political Utopia was real, then all kinds of possibilities opened up, not least of which was a club with a murderous mandate.

Was Matthew Easton involved in the society? Would more politicians die if the group wasn't stopped? Would Clare successfully go in, get the dirt, and keep the world safe for politicians? God, she hoped so.

Her cell phone rang. Cloutier.

"Finally," Clare said. "I was beginning to think you didn't care what I had to say."

"Can the dramatics, kid. I have other things to do all day than babysit your newborn ass."

"I'm glad your day was full. But I have news." Clare told Cloutier what she'd overheard that afternoon. "So what do you think? Is the group real? Do you think they're behind the murder?"

Cloutier grunted. "I think you watch too many cop shows."

"I don't watch any cop shows." That was a lie: she watched *Dexter*. But Clare didn't count that, because it wasn't formulaic or for morons.

"Then you read too many cheap detective novels. You know how rare it is for a group to pull off a murder in real life? They only need one dissenter — either before or after the fact — and the whole thing falls apart."

"Fine." Clare slumped in her desk chair. "I won't bother trying to penetrate the society."

"Are you stupid? Of course you should penetrate the society. We just think the murder was more likely the work of an individual member than the group as a whole."

Clare paused to process what he'd said.

"Um. Am I wrong here? You sound like you already knew about the society."

"The group has been on our radar since that Marchand case four years ago. We don't have positive proof of its existence."

"Thanks for telling me yesterday."

"Must have slipped my mind."

"Fine." Clare was furious. "So despite not having told me about it, you *do* want intelligence on the society."

"Intelligence." Cloutier emitted a sound that disturbingly resembled laughter. "Now it's a spy movie. Kid, we're not MI5."

"Information, then." Clare wondered how polite she was supposed to be when the man found every opportunity to belittle her. "Have you also considered that Utopia Girl might be someone like Brian Haas?"

"Of course we have. No secret society truly wants to be secret. They want buzz, people who want to be members but can't find their way inside."

Clare sipped her coffee. "You think there are others like Brian."

"On the outside looking in? I'd be shocked if there weren't."

"So should I look for people in the club, or concentrate on outsiders?"

"You should concentrate on understanding your job, first and foremost." Cloutier snorted, reminding Clare of a horse she had once ridden. "You're not a detective. You're not being paid for your theories, nor are they particularly intelligent."

"Can you remind me what my job *is*, then? You seem to have exhausted all the things it isn't."

"You're the eyes Inspector Morton can't have. Think of yourself as a clumsy surveillance device, like those robots the U.S. Army sends into hostile territory. Go to school; get friendly with the other kids. Gather all the information you can, then give it to me."

Why did he have to add "clumsy"? "Is there anything else you may have forgotten to tell me?"

"Vengel, stop pissing me off."

When she'd hung up with Cloutier, Clare Googled *Haas Communist* and came up with Carl Haas, who had run for federal office three times consecutively in the riding of Mississauga South. Each time, not surprisingly, he had lost by a landslide.

She threw Carl Haas's name into the search with Hayden Pritchard's. Despite giving a warm endorsement of Pritchard's candidacy for mayor, Haas was never pictured with the mayor, nor did the mayor seem to have any links back to Haas.

Brian's dad, it seemed, had a fervor that bordered on fanatic. A couple of articles drew references to a Communist Manifesto. Clare couldn't figure out if the manifesto was supposed to be Carl's own, or if it was a more formal doctrine endorsed by the Party as a whole.

Haas's pet issue was housing. He wanted to disperse low-income families throughout his and other affluent ridings. He thought the government should buy houses in good neighbor-hoods, and rent them out to families for what they could afford. He argued that the only way to truly equalize the starting blocks was to give rich and poor children alike access to the same play groups, neighborhood facilities, and public schools. Haas was willing to open his neighborhood to lower earners. The problem was that his prospective constituents were not.

Clare wondered what the big deal was about playing with rich kids. Were they smarter, or better athletes, or something? Maybe they had better morals. Where she'd grown up, everyone had had pretty much the same — nothing. She hadn't noticed anything missing, but she might have done if she'd been thrown in to mingle with kids who'd had newer toys and more expensive clothes.

Clare was willing to bet that the housing bill Brian planned to introduce in class was an exact replica of what his father had tried to get through real parliament. His father had probably also come up with that idiot scheme to force people to be charitable with their excess riches. Poor kid — Clare wondered what Brian would come up with if he was allowed to have ideas on his own.

Her phone rang. Clare didn't recognize the number, but it was local, and she answered.

"Did we have a date tonight?" It was Kevin, the reason she hadn't watched the news the night the mayor was being killed.

"Shit." Clare had forgotten they'd made plans for that night. "I got caught up in work. I'm so sorry. What time is it? Where are you?"

Kevin, to Clare's relief, laughed. "I guess I'll have to work harder to leave a lasting impression."

"No, you were great. I was looking forward to that wholesome evening you suggested. Dinner and a walk, right?" She looked out-side to see the light of day was fading. This time of year, that probably meant it was around seven-thirty. "We still have time for one or the other."

"What are you? Ninety? We still have time for both. And then if you're lucky, a repeat performance of the night we met. So have you eaten?"

"No." Clare moved to the bathroom and checked herself in the mirror. "But I need to shower first. I've been busy all day. I'm pretty sure I smell."

"Busy working?"

What had she told him, the night they'd spent together? She'd been drunk, but Clare was fairly sure she hadn't told Kevin that she was a cop. Then again, why would she have hidden it from him?

"Busy at school." She made the snap decision to run with her cover story. "And then homework. So where should I meet you?"

"How about if I come up there and help you get clean?"

"That could work." Clare shut down her computer, made triple sure that any bills or mail with her real last name were hidden. "Are you close by?"

"I'm dangerously close by." Of course he was in the neighborhood. They had agreed to meet at the Lamb to the Slaughter, the pub down the street where they'd originally met.

"Mmm," Clare said. "I like danger."

TWENTY-ONE
MATTHEW

"Jesus, Mom. You know that pisses me off." Matthew shoved his plate away from himself. "I could be prime minister of this fucking country, and you'd find something wrong with how I live my life."

"I just mean, wouldn't it be nice for you to settle down?" Anne Easton opted for a hurt look, which Matthew did not buy. "You're a good-looking man. You have a . . . well, a steady job, if not a particularly well-paying one. You're only a little past your prime. I'm sure there are lots of unmarried women who would find you a real catch."

"Thanks for the vote of confidence." Matthew smoothed his paper napkin on the cheap linen tablecloth. How could he have lived here for so many years without cringing at the tackiness of everything?

"I know you're holding out for a supermodel who's also a brain surgeon. But if you open your mind and look beyond skin deep, I think you'll find someone wonderful you didn't know you were looking for."

Matthew stood up. "I'd love to stay and finish dinner. I do enjoy an overcooked pot roast. But I worry that if I listen to this drivel for a moment longer, I might start to believe you about my own limitations."

"Sit down." Matthew's father spoke softly. "I won't have you insulting your mother's cooking."

"But you'll have her insulting your son." Matthew grabbed his wallet and car keys. "I wish it could be different, but I'm afraid I have to leave."

Matthew was shaking when he got to his car. It was ludicrous that his parents could still have this effect. The subtle little jabs, delivered with a smile. Were they designed to undermine his confidence? Or did his mother truly believe that she was being helpful? He wished he hadn't said that about the pot roast.

Matthew had no idea where he wanted to go. He was tempted to get onto Kingston Road, like he used to do when he was frustrated as a teenager, and take it all the way out of town until it turned into Highway 2. A few times, when he was really angry, he'd made it all the way to Kingston, and driven around the perimeter of the penitentiary, before stopping at Tim Hortons to load up with coffee for the drive home.

But now Kingston made him think of Elise, and Matthew pointed his car toward his own house. He thought of calling Annabel back — she'd left a needy-sounding message — but he'd spent the previous night at her place, and he didn't want to give her reason to think of him as her boyfriend. Plus she sounded like she had a cold, which Matthew didn't feel like catching.

He didn't want to go home. Ethan's comment the previous day was nagging at him, and their interactions since then had been forced. Was Matthew mean to women? He didn't think so. He didn't lie to them. He slept around, but they could, too. It wasn't the 1950s.

What he wanted was to go to a keg party in the backwoods and get absolutely soused, but his friends didn't have keg parties, and he could hardly crash his students' dorms. They were probably all studying anyway.

Maybe Elly wasn't busy. That was a fire he hadn't stoked in a while. He fumbled in his pocket for his cell phone.

"Elly's Epicure."

"You expecting a business call at this hour?"

"It's eight o'clock, Matthew. I get business calls right up to midnight."

"So . . . is this a bad time?"

"Not the best."

"Sorry," Matthew said. "Well, can you get away?"

"Doubtful. I have the kids to put to bed, then Emmett should be home around nine. I'll feed him, then I have to pop out to an event. The earliest I could be free is eleven."

"I'm tired listening to all that."

"Welcome to my life. Should we try for another night this week?"

"Yeah, maybe. What's the event?"

"It's a house party. You know Libby Leighton and Sam Cray?"

"Of course."

Libby rode a bicycle to work, and wanted to legislate in the biggest carbon tax any country in the world had ever proposed. Thankfully, she wasn't on the side of the government. She also changed issues with the wind, so her passion was likely to be short-lived. Her partner was a right-wing senator. They must have had some crazy chemistry between the sheets, because their politics alone should have been enough to drive them apart.

"What are they like to work for?"

"Challenging." Elly laughed. "They can't agree on anything, so I had to suggest that they separate the tasks for tonight's party. Libby chose the hot appetizers, Sam chose the cold. That kind of thing."

"Are they nice people?"

"Yeah," Elly said. "They're actually quite pleasant."

"Maybe I could meet you at the party. We could sneak out back and do it in the alley."

Elly snorted. "After the day I'm having, that sounds perfect. Unfortunately, I don't think it's practical. The staff like to go out back and smoke cigarettes. Not your students, of course."

"How about if I head there now and scope it out? Worst case, you can hop in my car and we can find a deserted parking lot. Just like university." When Matthew's options had been limited to ugly women.

"Yeah," Elly said. "Yeah, that would be great."

She gave him the address.

THURSDAY / SEPTEMBER 9

TWENTY-TWO
ANNABEL

"Penny. Hi. It's Annabel Davis. Did I catch you at a bad time?"

"I'm the editor of a national newspaper. It's always a bad time."

"There's another letter." Annabel sipped her tea and nearly burned her lip. "From Utopia Girl."

"Don't say that name out loud."

"Sorry."

"Walls have ears. Never forget that. Have you read this new correspondence?"

"No," Annabel said. "But the title —"

"Good. Don't. I want you to forward me the message immediately. Then delete it from your own computer."

"Do you want me to keep a copy as a backup? At least until we've passed it on to the police."

"It's not secure on your server. And I don't want you reading it down there where anyone can look over your shoulder. I have an office I can lock."

"Surely you don't think anyone who works here would —"

"I'm not accusing my staff of subterfuge. But we can't afford to play fast and loose with security, Annabel."

"I see your point. Should I come up to your office and read the letter with you? It was sent to me, after all." Annabel immediately regretted the boldness of her statement.

"Just carry on. I'm sure your regular workload is enough to keep you busy. I'll contact the police."

"Okay." Annabel didn't even resemble sassy. "Let me know if there's anything I can do that's helpful."

TWENTY-THREE
CLARE

I t was the third day of school. The second Poli Real World class, and Clare was late.

The night before had been incredible. Kevin came over, and Clare had barely offered him a beer before they were naked on her ugly sofa. (So much for wholesome, but it had certainly broken the ice.) After exhausting each other in Clare's living room and then in the shower, Kevin insisted that they go for a walk.

They headed south, toward Bloor Street and High Park. They stopped once for food, twice for coffee, and about twelve hundred times to make out like love-starved teenagers. After walking through parts of the city Clare hadn't known existed, Kevin had dropped her off at her door about an hour before her alarm was set for school.

None of that helped her head feel clear today. Clare felt like she'd been driving forever to find a parking spot, which was practically unheard of on a motorcycle — she could almost always find room between two cars. When she finally found somewhere to park, it was three blocks from class, with no coffee shop on the way. She contemplated a Starbucks detour — she thought she remembered seeing one on Harbord Street — but decided not to incur any more of Dr. Easton's wrath than she had to. At least her homework was done. Between six and eight that morning, Clare had drafted a bill suggesting the criminalization of cigarette production and sales. She knew it was unoriginal, and mildly hypocritical given that she smoked a carton a week. But it was the first thing that had come to her, and she was rushed. When she got to class, she placed her assignment in the pile with the others.

"Ah. Simpson. I hope you enjoyed a leisurely breakfast and a stroll before deciding to join us for class."

"Sorry I'm late."

"Are you late?" Dr. Easton glanced at his watch. "Oh! So you are. Well, that must be why we started without you."

Clare found the seat she'd been saved in the back row of the Commie section.

"Did you hear?" Brian whispered as Clare was pulling out her notepad. "The cops are interviewing the entire class."

"Why?" Clare's surprise was genuine.

"It's something to do with Libby Leighton. They're speaking with us one by one, and we're not supposed to talk to each other until the interviews are over. But how could we not? It's too exciting. I haven't been yet, but apparently they're showing us this business card. As in, real evidence."

"Who's Libby Leighton?" The name was familiar from Clare's late-night Internet session where she'd attempted to learn all things political. But she couldn't place it into any context. Maybe she needed another session. Maybe she needed some sleep. Her normally strong stomach began to feel queasy.

"You mean who *was* Libby Leighton? Wow, you're not from here, are you?"

Clare shook her head, glad that she and Kevin hadn't been drinking much the night before. Just the one beer at her place and then . . . ah, but back to reality.

Clare whispered to Brian, "Do you mean that she's . . ."

"Dead," Brian said it for her. "Murdered, is everyone's guess.

She choked and died at a party last night, and now the cops are here."

"Like Hayden Pritchard."

Brian nodded. "Less vomiting, I think. But yeah. Too close for comfort. Or coincidence."

"What does that all have to do with us?"

"Do you have something you'd like to contribute to the group discussion, Simpson?" Dr. Easton was glaring at her.

"No," Clare said. "I'm just talking to Brian. But thanks." Damn. That was out before Clare realized how rude she sounded.

"Fine. Then at least keep it down, so that those of us who *are* participating can hear each other."

"Absolutely. Sorry." There went her participation mark — along with her chance to blend in. Clare turned back to Brian, in a whisper this time. "Has anyone come back yet?"

"Two people have already gone. Jonathan's with them now."

Clare wondered why Cloutier hadn't been in touch about this new death. She pulled out her phone to check for messages or missed calls, and found the battery dead.

"So is everyone okay?" she asked Brian. "No one's missing from class, or anything, are they?"

"Everyone's fine," Susannah turned from the front row to say to them. "Can you guys keep quiet? I'm trying to prepare my rebuttal."

"Rebuttal?" Why did it feel as if everyone here spoke in code?

"For the bill we're debating. It's Jessica's." Susannah passed back the extra copy she must have been saving for Clare. "It's about hospital administrators being personally accountable if a patient dies waiting to be seen."

"Sounds personal." Clare glanced at the page. "Is it well-written?"

Susannah shrugged. "I find it convoluted and illogical."

Dr. Easton called upon the Commies, and Susannah stood up. She barely had a sentence out when the door opened. Jonathan came in quietly, but all eyes turned his way.

"They want whoever's next."

Dr. Easton consulted the class list. He was clearly going in random order, because he made a tick toward the bottom of the page and said, "You go, Simpson. There are people in the next room who will actually be pleased to hear your nattering."

In the next room, Clare found Detectives Morton and Kumar. She would have been thrilled to see Morton, to thank him for taking a chance on her, if she didn't feel like she'd screwed up royally by letting her phone battery die.

Clare shut the door behind her. "Is this about . . ."

Morton nodded. "Libby Leighton."

Clare's body sank limply into the chair across the table from the detectives.

"Was another letter sent to the *Star*?"

"Sergeant Cloutier has been trying to get in touch with you."

"My phone's been dead." Clare felt stupid even saying it.

"I see." Morton's eyes said he agreed.

Morton nodded to Kumar, who glanced toward the closed door before passing Clare a copy of the second obituary.

Libby Leighton: April 14, 1958–September 8, 2010

We are pleased to announce our second step toward a political utopia for the real world. Libby Leighton has been a drain on the public payroll for too long, and we're delighted to see her off into the next world.

Libby was a career politician, and we doubt that she would have had the skills to keep a job in the private sector. See, in the private sector you have to justify your wages or you get fired. In Libby's case, she thought that getting the job was where the work came in, and that once she was in, she had only to share her half-formed opinions while smiling for the camera.

For reasons we cannot fathom, the public kept voting for

Leighton time and again. Today, we have saved taxpayers the expense of a smug and useless tax drain. We have also moved one step closer toward the political utopia our professor — our leader — demands.

You're welcome.

This has been a message from the Society for Political Utopia.

Clare set down the page, and looked back and forth between the two detectives.

Morton spoke Clare's thoughts. "We think the killer is in this department, either as one of the students, or a professor."

Clare nodded. "By professor, do you mean Dr. Easton?"

"Not necessarily. It could be someone who wants him gone."

Kumar showed Clare a business card protected by a plastic evidence bag.

"SPU." Clare flipped the card over. "*Your death will be your greatest public service.* What's this?"

"We've been showing it to the students, trying to gauge their reactions."

Clare passed the card back. "Is it evidence?"

"Laura Pritchard found the card in her husband's belongings, but we're not telling the students that."

"Her girlfriend is in my class. Susannah probably knows about it."

"We know," Morton said, adding one more thing Clare was pissed at Cloutier for not briefing her on. "And for whatever reason, Mrs. Pritchard hasn't told her girlfriend that she found it."

Clare wasn't so sure she believed that. But okay. "What are you telling the students, then? When you show them the card?"

"We're saying Sam Cray found it, in Libby Leighton's belongings."

"Smart," Clare said. "Any strange reactions yet?"

"No. But you're only our fourth interview. Assuming you can

get that phone charged, Sergeant Cloutier will brief you once we've had a chance to consider everyone's statements."

Yeah right. Cloutier would hold something back, like he had when he'd briefed her in the first place. It was like he had something against Clare succeeding.

"It was good work — or inadvertent good luck — that you overheard that conversation yesterday."

So Cloutier *had* deemed it important enough to pass on. At least she was getting kudos — or inadvertent congratulations — for something.

"I got the sense that Dr. Easton was holding back," Clare said. "Maybe not lying to Brian directly, but he was cagy. And he kept looking back at me. Though I don't think he noticed me noticing."

"Right. Sergeant Cloutier said all that. We agree with Brian, by the way. We think Matthew Easton is the society's founder."

"Does Cloutier know that?" Clare felt her blood approach its boiling temperature. She was determined not to let it come to the surface.

"Of course he knows."

"Fucking jerk." There went her determination.

"Are you all right?" Morton eyed her strangely.

"I'm fine." Clare gritted her teeth.

"You were practically beating down my door for this opportunity. Don't make me think I made a mistake giving it to you."

"I'm sorry." Clare slumped in her chair. She felt disoriented. She needed sleep. "You're right. I'm sure Sergeant Cloutier either told me or he meant to."

"Fine," Morton said.

Clare straightened her posture. She had to show them she was serious. "So should my main focus, as well as gathering information, be to penetrate the society?"

"If you can. Although if Brian Haas has been trying to get in for years, it may not be as easy as you think."

"You should get back to class," Kumar said, looking at his watch. "It doesn't look good if you're longer than the rest."

"Okay." Clare got up. "I'm, um . . ." She was about to say she was sorry for her outburst, but thought it was better to leave on a positive note. "I'll do my best to get into the society."

"Good luck." Kumar tossed her a skeptical smile.

TWENTY-FOUR

JONATHAN

Jonathan loved the way the sun felt on his head. It was the first pleasant feeling he'd had all day. It had been a late night at work again, and when he'd finally fallen asleep he'd had nightmares.

"Are you dating Jessica Dunne?" A shrill voice came up from behind.

"Go away, Diane."

"I have something you might like to know about her."

"I'd like to know everything there is to know about Jessica," Jonathan said. "But I want to learn it from her."

"We're being targeted, you know."

"We?" Jonathan walked faster.

"The society. This year's society, to be specific. You have to wonder who wants us in the spotlight."

"We're not in the spotlight. We're being interviewed by the police because of some card they found."

"The card looks just like ours. Right down to the off-center letters from that discount printer we used."

"I know what our cards look like."

Jonathan turned abruptly at the corner of a building, and

Diane kept perfect pace with him, though it meant some scrambling on her part.

"What's your beef with me?" she said.

"Where should I start?" Jonathan threw his hands in the air. "I hate what you did to Dr. Easton in your first year. Your ideas for the society are small-minded and not nearly radical enough to be considered anything other than mainstream. I could go on, but why be cruel?"

"You don't think taking over the campus radio to get our message across is a cool idea?"

Jonathan wondered if it was a coincidence that the sun had gone behind a cloud as soon as Diane had approached him. "It's juvenile. Plus none of the rest of us agree with you that Jesus is the Way."

"You must agree that getting kids back into religion — making it hip and fun — is a better alternative than letting them run wild with gang violence."

"Must I?" Jon shifted his oversized knapsack. "Then you must agree that churches should take some of that money they extort from their congregations, and put up their fair share of property taxes."

"Hmm." Diane put a finger to her chin. "We'll agree to disagree. Are you willing to discuss the Tree-Huggers' support of Susannah Steinberg's Commies?"

"Have you considered changing your major to political journalism?"

"How did you know?"

"You'd make a better rabid dog than electable member."

"You're so sweet. Has Brian Haas approached you yet?"

"About supporting the Commies? Would you give it up already?"

"He wants into the society."

"How does he know who the members are?" Jonathan looked at Diane accusingly.

"He's approaching everyone. Even Dr. Easton."

"That's a little weird." Jonathan slowed his pace.

"He's desperate. Something to do with his father and some manifesto."

"What did you tell him?"

"Nothing. Obviously. Nor will anyone. He's not getting an invite, and that's final."

"Final according to you?" Jonathan made up his mind to help Brian.

"Final according to everyone. Brian has an agenda he wants us to follow. Plus, he's annoying."

"How is that different from you?"

Diane rolled her eyes. "Well, thanks for your time, Jon. You've helped me out a lot. Gotta run."

TWENTY-FIVE
MATTHEW

Matthew gazed out his weathered office window. At least he had a view across St. George Street, onto the older, more stately part of campus. Most of his colleagues had views of an ugly brick lab building.

And why did he care about stately? At what point in his life, from his basic middle-class upbringing to his — screw what his mother said — successful academic career, had he turned into this pompous ass, this pathetic man who aspired to the finer things but didn't care to open his wallet to pay for them? Not that his wallet held anything impressive, when he did open it. But he could afford to be more relaxed about his spending. And less pretentious about his taste.

He sent a text to Annabel asking if they could cancel dinner. She'd think the worst — she always did — but Matthew couldn't care about her paranoid jealousy right then.

A knock on the door.

"What is it, Shirley?"

The door opened.

"Why so welcoming?"

Matthew swiveled in his desk chair. "I'm working."

"Your computer isn't on."

"You can see the screen from there?"

"I can see the power bar."

"Oh. Well, I was gathering my thoughts to work."

"On your book?"

Matthew nodded.

"Well, I'll be brief. The police came by. Have they seen you yet?"

"They've seen me, and my entire Poli Real World class."

Shirley took the seat opposite Matthew's desk. "Are you in trouble?"

"Of course not. They're interviewing everyone."

"They were asking a lot of questions about you. Especially the small man. The inspector."

"What were they asking?" Matthew wanted Shirley to leave him alone, so his thoughts could scream in private. But he had to know everything she could tell him.

"Mostly basics. Like when did you start working here, how did the rest of the department react when you got tenure so early. That kind of thing."

"Okay." So they were interested in him. That wasn't good, but it was hardly a conviction.

"And then he asked me about the society."

"The society?" Innocence first, obviously.

"Come off it, Matthew. The society you founded the year you started working here. The political utopia whatsit."

"I don't know what you mean."

"I think it's wonderful, the way you challenge the students, make them see that they can make a difference. I haven't told you before because I can't officially condone it — the illegal parts, that is." Shirley paused, appearing to search Matthew for a reaction. "It's why you have tenure, Matthew. The society is why I fought so hard for you in that committee. Universities need original thinkers — both students who embrace it and professors who encourage it."

"Thanks." Matthew found room, in his spinning head, to feel flattered. Did she know about Elise? Surely the department head wouldn't have supported a group with links to the hospital murders, even if they had been mercy killings. Maybe Shirley was more radical than Matthew had given her credit for. And maybe she was fishing. "I mean, thanks for taking my side, helping me get tenure. But the society is nothing more than a rumor."

Shirley stared at the bookcase. "I'm here to help you, Matthew. Are you in trouble? Just tell me yes or no."

She made it so tempting. Was it time to give the whole thing up? The society, the secrecy, the rest. Or was he being ridiculous, crumbling at the first sign of pressure?

Maybe if he got to the police first . . . retracted his statement in favor of the truth . . . But why would they believe anything he told them?

"No," Matthew said. "I'm not in trouble."

TWENTY-SIX
CLARE

"Nice place." Clare couldn't tell if Cloutier was sarcastic or serious. "At least the beams are real, not slapped up to create that fake English pub look."

"I had to miss a caucus meeting to see you here," she told him.

"The Lion and the Shrew. It's not your local or anything."

Clare tugged at the label of her Bud. "Do I look like an idiot, or is that your preconceived notion?"

"Christ, kid. You still pissed because I couldn't read the briefing notes about that secret society?"

"Yup."

"You gotta loosen up. You ever try reading Inspector Morton's handwriting? The world missed out when he passed up med school."

Clare glowered. "So how did the interviews with my classmates go this morning?"

"Classmates." He grunted. "You planning to quit the force and stay in school after this case?"

"Did Morton and Kumar get any names for the society?" Clare wondered if Cloutier was being obtuse on purpose.

"Not officially." Cloutier took a gulp of draft. "Everyone

acknowledged hearing the rumors, but no one gave any clues about who they thought might be a member."

"So what did you call this meeting for?" Clare didn't care if she sounded disrespectful.

"To tell you who the inspector wants a closer look at. Kumar flagged four people — five, including the professor — who he thinks were lying about the society. Strange thing is, they were all at one or both of the events where the deaths occurred."

"How is that possible?" Clare pushed her beer away. She should have ordered coffee. "Are these kids just ridiculously well-connected?"

"Susannah Steinberg worked the benefit — this we already knew. Diane Mateo was at the Leighton/Cray house party — she says briefly, but how long does it take to poison a politician?"

"Sounds like the start of a joke," Clare said.

"Jessica Dunne and Jonathan Whyte worked as cater waiters for both events."

Clare poked at her cigarette pack.

"And the professor claims to have been at neither event. Though Mateo thinks she saw Easton's car parked in the back alley of Leighton's house last night."

"What does Dr. Easton say?"

"What do you think? He says no way he was anywhere near there."

"Did Kumar think he was lying?"

"No read either way."

"Hmm." Clare opened her pack, slid out a smoke, and started playing with it. "Is that normal? I mean, I thought Kumar could sniff out a liar three counties over."

"The guy's not God." Cloutier scowled. "He can't say 'Are you the killer?' to a bunch of people until we can make an arrest."

"My money's on Diane." Clare told Cloutier about Diane's failed campaign to get rid of Dr. Easton.

"Kids' stuff. Find me someone torturing puppies, okay. Being arrogant and whiny doesn't make someone a murderer."

"You said it yourself. This killer is cocky. They want to be known, but not necessarily caught."

"Doesn't fit what you've told me about Diane."

"So you're a profiler now?"

"I'm sorry, but did you even go to the training session that taught you how to speak to your superiors?"

"I was sick that day."

"Well, if you plan to advance in the force, you might want to go back and learn it."

"Thanks for the advice." Clare shook her head at the waitress, who was motioning toward her almost-empty beer.

"Have another, if you like. The station's paying."

"Have another yourself. I'm in the middle of a work day and I'm running on about twenty minutes' sleep."

"Not my problem." Cloutier motioned for the bill. "Look, Vengel, you're gonna have to get past your hostile perception of me. I might not like you all the time, but we're working together here. You're gonna need to trust me."

"Okay," Clare said slowly. She wished her head wasn't in such a fog. "I maybe was overreacting."

"Which time?"

"I don't think you're sabotaging my assignment." Clare was tempted to apologize, but, as with Morton, she guessed that Cloutier would rather see that than hear it.

"You want to smoke?" Cloutier said. "I'll go with you."

"You still have half your beer."

"I can live without it. I can see you're anxious for your fix."

Cloutier paid, and Clare led the way to the back alley, where her bike was parked.

"I'd worry about being overheard here." Cloutier glanced toward the open windows in the second floor apartments.

"So let's walk." Clare allowed Cloutier to light her cigarette for her, then waited as he lit his own. "We can go around the block and come back in the alley from the next street."

"You know your way around pretty good. You sure you're not

a regular at this place?"

"I've been here once, with someone I don't even know anymore."

"He still come here?"

No, he lives in Orillia, Clare thought, and is about to marry the stupidest woman in the world.

"Like I said, I don't know him anymore."

They walked around the corner, onto the residential street.

"I heard a rumor that Dr. Easton sleeps with his students," Clare said slowly, forming her thoughts as she expressed them. "Since he seems to be at the center of things, I thought I should maybe, you know . . ."

"What? You should sleep with him?"

Clare shrugged. "I mean, if I can, it would be helpful, right?"

"I never saw you as the seductress type." Clare thought she saw a grin tug at Cloutier's mouth. "Besides, I think most professors who sleep with their students are interested in the adoring young ingénue."

"I think I can find a way." Was it so ridiculous that Dr. Easton might find her attractive? There was already an undeniable tension between them. Clare just had to switch it from hostility to intrigue. "If he does head up this society, it might be the most direct route in."

"No arguments here. Just make sure you don't alienate him by trying too hard to get close."

"Can you stop treating me as if I know nothing about anything?" Clare stopped herself short of stomping her foot.

"Can you stop with the assumption that this case is all about you?"

"I thought we were negotiating a truce."

"We're still negotiating."

"Good to know." Clare shouldn't try to work on so little sleep. It was turning her into someone she wouldn't want to work with. She reminded herself of her end-goal — a career that wasn't a dead bore — and offered her most dedicated smile. "So who's the prime suspect?"

"There really isn't one." Cloutier tossed his cigarette into the road. "But I got some theories if you want to hear them."

Clare nodded.

"Typically, it's men who crave the spotlight. So because of the newspaper letters, your professor's a good start, as are Jonathan Whyte, Brian Haas, and maybe don't discount Susannah Steinberg."

"Men and lesbians?"

"You said it."

"But also typically, it's women who use poison," Clare said. "Does that point to Susannah, 'cause she's on both lists?"

"Maybe it does." Cloutier looked thoughtful.

"Maybe they're working as a group."

"You won't let that go, will you?"

No, she actually wouldn't.

TWENTY-SEVEN
ANNABEL

ancel? Cocksucker. In a text, so she couldn't catch him off-guard by asking why.

Annabel: *Know what? Let's cancel indefinitely.*

She'd left work at noon. Her cold had turned into a fever, and she couldn't see in straight lines. She'd snapped at her direct boss, the obituary editor, but at least he had a sense of humor about things, and no permanent damage had been done. Now this with Matthew — but he deserved it. He was likely cancelling to spend time with whatever student he was making a project of this year.

Her phone beeped.

Matthew: *Don't be angry. Swamped with work and have deadline with editor.*

Bullshit. He would have known about his deadline, if he had one, when they were making plans the other day.

Annabel: *Don't let me hold you back.*

Annabel stirred the pot on the stove. She could make her own damned chicken soup.

Her phone beeped again. She went to shut it off, but it wasn't Matthew. It was an instant message.

Utopia Girl: *Like my obituary this morning? In honor of Libby*

Leighton?

That was cute. Utopia Girl, hardened killer, needed external validation.

Death Reporter: *You didn't say anything about why you killed her.*

Utopia Girl: *Course I did. She was a smug, useless bitch.*

Death Reporter: *Most people don't have two separate reasons for killing two separate victims. Hypocrisy and inefficacy are just . . . different.*

Utopia Girl: *Both fit fine with my mandate.*

Death Reporter: *Your mandate?*

Utopia Girl: *The reason I'm killing politicians. Duh. Create a better world, politicians who work for us, not against us. Very hurt, Annabel. Thought you understood me better.*

Annabel got up to check on her soup. It was still only a bunch of bones, but it was beginning to get some nice flavor. At least she had a few taste buds left that were working.

She wanted to ask Utopia Girl how she gained access to the politicians. But at the same time, she didn't want to know, because if she had a clue she'd feel compelled to go to the police. The sooner she was caught, the less compelling Annabel's book would be to a publisher.

Jesus, was Annabel really thinking this way? Compromise the lives of a few politicians so she could leapfrog out of a life rut she'd created for herself. This whole plan seemed suddenly and amazingly selfish.

But she was sick; her temperature had been over 102, before she'd taken pills to bring it down. Two days ago, when her head had been clear, this plan had been a good one. She'd stick with it until she felt better, and could make good decisions again.

Death Reporter: *How many more people are on your hit list? Is it every bad politician you can get your hands on until you're caught? Or is there a master plan? A bigger reason?*

Utopia Girl: *You mean a smaller reason. Biggest reason would be the one you've outlined. Public altruism. Sacrificing my freedom for greater good.*

Death Reporter: *Fine. Is there a smaller reason?*

Her phone went quiet for at least a minute. Annabel wondered if Utopia Girl knew the answer. It would be disappointing if she was talking to some aimless crazy.

Utopia Girl: *Yes.*

Death Reporter: *Will you share it?*

Utopia Girl: *Not everything is free.*

Death Reporter: *Meaning . . .*

Utopia Girl: *Meaning work on it. Try to sort out the connection yourself.*

Death Reporter: *The connection between Leighton and Pritchard?*

Utopia Girl: *And the rest.*

Death Reporter: *They were both city councilors.*

Utopia Girl: *That's it. I'm aimlessly killing everyone who ever served on city council.*

Death Reporter: *They were both socialists.*

Utopia Girl: *Same notation, Nancy Drew. Every socialist, dead.*

Death Reporter: *Work with me, then. I'm not inside your head.*

Utopia Girl: *Precisely. When you can get inside me deep enough to know what my victims have in common, I'll confirm it for you.*

Annabel clenched her hands around her BlackBerry as if she was wringing its neck. She was sick of being treated like everybody's bitch.

Death Reporter: *Fantastic. So once I've solved the case, you'll help me solve the case.*

TWENTY-EIGHT
CLARE

She was clipping her helmet to her motorcycle when Clare heard a frantic voice saying her name. She wasn't sure if it came from a woman or a man until she turned around.

"Brian? What's wrong?"

"You missed the Commies' lunchtime meeting."

"And that's why you're so upset? I had a dentist's appointment. Trust me; I would have much preferred to have been with you guys." Clare hoped he didn't ask to see her teeth.

"Are you in their club?" Brian stared at his freshly polished shoes. "Oh, what am I saying? Of course you are. You're perfect for them."

"Perfect for what?" Clare was perversely flattered.

"The spu."

"What's that?" Clare pulled out her smokes from her knapsack. "Shit. You mean like on that card the cops were showing us this morning?"

"It's the Society for Political Utopia. Are you in it?"

"No," Clare said. "Should I be? I mean, how do I sign up?"

"You can't sign up. It's a secret society."

"Yeah?" Clare lit her cigarette. "Well, then I guess that's out."

"Do you have any idea what it means?" Brian followed Clare as she began to walk toward her next class.

"Nope." Clare offered her pack to Brian.

He wrinkled his nose at the cigarettes. "Do you really not care if you're in it or not?"

"Why would I?" Clare put the pack back in her knapsack. "I should let a group I've never heard of make me feel inadequate because I'm not a member?"

Brian's eyes watered; Clare worried that she couldn't push him far.

"Sorry, Brian. But why do you want in so badly?"

"My dad wants me in."

"What does he care?"

"In my last year of high school, SPU cards started showing up at rallies, and at the scenes of some less legal political stunts."

"So?"

"So my father is huge in the federal Communist Party." Brian's chest puffed out as he spoke. "But the Party has never been able to get enough funding to run a good campaign, which is why his great ideas have been left floundering in the dark."

"And he thinks that if you join the society, *you* can introduce his ideas, in a less legal, more active kind of way."

"He doesn't want me to break the law." Brian waved away the smoke from Clare's cigarette. "Just network, mostly. Maybe go less extreme in my choice of party, so I actually have a chance to get elected."

"And that's what you want for your life."

"Oh," Brian said. "We don't all get to choose. My mom says I'm like Jesus."

"Um."

Brian smiled. "I know what you're thinking. But I'm not a nutcase. I don't think I'm a divine religious guru or anything like that."

"Oh good."

"Some of us are born with our destinies predetermined. I'm lucky, in a way. I don't have to go through all that angst my peers do — no offense — trying to figure out who I am and find my own identity."

No offense taken. "Because your parents have already told you."

Brian nodded.

Clare couldn't believe what she was hearing.

"And I'll get married, of course. To a woman. Even though I'm gay. But probably not a woman with a motorcycle," he said apologetically.

Clare, once again, was not offended. "Your parents can't make you . . ."

"They're not making me. It's a sacrifice. I'm proud to make it. Proud that my life is going to mean something."

Well, okay. Who was Clare to say whose dreams were valid and whose weren't?

"So you don't know *anyone* who's a member of the society?" she said.

"I'm sure I *know* them, but I don't know who they are."

"We're not talking Bilderbergers, are we? How hard can it be to find out who the members are?"

"Thanks," Brian said. "Maybe I'm as dumb as my father thinks I am. I've been trying for three years to get some kind of clue. Now I'm in my last year here, and I'm no closer to penetrating the society than I was when I first arrived."

"You're not dumb, Brian." Clare was outraged that any parent would try to make their kid feel otherwise. "You would have found a way in by now. The society's probably not even real. Just an elaborate compilation of rumors."

"Rumors don't murder politicians." Brian kicked at a pebble. "Of course the society is real."

TWENTY-NINE
LAURA

aura fiddled with the radio until the CBC was loud and clear, broadcasting a beautiful new recording of a jazz trio from Vancouver. It was three p.m. Far too early to pour herself a Scotch, but there it was. The tumbler was the last of the set she and Hayden had registered for, when they were about to be married and crystal tumblers had been important. She couldn't remember the other glasses breaking, but they must have done, one by one, over time.

She wasn't bothered about the card she'd found at Hayden's house, nor even by what Penny had told her, about Laura being a suspect herself. What was under her skin was the second card; the one she'd found an hour earlier, as she was gathering clothes to take to the cleaners.

The Scotch was fabulous. It was a smoky blend that had been sitting in the cupboard since Susannah's parents' last visit. So maybe it wasn't solving her problem, but it was doing its best to make her forget that she had one. Laura reclined into the plush living room sofa and contemplated becoming an alcoholic.

The card in Susie's jacket didn't have that horrific message typed onto the back. But the rest was identical. A plain white background, with SPU printed inexpertly onto one side. Laura's mind went back and forth between coming out and asking Susie what it meant, or replacing the card — she hadn't made it to the cleaners — and not letting on that she'd found it.

She thumbed the card, flipped it over and back in her trembling hands. She needed a manicure. French would look nice. She needed to reverse the aging process. She didn't remember having this many wrinkles on her hands.

"What's that?"

Laura hadn't heard Susannah open the door.

"It's a Scotch. Can I pour you one?"

"I'm good." Susannah lifted a corner of her mouth. "Is this what you do all day when I'm in school?"

"I think Hayden's death is affecting me more than I've acknowledged." Laura smiled nervously. "Are you home for the day?"

"For a few hours." Susannah kicked her shoes onto the mat by the door. "I'm supposed to go hear a speech tonight, on campus."

"It's great to see you so into your schoolwork." Laura tucked the card under a couch cushion.

"I was thinking of missing the speech." Susannah gave her a sheepish glance. "I have tickets for the film festival. Someone gave them to me at the benefit — I think they were meant to be some kind of tip for my services. You want to come with me? That is, if you're not too drunk by then."

"What's the movie?" Laura was stalling; she didn't know how she felt about spending the evening alone with Susannah.

"It's something foreign and subtitled, which is probably why the tickets were given away in the first place. But I asked a couple of classmates, and they say the film's supposed to be excellent."

"Foreign and subtitled sounds perfect," Laura said. Because while the movie was playing, at least she could let her mind wander.

THIRTY
MATTHEW

"**F**uck me!" Matthew slammed his fist into the hood of his ancient Ford Escort. "Rusted piece of crap!"

"You shouldn't talk to your car like that."

He turned to see that know-it-all Clare, helmet in one hand, cigarette in the other. Matthew might have found the tight jeans and leather jacket compelling if they were hugging the curves of someone he could stand to speak with.

"Sorry for the language," he said through gritted teeth.

"Doesn't bother me." Clare took a drag, smiled like she found it delicious, then exhaled. "It's your car that might take offense. Would you do any favors for someone who treated you like that?"

"Don't you have someplace else to smoke?"

"Nope," Clare said. "Want me to take a look?"

"Be my guest." He moved aside to give Clare access to the hood. "Maybe it'll like you."

"I'll start by being nicer to it. Hello, Car." Clare set her helmet on the ground, tossed her fancy studded black jacket over the seat of her bike — what normal student could afford designer leather? — and crushed out her cigarette with a chunky black boot. She was completely unfeminine, and yet — forget about it. Matthew would die before admitting he felt any kind of attraction to her. She glanced inside the hood. "So what's the problem?"

"Are you talking to me or the car?"

"You, dummy. I know cars can't talk."

Could have fooled him. "It's acting like it has the whooping cough."

"You mean smoking and backfiring when you try to start it?" Clare poked her head under the hood and appeared to study the engine. "I know more about motorcycles than cars, but maybe I'll be able to help. The thing's pretty old, right?"

"Right." Forgive him for not driving the latest Bentley like her parents.

"Good. My dad's never owned anything newer than ten years old." She pulled a spark plug out of its socket and blew on it.

So her father was that kind of rich guy. And why did Matthew care? "Does your father collect old cars?"

"Huh? Yeah, I suppose you could say that."

Clare got down on her stomach and looked under the car. He liked the sight — he could at least admit that to himself — but she was back on her feet in a few seconds.

"You're not leaking anything, which is good. I'm gonna try cleaning the spark plugs — they're caked with gunk, which might be the problem right there."

"You mean it might be something simple?" Matthew didn't want to think about the cost of a tow unless he had to.

"Maybe." She looked dubious. "But there's a reason the plugs are so dirty. Have you noticed any small oil leaks recently?"

He couldn't remember seeing any spots on his driveway at home. "No."

Clare returned to the hood, pulled out the remaining spark plugs, and set them gently on the ground. "Do you have a rag? Or more ideally, sandpaper?"

He grabbed an old T-shirt from the hatchback. "Will this work?"

"Thanks." Clare took the shirt and started polishing a plug.

"So did you always want to be a politics professor?"

"Pardon me?" Matthew was caught off guard. "I mean, yes and no. As a child, I wanted to be prime minister. As I grew up, I realized that the academic route would be more practical."

"Why?" Clare blew on the plug, then appraised it.

Because his parents had laughed at his ambitions, making him believe they were out of his reach. "I'm too outspoken to toe any party line. And you can still effect change from the sidelines."

"Is that important to you?" Clare set the first plug down and got to work on the second. "Effecting change? It seems like a constant theme in class."

"It's more than important. It's why we're alive."

"All of us? Because I thought I was here to be loving and kind and leave things as nice as I found them."

"You should work on the loving and kind part," Matthew said under his breath.

"I heard that." Clare blew on the second plug, then set it down and picked up the third. "I'm sorry I pissed you off this morning. I don't know what got into me. I could hear myself talking but I couldn't seem to stop the words from coming out."

"It happens to the best of us." It was time to forgive her.

"So which party would you have joined?" Clare asked. "As prime minister."

"I would have started my own."

"Not too late." Clare went for the fourth and final spark plug. "You're only what? Around forty?"

"Thirty-seven." Did he look forty?

"Your job is the perfect recruiting ground. Let me know when you're signing up new members." She replaced the spark plugs in the engine. "Try starting your car now."

Matthew got into the driver's seat and turned the key. It coughed a bit at first, but the sound got smoother as the engine stayed running. He left the car on and got out to ask Clare if it was safe to drive away.

"Yep. You're good." Clare picked up her helmet and lit another cigarette.

"Listen, I appreciate your help. Are you in a hurry to get home?" Matthew wasn't sure what he was doing.

"Not especially. In fact, if you like, we can find some sandpaper and really give those plugs a scrub."

It would be a wonderful image if not for the sandpaper. "I was thinking more along the lines of a drink," Matthew said. "You've saved me a fortune in repair bills."

"Sounds fun. But listen, I'd help anyone out of a jam. You don't owe me anything."

"Maybe not. But I'm hoping that if I get you drunk enough, you might tell me why you forced your way into my class at the last moment."

"Huh?" She looked at him quickly.

"Come on. You know what I'm talking about."

"No." Clare's eyes widened. "I don't."

"On Tuesday morning, my department head got a call from the Registrar with a firm request to let you into the class. Poli Real World admission is normally by invitation only."

"Seriously?" Her eyes narrowed. "I thought that it looked like an interesting class. I didn't know anything about forcing my way in."

"Well, who do your parents know? The Registrar? The Chancellor? The late mayor?"

"They don't know anyone." She stared at her shoes. "It was late August when I decided to transfer to U of T. My dad's sick. Terminally. I came home from out east to be near him. I guess — maybe — is it possible that someone in Admissions would have taken pity on me?"

"My god. I'm sorry." Matthew felt like an ass. "Of course it's possible. Are we still good for drinks?"

"Sure." Clare met his eye tentatively. "Um, if you want me to drop your class, you know, say the word. I mean, I love the course. But I don't want to mess with your system. I can apply for it next year like anyone else."

"No," Matthew said. "No, I'd love for you to stay on. I just wish those bloody bureaucrats would have told me the truth in the first place."

"Yeah." Clare grinned. "Bloody bureaucrats. Someone ought to change the system."

THIRTY-ONE
JONATHAN

Jonathan liked the way Jessica's hand felt in his. It was small, and soft, and it betrayed a vulnerability that her words and actions did their best to hide. It was also a milestone; it meant she liked him back.

"Do you really think churches should pay property taxes?" Jessica said. "Or is it what you think Dr. Easton's opinion would be?"

It was well past four, but the sun was still strong. It felt like they had all the time in the world between now and the speech on campus they had agreed to attend together.

"Caught me." Jonathan smiled at his reflection in an art store window. "I care more about getting into the mind of an egocentric old man than I do about pursuing an unattainable utopia."

"Don't let Dr. Easton hear you call him old. I get the feeling he's sensitive about his age."

"Probably thinks he's past it," Jonathan said. "Which he kind of is, for sleeping with undergrads. Poor old Diane. You can practically see the venom dripping from her when she looks at him."

"Poor old Diane?" Jessica rolled her eyes. "I'm surprised her major is poli sci and not boring religions and the morons who subscribe to them."

"And yet you think her church shouldn't have to pay property tax?"

"I never said that. I just don't care."

"You might care if you were one of the businesses who pick up the tax slack in this supposed era of divorced church and state." Jonathan felt himself grow heated.

"You, on the other hand, do care." Jessica stepped aside to avoid walking over a grate, pulling Jonathan's hand and arm along for the ride.

"Are you afraid of something?" Jon said, as his arm stretched to its full capacity. She wasn't wearing heels, which was the only reason he could think of for avoiding the sidewalk grate.

"Yeah. I'm afraid of falling in, and landing on a subway track, and getting squished by the next northbound train."

Jonathan laughed. "We're nowhere near the subway line. Anyway, what's with *your* bill?" He poked her lightly in the shoulder once she'd returned to his side. "Can you say *personal vendetta*?"

Jessica frowned. Jonathan liked the way her lips curled down, like a child trying to solve a puzzle. "I know I didn't write my legislation well. But I think the essence is right. My dad would be alive today — working, thriving, happy — if the emergency system was set up to deal with emergencies."

"How do you know he'd be thriving and happy?"

"It's who he was. Why would that have changed?"

"Maybe we all have our end date. Maybe if we live past that, by some weird accident of fate, then our lives after that aren't so great." Jonathan wasn't sure where he was going with this thought line.

"Maybe the accident of fate is what took his life to begin with."

"So the hospital administrators should be thrown in jail as a result?" Jonathan pointed down Baldwin Street, where they were turning.

"Someone should be accountable."

Jonathan steered Jessica around an old fish crate that was

particularly smelly. "Sometimes crappy things happen, and it's no one's fault. The aneurysm already took your dad's life. Don't let it ruin yours, too."

"I know." Jessica's pale blue eyes were beautiful when she allowed her sadness to come to the surface. "I have to get past it. But he was such a loving person. I'm afraid that if I let go of the anger, I'll be letting go of him."

"You won't lose what matters."

"That's what my mom said." In front of one of the shops Jessica stopped to examine a display of cheap sunglasses. "About a week before she died."

Jonathan didn't know what to say. "You want to smoke a joint with me?"

"No," Jessica tried on a pair, vamped briefly for Jon, then replaced the sunglasses on the vendor's table. "Pot makes me paranoid. But smoke if you want. I have no moral objection."

"I wouldn't think so." Jonathan thought the shades had suited her, made her look like a softer, sexier Janis Joplin.

"What's that supposed to mean?"

"Wow. Touchy. It means that you seem like a live-and-let-live kind of person."

"Oh."

Jonathan opened the door to a small café, and held it open for Jessica. "In here. If you want to grab a seat, I'll get the drinks."

Jonathan stood in line, watched as Jessica chose a table in the corner, pulled out her netbook, and booted it up.

"I forgot to ask what kind of milk you like," he said a few minutes later, as he set her latte in front of her. "I went with two percent."

"My favorite percent." Jessica looked up from her computer. "Kensington Hideaway. This place has character. How'd you find it?"

"My mom owns it. We live upstairs." Jonathan took out his own laptop and began setting up.

Jessica leaned back in her armchair. "I would love that life."

"You would?"

Jon didn't know why anyone would trade a perfect life in Rosedale for the stress of not knowing where next month's rent was coming from. But he wasn't going to spill his mother's business woes. And he liked that Jessica at least thought that she wanted his life.

"When I was little," she said, "my favorite game was pretending I was a struggling businessman."

"You played a man?"

Jessica grinned. "Weird, right?"

"Yup. So how do you play struggling businessman? Is it like playing house, but with commerce?"

"I knew you understood me better than most people."

Wow. Did she just say that? Jonathan tried not to show her his heart leaping well past the ceiling.

"It was more like playing store. But there were always stakes. Like, I'd have a lemonade stand outside the house, and I'd pretend I needed a certain number of sales or my family would go hungry."

"That's cute."

Jessica laughed. "Yeah. Cute. Sometimes I'd be out there for, like, ten hours. I always met my quota though. It was so exhilarating, when I'd finally make it."

"Yeah, I bet. You must hate losing so consistently at *Who's Got the Power?*"

"No, it's refreshing. Too bad it won't last."

Poor girl had no idea.

"So you're counting on the home turf advantage?"

Jonathan smirked. "I'm counting on the greater skill advantage. Which disadvantaged country would you like me to be today?"

"I think Liberia."

"Fine." He slurped his hot chocolate. "I can use their lawlessness to screw you up. We'll still be in lots of time to hear Manuel Ruiz speak. The States again for you?"

"Yup. Although I admit I'm kind of fine to miss the speech

tonight. Manuel Ruiz is too smug for my taste."

"He's not my favorite guy either." Jonathan particularly hated the non-smoking bill Ruiz had successfully passed. It had cut his mother's revenue by half, when the law had first come in. "But Dr. Rosenblum wants us to hear him, and I have a lot of respect for her."

Jessica groaned. "I know. I'd feel like a fraud for pretending to have been there."

Jonathan took a forkful of the communal banana cake he'd brought with the drinks. "You want the computers side by side, so you can make sure I'm not cheating?"

"Across from each other is fine. If there was a way to cheat, I would have figured it out by now."

"You got it." Jonathan logged into the game. "Prepare to go down, Killer."

THIRTY-TWO
CLARE

The office smelled musty, like old paper, with a mild coffee overtone. Clare wanted to open the window, to look down upon the concrete quad that was deserted by this time of night, devoid of students bustling by. But she had tried the window, and it was stuck.

She glanced at Matthew's tweed jacket, hung too carefully on the back of his vinyl desk chair. Clare didn't know whether snooping around would be wise or stupid. Matthew had said he was going down the hall to use the washroom, and he had already been gone for what felt like ages.

Still . . . if she didn't search the office now, when would she have the opportunity? Clare took a sip of the wine Matthew had poured for her, then positioned herself in his chair.

She opened the top drawer first. She couldn't see anything special. Pens, small sheets of paper, a few business cards. She rifled through the cards, but found none resembling the SPU card Morton and Kumar had shown her.

The deeper drawer to the right held hanging files. On students? Clare was dying to see what was in there about her. But of course they weren't student files — they were course plans, with handouts and drafts of tests. Clare shut this drawer quickly in case Matthew might see her and think she was planning to cheat.

In the drawer beneath that, the file headings were arranged into chapters. Was Matthew writing a book? Clare had never slept with an author before. Did he even want to sleep with her, or was he being nice because she'd fixed his car? Either way, she was making a good inroad.

Clare thumbed randomly through the titles. *Chapter Twelve: Utopia and Controlled Substances.* Straightforward enough. *Chapter Two: Utopia and Party Politics.* Was there an audience for something that boring? *Chapter Seven: Utopia and Law Enforcement.* This was up Clare's alley. It didn't seem like much of a clue, though, so she replaced this folder with the others.

Final Chapter: Utopia and Death. Why no chapter number for this folder? Did Matthew not know in advance how many chapters would be in his book? Why did death have to be the last one? Or was this something different — unrelated to the book? Clare wanted a closer look. Not now — Matthew would be back any second, and Clare was beginning to realize that only an idiot would search a room under these circumstances.

She returned to her seat by the window. Her heart was thumping furiously. She gulped at her red wine. Pathetic. If she was this nervous upon finding nothing, how would she feel when confronted with a piece of real evidence?

As Clare drained her glass, the door handle turned. He was back.

"What's wrong?" Matthew stared at her. "You look like you've seen a ghost."

"Can we open the window?" Clare was dismayed that her anxiety was so obvious. "I tried, but I couldn't —"

"Of course." Matthew gently brushed past her and struggled with the window until it came unstuck. "Cheap fucking piece of glass. Are you okay?"

"Yeah," Clare said. "The air helps."

"Sorry to be gone so long." Matthew poured Clare some more

wine, and sat beside her on the couch. He took her hand. "You sure you're fine?"

"I am," Clare said, surprised by the warmth she was feeling from his touch. "I'm great. And thanks for dinner. I haven't had a meal like that since I lived at home."

"Is your mom a good cook?"

"No." Clare told the truth. "But she's better than I am. Living on my own, I tend to dine on coffee and Kraft Dinner."

"My mother is a terrible cook." Matthew had a great smile, when it came spontaneously. "When I went away to grad school, the campus cafeteria was a step up."

Clare smiled nervously. She wanted more than just his hand in hers. She hadn't planned on feeling genuine attraction.

"Hey." Matthew squeezed her hand gently.

"Hey." Clare tried to sound casual. She shifted slightly to face him.

"Are you seeing anyone?" He ran his free hand lightly down her arm until it rested on her outer thigh.

"No." Clare squeezed back. She wasn't used to this kind of quiet electricity.

"I don't want to make you uncomfortable."

Clare inhaled deeply. She was uncomfortable in the best possible way.

"Would it be inappropriate if I kissed you?"

The most unromantic words Clare had ever heard. And they turned her on now more than anything Matthew might have said.

She smiled. Squeezed his hand again. Nodded. "You can kiss me."

THIRTY-THREE
LAURA

Laura shrugged into her cardigan as she and Susannah left the Hart House Theatre. She liked that the evenings were getting cooler. It made her think of hot chocolate, and lit fireplaces, and curling up with a good mystery novel.

"I'm sorry," Laura said. "I can barely keep my eyes open. Will you drive home?"

"Hell, yeah. Can we drive with the roof down?"

"You sound like my son. Of course we can have the top down."

"So did you like the movie, despite those nasty subtitles?"

Susannah tossed the car keys up in the air and caught them, grinning. Their fifteen-year age gap felt huge, at the moment. Probably due to the lead in Laura's veins.

"What I saw was great," said Laura. "Unfortunately, I think I slept through half the film."

"Probably the Scotch you were pounding back this afternoon."

"You mean the one ounce?" So maybe it had been two.

Susannah unlocked the car with the remote. "I probably should have driven us here, as well. Hey, is that Brian? With a girl?"

Laura was about to say that she didn't know who Brian was when the young man in question approached them.

"Susannah. Hi."

"Hey, Brian. This is my girlfriend, Laura Pritchard."

Brian came forward to shake Laura's hand. The young woman with him stayed back. "Oh my god. It is such a pleasure to meet you. I'm so sorry about your husband. I mean, your ex-husband. I mean, your late ex-husband. That must have been horrible."

Laura shook the boy's hand. She wished Susannah would remember to introduce her by her maiden name. "Thank you, Brian."

"Wasn't that crazy tonight?" Brian said.

"Wasn't what crazy?"

"At the speech. You know, Manuel Ruiz —"

"Oh, we weren't there," Susannah said. "I know Dr. Rosenblum wanted us to go. But I had tickets to the film festival. Who wants to pass those up for some boring speech I can read about in the paper tomorrow?"

Strange, Laura thought. Susannah normally loved hearing politicians speak. Even those she hated — her vitriol fueled her interest, if anything.

But Laura was being ridiculous. What was suspect about preferring an exclusive film presentation where the actors came out for a Q&A after the show over listening to some pedantic politician?

"Yeah, I'm sure you'll be reading about this one in the paper. And seeing it on the news." Brian seemed about to elaborate when his date tugged gently on his arm.

"Maybe Mrs. Pritchard doesn't want to hear about Manuel Ruiz from us," Brian's date said. "You look exhausted. No offense."

"None taken." Laura was grateful. "And you're right. I am falling asleep on my feet."

THIRTY-FOUR
ANNABEL

Utopia Girl: *Wake up, Annabel.*

Death Reporter: *What do you want? I'm sick.*

Annabel looked at her alarm clock. 12:20. She'd fallen asleep without closing her blinds. From her bed, she could see the St. Lawrence Hall on King Street, past St. James Park, with the cathedral off to the side. The sight of these sturdy landmarks made her feel safe. She left her blinds open so the buildings would continue to protect her.

Utopia Girl: *I want to talk. I'm on a high.*

Death Reporter: *Fantastic. Any particular reason?*

Utopia Girl: *Got rid of another parasite. And on a date to boot. Well, not a "date" date . . . but you can imagine it presented a challenge.*

Did she want to be congratulated for her cleverness? Annabel wandered into the bathroom and stuck her digital thermometer in her mouth. She left it in while she typed her response.

Death Reporter: *Again? Thought you killed someone last night.*

Utopia Girl: *That should stop me tonight because . . . ?*

Death Reporter: *Who was it this time?*

Annabel pulled the thermometer out. A hundred and three

degrees. What the hell was that in Fahrenheit? She tried to do a mental conversion, but her brain wouldn't wrap around the challenge. Then she realized it *was* Fahrenheit. If it were Celsius she would have combusted already.

Utopia Girl: *Manuel Ruiz. The pious motherfucker who wants to make it illegal for pregnant women to drink and smoke? Make that "wanted" to make it illegal.*

Manuel Ruiz. The name was familiar, but Annabel couldn't specifically place the guy. That didn't mean much — her mind couldn't place much of anything at the moment. It suddenly occurred to her that this was the third death in four days. Was that even possible? Maybe she'd missed a week. But no — she checked the date on her BlackBerry — it was still the week of Labor Day, when all this had begun.

Death Reporter: *Why are you working so fast?*

Utopia Girl: *Taking advantage of opportunities. Plus I don't know how long I have.*

Damn. Annabel hoped like hell this wasn't one of those cases where someone had a brain tumor, and started doing horrible things right before they died. That would be her luck — to get a scoop like this and then lose it before anything could come of it.

Death Reporter: *Are you dying?*

Utopia Girl: *Hadn't thought of that. Hope not.*

Annabel had no idea how to interpret that answer.

Death Reporter: *Most serial killers start slow, and even at the end don't build up to the pace you're going. There must be a reason.*

Utopia Girl: *Agree. There must be. And maybe don't call me a serial killer.*

FRIDAY / SEPTEMBER 10

THIRTY-FIVE
CLARE

"Another murder?" Clare said dumbly into her paper coffee cup. Of course another politician was dead. She hadn't found the killer, solved the case, and proven herself a brilliant undercover cop yet. Clare snorted at the memory of her own naïvety. Had it only been three days?

"Ruiz wasn't as famous." Cloutier seemed personally relieved. "He was well known in his circle, obviously. But your average guy on the street couldn't have told you his name."

"Meaning you? I'd heard of him." Clare took the third obituary from Cloutier.

Manuel Ruiz: April 25, 1966–September 9, 2010

We are pleased to announce our third step toward a political utopia for the real world. In the middle of a patronizing speech, Manuel Ruiz dropped dead, facilitated by — you guessed it — that poison that prefers to remain anonymous.

Ruiz thought that we as a public were ill-equipped to live our lives. Each bill he introduced was designed to protect us from ourselves.

He got a law through that banned Rottweilers from the city limits. Nice, right? No more little kids getting bit. What about the breeders who were put out of business overnight? He implemented a city-wide smoking ban. Clean air, fresh lungs for everyone. Cafés and restaurants closed down, and did Manuel think to allocate any portion of their exorbitant property taxes toward helping them stay afloat? Nope.

What was next on Ruiz's agenda? Would motorcycles have become illegal because the Hells Angels control drug trafficking?

You're welcome.

This has been a message from the Society for Political Utopia.

Clare looked up. "It's looking more like the whole group could have done this, right?"

Cloutier grunted into his coffee.

"No? You won't acknowledge that it's possible?"

"Sure, it's possible. Until we have a convicted man in jail, Bigfoot could have come down from his mountain to do these politicians in."

"Meaning you think I'm out to lunch."

"Meaning confirm the identities of the group members, and we might find ourselves closer to the answer."

"Can't we bring in all the people we suspect? Like, one at a time, we can hold them for twenty-four hours. Then if someone dies while they're in custody, bingo, eliminate that person as a suspect. And if someone dies while we're holding each one, then it's either none of them or all of them."

"No." Cloutier smiled. At least he got that Clare was joking, as opposed to just thinking she was stupid.

"Is Susannah Steinberg alibied for any of the murders?" Clare asked.

"Only last night's. By her girlfriend. A night at the movies."

The coffee shop was crowded this morning, and Clare glanced around anxiously. They were nowhere near the university campus, but she worried that she might be recognized.

"Is Laura Pritchard still a suspect?"

"We haven't ruled her out. She brought in that business card, remember."

"Wouldn't that help the case for her innocence?"

"Yes and no. Neither of the other victims seems to have been sent these cards. Mrs. Pritchard could have obtained a card from Ms. Steinberg, if she's in the society like we think she is."

"And what? Tried to frame her girlfriend for her husband's murder? Then killed a couple of other random people, to deflect attention from herself? And *not* had cards delivered to them?"

"It's looking like more of a long shot," Cloutier said. "But if Sasquatch is on the list, the wife who inherits the pensions is too."

Clare drummed her fingers on the laminate table top. "What about the girlfriend of the wife? Susannah's politics are pretty strong."

"The motive may have less to do with politics, and more to do with something personal. As I'm sure you already know, because now you're a political genius, Manuel Ruiz was not a far-left socialist like the others."

"He wasn't a radical right-winger, either." Clare thought there could still be a political connection. "Did last night's event use the same caterers?"

"Nope. The speech wasn't catered. Just a coffee bar set up at the side of the room." Cloutier tasted his date square and shuddered. "You like these things? My wife told me I have to start eating healthy, but that is fucking foul."

"I love them." Clare had finished her own donut, and was starving.

Cloutier shoved the paper bag in her direction. "It's all yours."

Clare broke off a small piece and chewed. "So how did the killer get the poison to Ruiz? Was he drinking a coffee from the venue?"

"He had a glass bottle of cranberry juice. His assistant brought it with him."

Clare swallowed hard. Bits of date square clung to her throat on their way down. "To avoid an outcome like this one?"

"Probably."

"I guess his juice wasn't being guarded the whole time. Any luck finding out what kind of poison?"

Cloutier looked like he was about to tell her, for the millionth time, to focus on her own job, but then something in his face changed, and he humored her. "No word on specifics, but I'll tell you what we know."

"Cool."

"The symptoms, combined with the fact that we're fairly sure it's ingested by swallowing, shortlists anthrax, cyanide, nitroglycerin, and a few others that are less common but easy to come by."

This was all Greek to her, but Clare was thrilled to be put in the loop. "What about antidotes?"

"Excuse me?"

"Doesn't it make sense to stock an emergency kit at all future political events, with antidotes for the most likely poisons?"

"Yeah." Cloutier grinned. "I'll suggest that."

Did he like one of her ideas?

"Is the *Star* still willing to keep all this quiet?" Clare asked.

"Hell yeah. The inspector says Penny Craig is eager like a teenage virgin for that exclusive."

"Really? Those were Morton's words?"

"You know what I mean. There's no problem getting the paper to shut up."

"I guess this rules out Matthew Easton." Clare felt herself filled, unjustifiably, with relief. "I was with him the whole night."

"Yeah?" Cloutier snickered. "How's that going for you?"

"It was fun. It started with drinks, then he took me for a great Italian meal, then we had sex on his desk." Clare grew warm recollecting it.

"That broken car thing worked?"

"Like a charm. I don't think academics are particularly blessed with common sense. Anyway, now that we know Matthew isn't Utopia Girl, am I wasting my time getting close to him?"

"Are you kidding? We think he's their leader. Stay as close as you possibly can."

"Right," Clare said, more than pleased with this directive. "So where did this speech take place?"

"On campus."

"By campus, do you mean . . ."

"University of Toronto. You didn't know the speech was happening?"

"I heard a couple people talking about it." Clare tried to respond to the actual question, not the accusation in his voice. "But I got the impression they were going under duress, for a class that I'm not taking. I had no idea it was on campus."

"I guess you can't be in two places at once. Good work getting close to your professor."

"Oh." Clare felt her heart sink. "I guess — if the speech was on campus — we have to put Matthew Easton back into the equation. And maybe move his position up on the list."

"You weren't with him the whole night?"

"He took a really long washroom break."

"How long?"

"Like, twenty minutes or more."

"What time was this?"

"God, I don't know. Maybe nine or ten."

"Ruiz died at 8:45. Could it have been that early?"

"I guess." Clare tried to remember. "I wouldn't have thought so."

"What was the light like outside?"

"It had just gotten dark when we went into Matthew's office

building."

Clare waited while Cloutier performed the mental calculation.

"The timing works, kid." For once, Cloutier's eyes held more concern than derision. "You sure you want to be doing this?"

"I'm sure." Was he kidding? Things were just getting interesting. "Hey, while he was gone, I searched Matthew's desk drawers."

"You what?" Cloutier looked at Clare blankly.

"Not for too long — I didn't know when he'd be back — but it looks like he's writing a book about utopia. I think it would be great if I can get back in, and figure out what his angle is."

"You're kidding, right." Cloutier set down his coffee and folded his hands on the table.

"Kidding? No. You don't think it would be interesting?"

"Of course it would be interesting. But please tell me you didn't search the man's office when he could have returned at any moment."

"I was careful!" Clare knew Cloutier was right.

"You could have blown your cover in an instant. All to find essentially nothing."

"I'm sorry." Clare stared at Cloutier's hands.

"I don't know what to make of you. You have these moments of brilliance, then you completely negate them with grand gestures of stupidity."

"Brilliance?" Clare looked up at him. "Because I can work on the stupidity. Take more time. Think things through."

"I don't know if you can." Cloutier looked sad. "This is why I wanted someone older, who's already made those mistakes."

THIRTY-SIX
ANNABEL

T he downtown core was mean and gray. Annabel's walk to work, normally her favorite part of the day, loomed like a gloomy chore.

This cold was going to do her in. It was warm out — still technically summer — and here she was bundled up in her warmest fall sweater and scarf. Annabel wasn't one to look for omens — oh, who was she kidding? She was as superstitious as they came. She couldn't help but come to the conclusion that the universe did not want her mingling with Utopia Girl.

But what could she do? She was in it this far. Backing out would only piss the Girl off, make her send her letters to someone else, maybe expose Annabel's involvement and cost her her job in the process. The universe should learn to give its omens at the outset, before a person became so heavily involved in a project.

Her phone beeped inside her purse. Like an addict, Annabel looked around furtively before pulling it out.

Utopia Girl: *You at work yet?*
Death Reporter: *I'm walking there now.*
Utopia Girl: *Late start? Not so admirable.*
Death Reporter: *Shut up.*

Utopia Girl: *Good one. Still sick, I take it.*

Annabel wrapped her scarf more snugly around her neck. Her fever had broken, but she wasn't a hundred percent yet.

Utopia Girl: *You've been missing a lot of work lately.*

Death Reporter: *I missed one afternoon. Big fucking deal. And how do you know?*

Annabel felt herself breathing faster. Who knew she'd been off work? Penny? Matthew? Had Utopia Girl been following her, spying on her? She could be anyone, anywhere. And she could poison a public figure without anyone witnessing a thing.

Utopia Girl: *Relax, Drama Queen. You had your email on auto-reply.*

Annabel let out her breath. Of course she had.

She caught her reflection in the window of a small café. She looked huddled, and fragile, and old. Did other people see her that way? She wouldn't have thought so — not normally. But maybe she projected those things from the inside — maybe that's why no one Annabel knew gave her any kind of credit or respect.

Even Utopia Girl seemed confident that Annabel could be pushed around. Over the fucking Internet. She had to change things, starting now. She had to grab the reins of their virtual relationship, and not relinquish control no matter how hard Utopia Girl resisted.

Death Reporter: *Do you move in the same circles as these politicians?*

Utopia Girl: *I don't stand out at the events.*

Death Reporter: *Are you a fundraiser? A caterer? A wife or daughter? A politician yourself?*

Utopia Girl: *What do you think? LOL, maybe I'm another reporter. Maybe we're friends.*

Death Reporter: *None of my friends are reporters.*

Utopia Girl: *At least you have good judgment on some things. What if I said I was witnessing these crimes, but prefer not to turn the killer in?*

Death Reporter: *I would say that makes you as disturbed as the killer. And an accomplice, too.*

Utopia Girl: *I think the term is "accessory after the fact." Which is maybe what you should worry about being considered. But that's not what I am. I am all killer, all the way.*

Annabel nearly bumped into a man in a middle-grade business suit hurrying along the sidewalk as she typed.

Death Reporter: *Do you work as part of a team?*

Utopia Girl: *Interesting question. I think I'll say yes.*

Death Reporter: *A team, like the society that signs those obits?*

Utopia Girl: *That's the implication.*

Annabel sneezed, and used her scarf to wipe her nose and face. It was kind of disgusting, but the scarf was designer, so she didn't toss it immediately in the garbage like she would likely have done with a cheaper brand.

Death Reporter: *Are you the team member who poisons the victims?*

Utopia Girl: *Wish you'd stop calling them victims. Diminishes their culpability. And no comment.*

Oh, screw it. She wasn't sick anymore — a couple of sniffles was hardly worth coddling herself for. She ripped the scarf from her throat, and stuffed it into a sidewalk trash bin.

Death Reporter: *Fine. Do you plan to stop killing after you've knocked off all culpable parties on your list? Or do you like it? Are you getting a taste for murder?*

Utopia Girl: *No, I don't like killing them. It's what has to be done. Will stop when the mandate is complete.*

Death Reporter: *Then what? A life of normality?*

Utopia Girl: *What the hell's that? LOL. You seriously think I would qualify?*

Death Reporter: *In your mind you might be perfectly normal.*

Utopia Girl: *Shit. I'm not that crazy.*

Death Reporter: *The less crazy you are, the more evil you must be.*

Utopia Girl: *It's all a sliding scale. And who defines morality? Am I evil because I'm trying to save the world? Or because my method doesn't jive with conventional sensibility?*

It was amazing what people could rationalize in order to sleep at night.

Death Reporter: *If your motive was so pure, you could share it with me without all this rigmarole.*

Utopia Girl: *Good word. Rigmarole. Makes you sound older, like sixty-five. Where were we before you got judgmental?*

Death Reporter: *Your future.*

Utopia Girl: *Right. I see my future holding one of two things. If I feel vindicated after the eliminations, then I go on and live a productive life. And hopefully our political climate is dramatically improved. If everyone dies and I still feel like the world is crap, then I'll write one more obituary.*

Death Reporter: *You mean yours?*

Utopia Girl: *Great story, right? I'd be dead and you'd be famous.*

Death Reporter: *And if you get caught?*

Utopia Girl: *Your second best scenario. I'll give you an exclusive from my prison cell.*

Death Reporter: *Why me?*

Utopia Girl: *Your job. Believe it or not, I wanted that first obituary printed.*

Death Reporter: *So why not my boss, the actual obituary editor? I'm only the assistant.*

Utopia Girl: *Sometimes it's about who you know.*

Death Reporter: *Who do I know?*

Annabel was drawing a total blank.

Utopia Girl: *Not going to spoon-feed you.*

THIRTY-SEVEN
LAURA

Laura slid her fingers around behind the seat cushion, but found nothing. She lifted the cushion; still nothing. She raised each of the other two large cushions in turn. After feeling along the rim at the back of the sofa, then peering at the floor underneath, she acknowledged that the SPU card was gone.

"Looking for something?"

Laura turned quickly, and saw Susannah leaning against the banister. She must have just come downstairs.

"I think I dropped my earring."

"Oh." Susannah remained leaning with her arms folded. "Well, good luck."

Laura tried to seem unconcerned as her heart began thumping audibly. At least, it was audible to her. "It may have fallen out somewhere else."

"Which pair is it from?"

"Um. They're gold . . . with . . ."

"Oh, give it up. You're a terrible liar. Is this what you're looking for?" Susannah produced the SPU card from the back pocket of her jeans.

Laura stared. She felt the life drain from her face.

"Where did you find it and what do you think it means?" Susannah spoke calmly. She looked half-amused, but then she sometimes looked that way when she was extremely angry.

"Um. I . . ."

"Good words you have."

"In your blue jacket," Laura said, a moment later, "with the mustard stain. I was taking a load to the cleaners."

Susannah put the card back in her pocket and folded her arms again. "So that's the first part answered. But actually it's the second question that has me more curious. What could you possibly think this card might mean, that you would thrust it under the couch cushion as soon as I walked in the door?"

Laura didn't know what the right answer was — nor what the truth was, when it came to that. Did she think Susannah was the killer? She had no idea.

"I alibied you for last night," Laura said finally. "In case anyone asks. The police phoned when you were in the shower. They wanted to know what both of us were doing when Manuel Ruiz died. I told them we were at the movies. I didn't say I'd fallen asleep."

"Oh, that's rich." Susannah uncrossed her arms and moved them to her hips. "So what you really think happened is you fell asleep, I snuck out of the theater to kill Manuel, then crept back in time to wake you for the credits."

"I . . ." Laura was horribly confused.

"I suppose I probably drugged you, to make sure you didn't wake up and notice I was gone. Nothing to do with the Scotch you were pounding back in the afternoon, when one glass of wine is normally enough to do you in."

"I'm sorry," Laura said. "But when I found this card . . ."

"When you found this card what? I don't understand the significance."

"I found another one," Laura said. "It was identical. Only it was in one of Hayden's suit pockets and it had the words *Your death will be your greatest public service* typed onto the back. Oh,

Susie!" Laura looked at her girlfriend and was stricken with remorse. "You don't think the killer gave you a card, too? Your life could be in danger."

Susannah rolled her dark brown eyes. "I'm not the next victim. Even if I were famous or important enough, there's a simple explanation. I'm in a club. This is our calling card. The cops showed us one like you described, with the same message on the back, but it was found at Libby Leighton's house. I guess all the dead politicians are receiving them."

Laura was still having trouble finding words.

"So that we're straight, are you trying to say that when you found this card in my pocket you thought I was the killer?"

"No! I didn't *think* you were."

"You were just afraid I might be." Susannah brushed past Laura, and grabbed her keys from the hall counter. "I'll be back this afternoon. If somebody dies while I'm at school, tell the cops you saw me cackling over the body as I gently laid my calling card beside it."

THIRTY-EIGHT
CLARE

"Thank god I found you." Clare rushed up to Matthew as he walked through a grassy quad in the middle of campus. She touched him lightly on the arm, then pulled away. "Sorry. Forgot we're in public."

Matthew cracked a smile. "They can't fire me for letting a student touch my arm."

"Good to know." Clare stepped into pace with him. "I also don't want you to think I'm placing too much importance on one night of fun."

Matthew frowned. "What if that one night had importance to me?"

"Then that's cool." Clare was strangely moved, before she reminded herself not to be. "But that's not what I'm here to ask you about."

"Enlighten me, then." Matthew lifted his eyebrows.

Clare inhaled deeply. "I have a seriously outrageous favor I need to ask you."

"Outrageous can work. What do you need?"

"Is there any way I could crash out in your office for a couple hours? I have a wicked headache — I think it's a migraine coming on — and I don't want to go home and miss my class this after-noon."

"Of course you can use my office. I'm heading there now, then I'm off to teach my introductory class. I'll grab some notes, and the room's all yours for the rest of the morning."

"Thank you." Clare kept pace with Matthew as he led the way out of the quad and onto the busy St. George Street. "I promise I won't make this a habit."

"Getting a migraine?" He stopped walking to analyze traffic, then began to cross the street.

"No." Clare followed. "Taking advantage of your — of our — you know."

"Ah." Matthew's tone was light. "You think I'm only being decent to you because of that number you did on my cock last night."

"No — I —"

They climbed the steps to Sidney Smith Hall.

"You must be sick." Matthew held the door open for her. "I don't get the impression that you're often at a loss for words."

"I'm in a lot of pain." Clare winced.

They rode the elevator to the poli sci floor. In the hall outside his office, Matthew introduced Clare to a gray-haired woman who was walking by.

"Shirley, this is Clare. She's one of my students. I'm letting her sleep off a headache in my office for the next couple of hours. Clare, this is Dr. Rosenblum."

Shirley nodded at Clare. "Pleased to meet you. Clare Simpson, by any chance?"

"That's right." Clare wasn't sure she liked having her cover name on the tip of the department head's tongue. "Um, how did you . . . ?"

"I received the call from the Registrar on the first day of school. Asking if there wasn't one more spot in Dr. Easton's cel-ebrated class."

"Oh. Well, um. Thank you. For whatever strings you pulled. I love the class."

"As long as that's all you fall in love with." Shirley glanced pointedly at Matthew.

"Shirley, please!" Matthew's voice rose in pitch. "The girl has a headache. I'm not going to be in the room with her."

Shirley gave them both a half-smile. "Fine. If you need anything while Dr. Easton's out — you know, an aspirin, or answers to any questions you might have — my office is down the hall."

"Thanks." Clare squinted, then shielded her eyes from the bright overhead light. "I just took two Advil. I'm sure a dark room and some quiet will do the rest."

True to his word, Matthew spent less than five minutes in the office before leaving Clare on the sofa with the lights out. She waited another ten minutes in case he returned, then she got up and went to the filing cabinet she'd been dying to search since the previous night.

She didn't turn the light on. Dr. Rosenblum had made a point of saying she'd be around, and there was more than enough daylight coming through the dirty window.

Clare sat at Matthew's desk, and opened the top drawer. She flipped through the business cards one more time. Like the previous evening, she found no match for the SPU card. But one did jump out: Elly Shore, from Elly's Epicure.

Clare was almost positive this was the firm that had catered the first two events, where Hayden Pritchard and Libby Leighton had died. But why would Matthew have the card? She wrote down the phone number and stuck it in the pocket of her jeans.

She pulled out the folder marked *Final Chapter: Utopia and Death*. Clare had never written a book before, but it seemed strange to her, in this age of computers, to have chapters arranged in such a primitive fashion. Inside the folder were a bunch of newspaper and magazine clippings, with dates and publication names written carefully in pen. There were several articles about euthanasia, a few on abortion, and one philosophical discussion about the morality of murder. She scanned the bylines, but none were Matthew's own.

She skimmed the articles for content. The article about murder made no sense — some ethics professor jerking himself off in a lame attempt to sound important. The rest were more interesting to Clare: the bombing of an abortion clinic, the subsequent fire set at the pro-life headquarters, the man who was sentenced to ten years in jail for the mercy killing of his daughter. Nothing about Elise Marchand, and Clare wondered if she should take its absence as a clue.

But she was reaching. None of this necessarily reflected Matthew's own views, which were what Clare had been hoping to get at. She replaced the articles and the folder, and returned to the couch to gather her thoughts.

Maybe she'd been looking for the wrong sort of information. If there was a society, then Matthew was probably its leader. Brian Haas and Inspector Morton both thought so independently, and Clare agreed intuitively with their reasoning. If there was a society, then there also must be some kind of paperwork. Minutes of the meetings, proposed schemes, a list of members. This paperwork was probably with Matthew, as opposed to with one of the members, and Clare guessed it would be here, rather than at his house. At home he had a roommate whom he'd mentioned. His office was his lair.

Matthew hadn't seemed at all put out when Clare asked to crash in his office, which probably meant that the society paperwork was well hidden, locked away, or both. But where? Clare had been through all of his drawers, and there was nothing that required a key.

Would he have the society stuff in his briefcase? He did guard the thing rather closely, and Clare had watched him use a combination to open it. Still, four years of society activity probably meant that there was more paperwork than anyone would want to constantly carry around. Clare was sticking with her original guess: there was something tangible here in this room.

She checked her phone. Matthew had been gone for half an

hour. His class was two hours long; she had plenty of time.

There was a vent on the wall. Clare studied it, but the screws were rusted over, and she didn't think anyone had opened it in recent history. She looked under the couch: nothing. Clare pounded her fist against the side of her head. It couldn't be this difficult.

Clare's phone rang. It was still in her hand, and it startled her.

"Susannah's in the club."

"Hello to you," she told Cloutier.

"Can you talk?"

"No." She glanced at the door. "I'm lying down. I have a headache."

"You're taking the day off for a bloody headache." Cloutier's voice sounded like it could explode right through Clare's tiny phone. "You seemed fucking fine to me this morning."

"I'm in Dr. Easton's office. He let me use his couch."

Cloutier's tone changed. "No shit? You alone in there, or you in for an afternoon romp?"

"Alone. But I really can't talk. I have to get some sleep before my next class."

"Fine. Don't say anything. But listen: Susannah's in the secret society."

"Thanks for understanding. I'll call you after school."

"She came in half an hour ago. To her local station."

Clare was silent.

"Listen, she came in voluntarily, allegedly to tell us all she knew. Gave us a list of all the club members dating back to the origin of the society. But Laura Pritchard, or Sutton, or whatever, had already put two and two together. She knew Susannah was in the club. Susannah came in about an hour before we got a phone call from Mrs. Pritchard."

Did Laura Pritchard suspect her girlfriend of murder? Or was it the other way around?

"Mrs. Pritchard was careful not to accuse Steinberg of anything, but the inspector thinks she's worried. Anyway, I get it;

you can't talk now. Call me as soon as you can. I have a list of names."

"Okay."

"And search that room like crazy. The professor is on the list." Cloutier hung up.

Of course Matthew's name was on the list. But why did Morton and Kumar have to find out before Clare made the discovery? Clare had to find something while she was in here. If this case was cracked and it had nothing to do with her, it would be back to the uniform, the break and enter calls, the paperwork, the excruciating routine of it all, for years and years to come. If she could even stand it.

Clare put her phone away and sat on the couch. *Where?* Where in this room would Matthew think was the perfect spot for his perfect secret?

She got up again and studied the vent. In her favorite TV show, the vent was where the killer hid his trophies. She poked at the screws keeping the grate in place. The rust felt real. She pulled her Swiss Army knife from her knapsack, and used one of the blades as a screwdriver. She glanced at the door, but glancing wasn't going to help her if Matthew or Shirley walked in and wanted to know what she was doing.

Clare worked fast. Though the screws were difficult, especially with the wrong tool, she got the grate off the vent and put her hand inside, feeling around the ledges beside the opening. Nothing. She got a small flashlight from her bag, and shone it inside the vent. Nothing in any direction. She refastened the cover — hopefully making it look as though no one had touched it — and sat down again on the couch.

Motherfucker. She could picture Matthew grinning at the futility of her efforts. Like a child with a magic act, he would be thrilled that someone searching for his treasure could be so close and yet so far.

And then it was so obvious. Child — magic trick — presto.

Clare checked the time, and ascertained that she had a

conservative forty-five minutes before Matthew's return. She went to Matthew's desk, and looked and felt around until she found the hidden drawer.

The drawer wasn't even that well hidden. It opened from the back of the desk, which was the side facing out. It would please Matthew, Clare guessed, to know that a student or colleague sitting opposite him — like Clare herself, the previous night — would be staring right at his secret, without knowing what it was.

Of course there was a trick to opening it. A lock (easily picked) under the belly of the desk released a latch that allowed the trick drawer to slide open.

Clare could happily have sat there triumphantly for her remaining minutes of safety. But ambition brought her back to the moment, and she pulled the papers out carefully, one by one, and committed as much as she could to memory.

THIRTY-NINE
JONATHAN

"Why don't you want a game?" He was bugging her, he knew, but Jonathan was restless. They were doing homework in the kitchen of his mom's café. Technically Jonathan was the on-duty cook, but this time of the afternoon, most people ordered from the prepared snacks and sandwiches out front.

Jessica barely glanced up from her chemistry text. "To be honest, I'm freaked out by all these murders."

"To be honest."

"Right."

"Trust me."

"Okay."

"You know that I'm a religious man."

"No, you're not. What are you talking about?"

"Things people say when they're lying."

Jessica closed her text. "So what am I lying about?"

"You're not distracted by these murders. Why would you care?"

Jessica was quiet. "Of course I care."

"You really want a game. But you're petrified that you can't win. Against me — some slacker who doesn't understand organic chemistry."

"Jonathan, what are you talking about?" Jessica stuck her book in her bag and sat facing him. "Did you smoke one of your funny cigarettes?"

"No!" Jonathan wasn't sure why he bothered with indignation; her question wasn't unreasonable. "Hey, why don't we get away this weekend? Skip out on work and go to Niagara Falls."

"What's in Niagara Falls?" She was still assessing him like he had two heads, but at least she was smiling now.

He wanted to get her drunk and marry her, but of course he couldn't tell her that. "Some grubby bars, some tacky wax museums, those scary haunted houses . . ."

"It sounds like fun, in a creepy kind of way. But how about next weekend? I don't want to miss work tomorrow night."

Missing work was exactly what Jonathan wanted to do. "Next weekend's cool." He put on an oversized smile. "So come on. How about a game?"

"Oh, fine. I'm obviously not destined to get any studying done."

Jonathan ran upstairs to get his laptop, and Jessica pulled her netbook from her shoulder bag.

"Elly's going to kill me," Jessica said when he returned. "I just remembered I have that dinner with my family tomorrow, and I'm pretty sure everyone I could call as a replacement waiter is already working."

"Call in sick."

"It's the same dinner I was supposed to be working. I'd like to keep my job if at all possible."

"Why? You don't need the money."

"What makes you say that?"

"You're, like, loaded."

Jessica frowned. "My grandparents are loaded. I'm not."

"Same thing."

"No, it isn't. They'd give me anything I asked for — my brother feels no qualms about sponging off them indefinitely. But

I'd way rather make my own money."

"What about Brian, for your shift tomorrow?" Jon pulled out a stool and set up his computer on a giant wooden baking table.

"Does it matter that he's not a society member?" Jessica was leaning lazily into a large bag of flour.

"Not to Elly." Jonathan opened the software for *Who's Got the Power?*

"I think your mom's cool," Jessica said. "Running this café, working hard and loving it. What does your dad do?"

Jonathan shrugged. "You want the real story, or one of the ones I made up for myself when I was a kid?" He made his opening move as Israel, which was to set up an army training camp in the Sudan.

"You did that too?" Jessica, as USA, countered by confirming South Africa as an ally. "After my parents died, I used to invent all kinds of crazy fantasies that meant they were still alive. Somewhere else. Waiting for the magic password or whatever to be allowed back into our lives."

"Like what?" Jonathan's hands froze on his keyboard, and he looked at her.

"My dad loved to play the piano, so I'd sit at the piano in my grandparents' house — the same one he learned to play on as a kid. His sheet music was still in the bench, with pencil markings all over it. I told myself that if I played his old lessons in order, from his beginner books to the classical pieces he played as an adult, he would walk through the door and explain that there had been this huge mistake, that he wasn't really dead."

Jonathan smiled sadly. "And when that didn't happen, were you crushed?"

Jessica shook her head. "I started again from the beginning. I told myself that I must have gotten the order wrong, or missed one note that made the whole thing not work. Like some magic spell that required perfection. I tried again, and again, and again, and — oh my god, you're going to think this is stupid."

"You still do it sometimes?"

Jessica nodded. "It's your move."

"I still do, too." Jonathan patented a line of Kosher food, and organized international distribution. "Only in my case, it genuinely is stupid, because my dad left by choice. He's probably alive somewhere and thriving, with a family he actually cares about."

"Is that your worst-case scenario?" Jessica made a broad move to the north, effectively commandeering the armies of Namibia, Botswana, Zimbabwe, and Mozambique. It was a good start. If Jon didn't watch out, she might take this game.

"Of course. Much better he's dead in a ditch, or captured by terrorists, or basically anything that means he'd be here if he could." Jon sent a group of intelligence officers down to Jessica's territory to garner as many mercenary soldiers as he could. "But my favorite scenario — the one I can't give up on, though I'm way too old and should put it the fuck out of my head — is of my dad in this old house, painting the walls, fixing things up, and after years of struggling to come to terms with what he did to us, he wants my mom and me to live in it with him."

Jessica looked at him for a long time, twirling a strand of hair around her finger. "I have no idea what move to make next."

"So take your time." Jon looked at her, gorgeous even lounging in the flour. "I could stare at you all night, and not get bored."

FORTY
MATTHEW

Matthew walked through the hollow metal steel doors and heard the guard lock them shut behind him. He could see why prisons seldom succeeded in rehabilitating their inmates. The décor was depressing, and the hallway held the distinct aroma of urine.

He was led to the room where he would be allowed a half-hour meeting with Elise. It smelled, not displeasingly, of curry. Matthew wondered if an earlier visitor had brought a family member a meal, or if the prison cafeteria planned to serve Indian food for supper. Luckily for him, the question was academic.

Elise was pale. Her light brown hair, once vibrant, hung dank and lifeless past her shoulders. She'd put on weight around her middle and in her face, though her upper body remained thin. Gone was the springy step of the optimistic undergrad; it had been replaced by an apathetic shuffle.

"Look who finally came." Elise lifted her eyebrows in Matthew's direction, and took a seat on the other side of the metal table.

"I brought you these." Matthew reached into his briefcase and pulled out a small gift box, the contents of which had cost him almost fifty dollars.

"Are those . . . ?" Elise's eyes lit up involuntarily.

"William Ashley champagne truffles," Matthew said.

Her eyes clouded over and went dull again. "You think I can be bought."

Matthew set the box on the table in front of her. He'd had to unwrap it to let the guard on reception take a look inside, and he'd re-wrapped the box crudely, as well as he could in the awkward space of the entry hall. "All I want from you is conversation."

"And to remind me of the life I can't have back. Thanks. I'll be sure to call you next time I'm beginning to come to terms with my surroundings."

Matthew stared at her with pity. How could anyone come to terms with these surroundings?

"It's not as bad here as you think. There are no men, which can be pleasant."

"I'm sorry, Elise." Reluctantly, Matthew pushed back his chair and picked up his briefcase. "I did the wrong thing four years ago, and I guess I'm doing the wrong thing now."

"Oh, stop feeling sorry for yourself and sit down." Elise challenged him with her eyes.

"So you *are* glad to see me?"

"I'm not sure. On the one hand, you're a visitor. This beats lying on my bunk writing letters I'm never going to send. On the other hand, where the fuck have you been for four years?"

"Did you not get my letters?"

"Both of them? Yeah, thanks. You didn't come to my trial."

"I know," Matthew said. "I was a coward. I want to change that."

"You want to rewrite history?"

"I have a student who may be in trouble. The same kind of trouble you were in. Only this time it might be worse."

"How could it be worse?"

"There's no gray area morally," Matthew told her. "These victims don't want to die."

"Are you helping with the crime?"

"I don't think so."

"Are you sleeping with the student?"

"I sure hope not."

"Do you even know which student you're talking about?"

"No."

"So how is it the same?"

Matthew told Elise about the society card found in Libby Leighton's personal effects. "I'm right in assuming you're not involved?"

"From inside these hallowed walls?" Elise gestured at the concrete and steel around her. "I'm not a fucking magician, am I?"

"I used to think you were."

"You and your innuendo." Elise snorted.

Matthew smiled sadly, tried to remember when and how he had once found Elise attractive. Would anyone find her that way again? Maybe Bubba at the prison mixer.

"So how can I find this person? What should I be looking for?" Matthew asked.

"Anger."

Elise began to tear the wrapping paper from the expensive little box. She'd always enjoyed this step. Matthew was glad he'd taken the time to wrap it up again.

"But you weren't demonstrably angry," Matthew said. "Not until all of this."

"I was an idealist. This person is nuts."

"Do you regret killing those patients?" He had never asked her this before.

"That's so complex." Elise finished removing the gift wrap and sat staring at the chocolates. "Yes? No? Morally, I think what I did was fine." She opened the chocolates and took a small bite from one. She didn't offer one to Matthew, and he didn't ask. "I'm not eaten up with guilt, which is why I'll never be eligible for parole."

"You could lie to the parole board."

"And have done all that for nothing? For a grassroots underground leader, you kind of really don't get it."

Elise popped the rest of the truffle into her mouth, and glared silently at Matthew as she let it dissolve.

"Will you explain 'it' to me, then?"

"I can't. Our time is up."

"We still have twenty minutes." Matthew glanced at the clock on the wall.

"I mean *your* time is up. I've given you enough of me today."

"Can I come back?" Matthew didn't understand why she suddenly wanted to be rid of him.

"If you bring chocolates."

Matthew was worried. "Um, I can't afford to always . . . you know . . ."

"Relax. I was joking. But maybe you need to reassess how deep that remorse is."

"You can't put a price tag on guilt," Matthew said. "Which is why I won't try."

"Oh, Matthew." Elise threw back her head in mocking laughter. "One thing I don't miss about you is how fucking cheap you are."

Elise put her hand up for the guard, and Matthew watched her shuffle away.

On the drive home from Kingston, he played the CD Elise had made for him, back in the early days of their relationship. The Beatles' "Revolution" was Track One. He tried to sing along, but he ended up with tears falling violently from his eyes. He had to turn the music off so he could see the road.

He'd screwed up so badly. He had led Elise, encouraged her in all her crazed passion, then dropped her when it had mattered most. Pretended not to know her. Dissociated for the sake of his career. Who the hell had he become?

When he got back to the city, though it was Friday evening and no one was around, Matthew decided to stop by his office. He let himself in, and opened the secret drawer where he kept the SPU paperwork. But something was wrong. It was the smallest of details — the box of society cards he kept on top of the papers was only slightly askew — but someone had been in this drawer. Had Shirley — the only other person in the department with a key to Matthew's office — been poking around for information? Or had Clare — crafty little whore — not had a headache at all?

FORTY-ONE
CLARE

Clare tossed her cigarette onto the sidewalk in front of the donut shop, and didn't bother to squish it out with her boot. Let it burn. Let the wind pick it up and drop it burning into a nearby tree, and let a fire devastate the whole damn neighborhood.

She watched Cloutier get into his lame old Hyundai and drive away. Who the fuck did he think he was? Clare had gone in hard, come out with some serious information, and Pete fucking Cloutier could only shrug his big dumb shoulders and ask if she'd found out anything he hadn't already learned that afternoon from Susannah Steinberg's statement.

She'd given him a list of society members, past and present. Yeah, Susannah had done the same, but what was her reason for that? Wasn't it at least mildly reassuring that Clare had confirmed the list more conclusively?

She'd figured out — she was fairly sure — where the next meeting was going to be held. Two days from now. Cloutier said two days was the equivalent of two years in investigation terms — did Clare plan to sit around and do nothing until then, with a killer on the loose? Yeah, and she planned to start sucking her thumb again, too.

And she'd figured out why Matthew didn't have any clippings of Elise's story in his "Utopia and Death" file — he must have had everything ever written about her locked away in that secret drawer. Cloutier said he'd make a note of this, but he didn't see it as relevant to the current case.

She started her bike. When she was sent back to uniform — which was inevitable; this mission was doomed — she wasn't going to smile and be okay. She would tell Cloutier exactly what she thought of him, which was that he was a sleazy unfair fuck-face who wouldn't survive a day undercover himself. Then she would quit. She would have to — it would be a million years before she was given another undercover assignment, and Clare could not endure another sob story about ugly stolen jewelry without screaming from boredom.

She raced along Bloor Street, weaving her motorbike in and out of traffic so that she didn't have to slow down. She hadn't had too much to drink, but she intended to. It was Friday night, and she had no plans except to get hammered out of her brains.

Clare parked her bike at home, but didn't bother going inside her apartment to freshen up. She either looked fine or she didn't. Her jeans were tight and that was all the men around here noticed.

She lit a smoke, and walked the half block to the Lamb to the Slaughter.

"Hey," Sandy greeted her. "Why do you look like you want to kill someone?"

"I'm pissed off at one of my professors." Clare figured this was close enough to the truth. "I decided to get drunk instead of finishing his damn assignment."

"You're in school? I thought you were a cop. Or a mechanic."

"I was." Clare didn't clarify which one. "But I sucked at it, apparently. I quit and went back to school."

"Good move. You want a Bud?"

"And a Jack." Clare set her helmet on a bar stool, and sat on the one beside it.

"Seriously?" Sandy eyed her.

"I'm pretty fucking angry."

"Man. Did your professor try to molest you or something?"

"No such compliment." Clare snorted. "He treats me like I know nothing about anything."

"So you want to prove him right." Sandy gave Clare the beer and started drying a tumbler for the Jack. "You want ice in this? Maybe some Coke?"

"No."

Sandy poured a little more than an ounce, and set the Jack Daniels beside the beer. "Hey, you know that guy you took home the other night?"

"Kevin."

"Right. He was in here last night asking for you."

"He was?" Clare wondered why he wouldn't have just called her.

"I didn't give him your number. Obviously. Because I don't have it. But he left his for you. I also told him you're a regular. I hope that's okay."

"It's fine."

Clare tasted her Jack. Strong, but the burning sensation felt good. She had another, larger sip, and screwed up her face as it went down.

Sandy opened the drawer beside the till. "I'm sure his number's in here somewhere."

Clare got up and went to the jukebox. About twelve Elvis songs were lined up. She put in a toonie and added some Bon Jovi, Britney Spears, and Bonnie Raitt — the jukebox was alphabetical by first name, and she was too lazy to move past the Bs. She returned to her seat right as Sandy was pulling a piece of paper from the drawer.

"Victory," Sandy said. "Here ya go. Your lucky night."

Clare frowned. "I'm not going to call him."

Sandy's face fell. "I thought you said you liked him."

"I do," Clare said. "But he lost my number. How important

could I be to him?"

"Not 'The Rules.'" Sandy poured herself a small glass of draft and leaned on the bar opposite Clare. "You're a free-wheeling biker chick. 'The Rules' are for those manicured little *Cosmo* girls with nothing interesting to say. Another Bud?"

Clare looked at her empty. "Thanks."

Sandy set Clare's second beer in front of her. "Come on. The guy's adorable. Why won't you call him?"

"Cute, isn't he? We went on a date the other night." Clare sipped her Jack Daniel's again. She decided this time that she hated the taste, so she downed it. "Do a shot with me."

Sandy lined up two more Jacks, this time in shot glasses. "You realize that you're not hurting your professor by getting drunk tonight."

"I get that. What are you, someone's mom?"

"I have a six-year-old. Want to see a picture?"

"I'd love to," Clare said.

"Another day." Sandy handed Clare her shot. "When you're less angry. Cheers."

They drank.

"So what do you think about that dead mayor?" Clare started to work on her Bud label.

"And the rest. There's three of them dead now in under a week." Sandy moved down the bar to set new beers in front of the two men at the end. She touched the computer screen a few times, and returned to Clare. "It would never happen in the States. Their politicians have too much security. You think Toronto cops will amp up security now?"

"Probably not. They're so fucking stupid."

"Wow. You hate everyone."

"I don't hate you."

"That's because I'm your lifeline to liquor. As soon as last call hits — bang! — you'll hate me, too."

Clare grinned. "Let's do another shot."

"At least you're smiling. Which is good, because here comes

Kevin."

"Where?" Clare spun around.

When Kevin's eyes met hers, they lit up unabashedly. It would have been sweet, had Clare been in a better mood and remotely glad to see him.

"Hey! I was in here last night. I lost your number, or I would have called."

"It's only been two days."

"Yeah, but we had a great time." Kevin moved Clare's helmet to sit on the stool beside her. "We did, right?"

Clare found a smile that she knew came out as phony. "We did. It's just . . . I don't know if I can do a serious relationship right now."

"Who said anything about serious?" Kevin ordered a Bud for himself.

"Oh my god. One day you want to take a long walk through the city where we spill our souls to each other, and two days later you only want a casual hook-up? I can't fucking read you."

"Relax." Kevin was laughing. What was so damn funny? "We can take it as fast or as slow as you want. I like you that much. You want me to fuck off and call you in a few weeks?"

"Yeah? That sounds perfect." Shit. Why didn't her speech filter work like a normal person's? "I'm kidding. Of course you can stay."

"Great." He shrugged his coat off, and slipped it over the back of his stool. "So how have you been since yesterday morning?"

"Actually." Clare drained her second beer. "I'm not having the greatest day."

"I never would have guessed." Did he plan to stop smirking soon? Ever? "Are you angry at someone in particular, or is the world just not going your way?"

Clare ordered another beer from Sandy. "I go back and forth. Sometimes I think it's the world, and sometimes I think it's this asshole Cloutier."

"Cloutier? Is he your French mystery lover?"

"No." Why was she talking? Clare hoped she didn't put the

whole investigation in jeopardy. "He's my anything-but-mystery hater. He's my boss, and he treats me like I'm four years old and stupid."

"I thought you were pissed at your professor." Sandy showed up with Clare's third beer.

"Yeah." Clare had to shut up. Angry and drunk didn't work so well with undercover. "It's all kind of intertwined and complicated." She turned to Kevin. "So tell me about *your* day. Do you have any weird and wild electrician stories?"

FORTY-TWO
ANNABEL

Annabel flipped her cell phone shut and wondered why she bothered. She closed her umbrella — was there a graceful way to do this, without water flying everywhere? — and got onto the streetcar. She would show up unannounced; she had no choice.

Annabel found a seat near the back with as few people around her as possible. It was nine o'clock at night, and though the car was half-empty, it still felt overcrowded. She hated public transit. She lived and worked downtown, and could walk to anywhere worth going. If she left the downtown core, it was usually with Matthew or Katherine, both of whom had cars. At worst she'd take a cab.

But today she was feeling crunched for cash — a notice slipped under her door had informed her that her condo fees would virtually double the following month — so she figured she'd better save twenty bucks everywhere she could.

The man behind her coughed. It was loud, phlegmy, and actually more like a hork. Annabel turned and glared at him, but he seemed oblivious to her scorn. Fuming, she stood up and moved to the center of the streetcar, where she could stand with her back to the window and observe anyone who tried to get too close.

By the time she got off the streetcar in the Beaches, Annabel was shaking. She would not be at all surprised if people who commuted by public transit suffered from earlier deaths, or at least a high rate of anxiety. As she began to walk down Matthew's street, alone and uninvited, she wondered if she was making a huge mistake.

At least the rain had stopped. She tried phoning again. She could see Matthew's house. By showing up unannounced, she would be breaking one of the cardinal rules of a non-exclusive relationship. But while she didn't want to lose him, she also feared for his safety.

No response. She put her phone back into her purse, and strode purposefully down the sleepy residential street.

Was she being followed? She glanced behind her but didn't see anyone in the half block between herself and Queen Street, where she'd gotten off the streetcar. She was probably just feeling jumpy. She'd be at Matthew's place soon. He might not be glad to see her, but he wouldn't turn her away.

Would he? Annabel didn't know if she could handle the rejection if Matthew refused to let her inside his house. She would definitely be taking a cab home — that had been her first and last streetcar ride of the century. Anyway, if he turned her away it was his problem. Annabel was coming over to do him a favor, not to be some clingy girlfriend who didn't get the point. She could live with not sharing information with the cops. But if Matthew was involved — if Utopia Girl was one of his students — Annabel couldn't justify keeping him in the dark.

She'd arrived at his house. Annabel took a deep breath, then ran up the stairs and rang the doorbell before she could change her mind.

"Ethan!" She hadn't counted on Matthew's roommate answering the door.

"Annabel!" He seemed equally surprised. "Does Matthew know you're coming?"

"I couldn't reach him. But it's important."

"I'll go . . . see if he's . . . awake. One sec." Ethan moved to close the door.

"Um . . ." Annabel didn't want to admit that she was too afraid of an imaginary killer to be left alone on the porch.

"Oops." Ethan opened the door and gestured for Annabel to enter. "Sorry. Don't know what I was thinking. Of course, come in."

"Thanks." Annabel waited in the front hall while Ethan ran upstairs and spoke with Matthew in a low voice.

A few minutes later, both men came downstairs together. Matthew wasn't tucking in his shirt, which was a good sign. He rushed over and gave Annabel a hug.

"Come in. I'm sorry my boorish roommate has never heard of hospitality. It's great to see you. Would you like a drink?"

"Yeah." Annabel relaxed in the warmth of his arms. "And then we need to talk. I think — Matthew, I'm sorry for coming over unannounced. I've been trying to call but — I'm worried that you're in some kind of danger."

"Danger?" He smiled like this was an amusing and faraway concept. For the first time, it occurred to Annabel that Matthew might *be* Utopia Girl. The connections were certainly all over the place.

But she had to press forward. "I've been receiving these letters."

FORTY-THREE
LAURA

Laura thrashed and twisted until her sheets were a mess at the end of her bed. She looked at the clock. 4:15. She had to chair a Brighter Day meeting about its inner city mentorship program in six hours. She'd be useless without sleep, but what was the point of lying there? Susannah hadn't come home since she'd left for school that morning, and Laura was flip-flopping wildly between guilt (for suspecting her) and terror (that Susannah might be a murderer).

She put on her Burberry-lined slippers and padded downstairs. She made coffee. She turned on the news. There was something comforting about wars raging in faraway places. A suicide bomber blows up a schoolhouse in Israel, and Annie the Anchorwoman still has perfect hair and makeup, and helpful answers to the difficult questions that must be forming in viewers' minds.

No local politicians seemed to have died so far that night, which was good. And here was the front door opening now.

Susannah crashed into the hallway and stumbled into the staircase.

"Are you drunk?" Laura had seen Susannah tipsy two or three times, stoned once, and drunk exactly never.

"Yup." Susannah sat on the stairs and faced her. "Drank them out of Jim Beam at Jake's. That's when I switched to cc."

Laura winced in sympathy, anticipating the pain Susie would be in when this wore off.

"The bars close at two. Where have you been the past three hours?"

"Walking. I'm probably going to break up with you."

"Let's get you to bed first. You can break up with me in the morning."

"It's already morning."

"I'll get some ibuprofen."

"On second thought, I think I'll break up with you now. Thanks for the offer, but I'll get my own ibuprofen. I'm not sure I can trust you not to poison me."

Laura wasn't sure whether she wanted to laugh or cry.

"And I'll be sleeping in the spare room tonight. So don't think you can convince me with any cunning cunnilingus."

Sex was the farthest thing from Laura's mind. She'd never understood how some people could enjoy the mixture of intimacy and anger. Or guilt. Or fear. Or any negative emotion, for that matter.

"The spare bed isn't made up. Take our room, and I'll sort myself out later."

Susannah stood and began fumbling her way up the staircase.

"I'll use my sleeping bag. Ha ha, and for once I'm not talking about you."

Laura followed her upstairs.

"Why are you following me?" Susannah turned around to scowl at Laura, and nearly lost her footing. "What part of 'we're breaking up' did you not understand?"

Laura attempted a smile. "The part where you were too drunk to mean it. But I can see you're angry. We can talk in the morning."

"Okay. We'll talk about me moving in with a friend. And by friend, I mean someone who doesn't think I'm a killer."

SATURDAY / SEPTEMBER 11

FORTY-FOUR
CLARE

Clare stared at her wallpaper. She wasn't sure which hurt more: its vivid blues and yellows or her cell phone ringing in her ear.

"Are you alone?"

"Good morning to you, too," she told Cloutier.

"You hungover?"

"Maybe." Clare squinted at the sunlight.

"Can you talk?"

She got up and pulled the blinds shut. Lovely day and all.

"Yeah, I can talk. I'm alone." Was she? There was no one in the room with her.

"Good."

She lit her first cigarette of the day. Where was her glass of water?

"Please don't tell me someone else is dead," Clare said.

"Nope. Killer seems to have taken a night off. Were you with the professor last night?"

"I don't think so." Clare began to recollect pieces from the night before. Was Kevin here? She should be careful what she said. "I'm pretty sure I'm mad at you."

"Just pretty sure?"

"I had some drinks."

Cloutier groaned. "Don't tell me you went and got drunk because I didn't pat your head hard enough."

It did sound kind of stupid, in the painful light of morning. But then she remembered how dismissive he'd been with her first bit of solid evidence, and her anger came back in full force. She gritted her teeth, and said nothing.

"Good work, Clare. Keep it up. Knew you could do it. Is that what you want to hear?"

"I'd prefer it if you meant it, but it's along the right lines."

"Fucking hell. I never took a babysitting course."

"Why did you call?"

Clare looked around for her glass of water, and found it half-full on the milk carton she used for a bedside table. Chalk up one more point for authentic-looking student décor. She gulped half of the water down in one sip.

"The inspector's interested in Diane Mateo. You friendly with her?"

"Not really." Clare knew she shouldn't have played along with Jessica in the subway. Common decency aside, it was foolish, in her job, to alienate anybody. "I don't think Diane is friends with anyone."

"Then it should be easy to get close to her. Her alibi for the Ruiz killing doesn't check out."

"She wasn't home studying? I thought her two roommates confirmed that."

"Home studying, maybe. But not all night. According to Jonathan Whyte, she was at the speech where Ruiz died."

"Why would Diane lie about something so obvious?" Clare thought it more likely that Jonathan was wrong.

"Right. Why?"

Clare's bedroom door opened, and Kevin walked in, wearing nothing and carrying two cups of coffee.

"I have to go." Clare held up one finger and smiled at Kevin.

"A delicious man has just brought me a coffee."

"You said you were alone."

"I thought I was." She clicked to end the call, and turned to Kevin. "Now this is the way to wake up."

"You don't have a hangover?"

"I do," Clare said. "But the sight of you naked makes it that much more bearable."

"Was that your boss, or your professor?"

"God, what did I tell you last night?"

"Nothing." Kevin cleared a spot on Clare's bedside milk crate, and set a book down as level ground for both coffees. "Only that you were pissed off at both of them."

Clare hoped that was all she'd said.

"This was my boss. He kind of apologized."

"Do you forgive him?"

"Yeah." Clare sipped her coffee, but it made her throat hurt. "For now."

FORTY-FIVE
LAURA

Laura stared blankly at her tomato plant. She set the pruning shears down. She didn't care about side shoots at the moment.

Susannah was gone. She hadn't taken all her things yet, but she'd made it clear in the morning that she'd meant what she'd said about leaving.

Laura didn't know what to feel. If Susannah turned out to be innocent — which of course she would; she wasn't cruel or heartless — then Laura may have made the biggest mistake of her life.

But that damn spu card kept nagging — and another one had been found at Libby Leighton's house. Susie must, at the very least, know the killer. Until Laura knew the truth, how could they share a bed, or a life?

Laura sipped the coffee she'd brought with her into the garden. It was rich and dark — she'd used the espresso machine instead of the family-sized brewing pot.

She eyed the garden hose, curled up like a sleeping snake at the side of the house. It had rained heavily on Wednesday, and then lightly the night before; the watering could wait a couple of days.

But what could she do? Not gardening, clearly. She set the

shears down on the patio table, picked up the phone, and fished out the phone number she'd been carrying around in her pocket.

"Is it too late to change my mind about playing detective?"

"Laura!" Penny's voice held something unusual. Was it warmth? "You sound like you're two inches tall."

"That's about how high I feel. Susie left." Should she be saying this? "I need a project, and pretending we can find out who killed Hayden seems about as good as any."

Penny laughed. Sincere? Ah, who cared? "I hope we won't be pretending."

"If you want to come over, I have another card I can show you," Laura said.

"What a perfect start to the weekend." Laura imagined Penny clapping her hands with glee. "I have plans for today. But this evening works. Are you still in that quaint little cottage on Amelia Street?"

"I am." Laura was quite sure Penny had never been inside her house.

"On second thought, why don't we meet at my office around five? We can start by poking through the archived articles."

"What for?" Laura took a small sip of her coffee.

"Connect the victims. We have a much more sophisticated system than typing some names into Google."

"You sound like you've done this before."

"I began my career as an investigative journalist," Penny said. "You'd be surprised how similar that job is to an amateur sleuth's. Will I see you at five, then?"

"See you at five."

Laura picked up the shears. This plant wasn't going to prune itself.

FORTY-SIX
CLARE

"Did I tell you how much I hate hangovers?" Clare said, as she propped open the hood of a Volkswagen Passat.

"Hair of the dog," Roberta said. "There's a beer in the fridge if you want one."

"Do you have any Jack?"

"That what you were drinking? Thought you couldn't stand the stuff."

"I was blowing off some steam."

Clare got into the car and drove it gently up the ramps. Then she climbed out of the driver's seat and jumped down.

"What's wrong now?" Roberta frowned at the alternator parts she had spread out in front of her.

"I don't know. Everything. But at least I didn't wake up alone."

"Ah, youth." This sounded funny coming from Roberta, who didn't strike Clare as having an age. "Is he someone I know?"

"Kevin? No. I've seen him a couple times. I'm trying to hold him back until I finish the case."

Clare placed a chock behind the Passat's rear tires.

"You got involved with a new guy while you're on the case? I thought you were getting busy with your professor."

Thinking of Matthew made Clare smile. So maybe he was implicated in one of the biggest murder cases the city had ever seen, but Clare wanted more of him. There was something so . . . sexy . . . about the way he'd slipped her clothes off, the way he'd treated each part of her body like it was the most beautiful thing he'd ever seen.

"I met Kevin the night before I got the assignment. Problem is, I don't know what I told him about what I do for a living. I'm going with the cover story, but I'm not sure he believes me."

"Lots of drunken nights for you lately?"

"Just the two." Clare started removing screws on the plastic underbody cover.

"How's your case going?"

"I keep making stupid mistakes."

"Why?"

"No idea." Clare set the cover aside, and put the last couple of screws into the old coffee mug she was using to store them while she worked. "Maybe I want this too badly."

"Want what?"

"A permanent transfer."

Roberta picked up the voltage regulator and began to open it up. "Why shouldn't you want that? You'd make a great undercover. You're creative. You get along with people. And you're fucking intelligent."

"Tell that to my handler."

"Show that to your handler."

"That's the problem. I get stupid around him. I either come across as completely ditzy, or I get angry and say things I shouldn't."

Clare assessed the car, trying to decide whether to go at the oil filter from underneath, or remove the coolant reservoir from its housing and come in from the top. Underneath seemed like less work, which was a good thing when her brain was fried.

"What do you get angry at?" Roberta asked.

"Myself, probably. For sounding stupid in the first place."

"Well, there's your problem." Roberta studied the brush she'd taken from the regulator. "You're thinking about yourself too much."

Clare frowned. "Are you saying I'm self-centered?"

"You? Never."

"Come on, Berta. I'm being serious."

"Terribly sorry. Okay, no, you're not self-centered. *Usually.* But I think you might have your head flipped around on this one. Try focusing on the task, instead of on your own performance."

"I *am* focused on the task." Clare found a drainage pan, and stuck it under the filter. "If anything, too much so. I can't fall asleep at night, because scenarios about the case play themselves over and over again in my mind."

Roberta was quiet. Was she waiting for Clare to say more?

"Maybe I could have that beer now."

Roberta opened her fridge. "Maybe I should have one with you."

"Alternator pissing you off?"

"Confusing me." Roberta opened a beer and passed it to Clare. "It's not a brush problem, like I thought it was."

"You? The great mechanic? Confused by a mere alternator."

Roberta cracked a beer of her own, and shut the fridge. "A mechanic is only as great as her latest repair job."

"My dad used to describe you as gifted," Clare said.

"Used to?"

"When you worked for him. He said you could get right into a headspace that let you solve almost any problem."

Roberta smiled, and Clare thought she was trying not to appear flattered. "Your dad was a good teacher."

"*Was* being the operative word."

Clare got back on the ground and found the drain plug on the oil pan. She slid another drip tray under it, and opened the plug. She loved the way the oil came gushing out, liberated from its former dirty prison. She lay there, watching it, for a full minute. Then she got up, to give the rest of the oil time to drip out.

"Don't be stubborn, Clare. It was cute when you were twelve, but it's time to throw that out."

"You thought I was cute when I was twelve?" Clare went over to the sink and washed her hands.

"You were great." Roberta took a healthy glug of beer. "Eddie had just walked out. I was all alone trying to bring up that hell-raiser of a Lance. And I was pulling out my hair figuring how to make the trailer payments each month. Then your dad gave me that job — and whatever he says, I did *not* start out as a gifted mechanic — and you came around the shop like a crazy little monkey, maybe knowing a bit too much about cars for my comfort, but always — *always* — you could get me to laugh."

Clare picked up her beer and took a long sip. It was funny how people's memories of the same situation could be so completely different. "I was terrified of you."

"Of me? Why?"

"Your big red hair, maybe? Your arms, with their man-muscles?"

"You think you're funny." Roberta flexed a muscle and eyed her own arm appreciatively. "So what's your new guy like?"

"Sexy," Clare said. "I could do him every night and not get bored."

FORTY-SEVEN
MATTHEW

Matthew rolled around lazily to look at the alarm clock. Noon. He hadn't stayed in bed this late for years.

He turned back toward Annabel. "So what do you want to do today?"

"You're kidding, right?" Her lips curled in irony.

"Why would I be kidding?" He took her hand and smiled to think of what it had recently done for his cock.

Annabel laughed. "If we were at my place, you'd have been gone before I woke up. Where did this spending the day part come in?"

"When you trusted me with all that stuff last night. It meant a lot to me."

Matthew brushed a fallen strand of hair behind Annabel's ear. She looked so pretty this morning, the way the sun caught her blond highlights.

"So my reward is a whole day of Matthew." Annabel rolled her eyes, then looked at him. "Do you really think Utopia Girl is one of your students?"

Matthew sighed. "I was worried already. What you've shown

me cements it."

"Worried already? You mean you know which student?" Annabel's eyes shot wide open. "I should have come to you before. We might have saved a life, or even two."

"I don't know which student."

"Oh." She relaxed. "Then what made you think one of your students was involved?"

"Well . . . You know how those letters have been signed by a secret society?"

"Of course," Annabel said. "But I thought that was a smoke-screen. Are you telling me the society is real?"

"It's very real. I founded the SPU when I first came to U of T."

"You founded a secret society?" Annabel took her hand away from Matthew's, and used it to prop up her head. "That's really cool . . . or it could have been, if, you know . . ."

"It was supposed to give students a sense of their own power. Each year, I've chosen the handful of kids who — not to be immodest — remind me of myself at their age. Only instead of feeling unimportant and not listened to, like I did, I wanted these kids to see that what they say and do can make a difference."

"Matthew, that's amazing."

He shook his head. "I got sidetracked by my own ego."

"Who wouldn't?"

"A stronger person? I'm supposed to be their role model, and instead I led them into murder." He wanted to tell Annabel about Elise. But of course he couldn't. He'd lied to the police, and he sure as hell didn't want that case reopened.

"You didn't do it on purpose. Did you?"

"Of course not."

"So don't blame yourself for your good intentions. Take con-trol of now. Maybe together we can solve this."

How adorably naïve. And somehow that thought led Matthew to think of Clare. He'd enjoyed her so much, that night in his office. She was innocent like a student, but tough like a — shit. That's why she'd been snooping.

"When did you get the first email?" Matthew said. "That first fake obituary, about Hayden Pritchard."

"Tuesday morning. I opened it when I came into work."

"And when did you contact the police?"

"What? Why do you care?"

"Humor me."

Annabel shrugged. "My direct boss was out for the morning, so I showed Penny right away. She called the police, and two detectives were interviewing me in under an hour."

"What time do you think the cops left the *Star* offices?"

"I don't know." She looked at him strangely. "I got to work a few minutes before eight. They were probably leaving around nine-thirty or ten."

About an hour before Shirley had informed him he had an uninvited guest in his utopia class.

"That little bitch is a cop."

"What little bitch?"

"Clare."

Matthew got out of bed and looked at his face in the en suite bathroom mirror.

"Who's Clare?"

Annabel got up as well, started gathering her clothes from various locations on the floor.

"A student of mine. I think she's an undercover." Matthew splashed water onto his face. "You want to go over to the island today? Rent a couple of bicycles, act like tourists?"

"Why not? Let's pretend for a day that you actually like me."

"What?" Matthew returned to the bedroom, an open can of shaving cream in his hand.

"I know we can't do this forever." Annabel slipped a leg into her thong. "But sure, for today, let's pretend."

"Annabel!"

Why today, of all days, did she want a meaningful relationship discussion?

"Don't be upset. I like you. I'm not mad."

"Then why are you being insecure?" Matthew set down the shaving cream and sat on the unmade bed.

"I'm not *being* insecure. I'd be foolish if I *was* secure."

"You think I'm using you for sex?"

"No." She did up her bra. "I think you like me, as much as you're capable of liking someone."

"But — last night — this morning — didn't we have such a good time together?"

"Yeah." Annabel wriggled into her J Brand jeans. "I shared some information, then we had better sex than we've had in two years."

"And what do you mean, as much as I'm capable?"

"I mean, until you like yourself, if you ever do, how can you have any respect for someone else who does?"

Matthew sighed. "What have you been reading?"

"Look, for whatever reason, I still want to date you." Annabel sat beside him, half-dressed, on his bed. "So let's do it. Let's go to the island. Rent some bikes. Pretend we're in love."

"Okay."

Matthew was turned on by Annabel's new attitude. It was a shame she had to be slipping away for him to see it.

FORTY-EIGHT
CLARE

Clare toyed nervously with her lit cigarette as she stared at herself in the mirror. Garth Brooks was in her CD player, but even "Friends in Low Places" couldn't make her feel comfortable about the party that evening. Who was she to mingle with lobbyists and politicians? And what if someone died tonight? Cloutier would blame Clare in a heartbeat — he would jump at the chance to get her pulled from this case.

She had no idea if the dress she was wearing was fancy enough or over-the-top or plain wrong for any number of reasons. The lady in the consignment shop had assured Clare that it was black tie appropriate. And the fit was good — it even made her look like she had breasts that were larger than her paltry B-cup. Still, when she looked in the mirror, it didn't feel like herself looking back.

Her phone rang.

"Clare? Matthew."

"Um." She drew a blank. "Oh right. Dr. Easton."

"I think you're all right to use my first name."

"Yeah. Sorry. I'm distracted." She frowned at the mirror.

"Did I reach you at a bad time?"

"No," Clare said. "I'm trying on a dress for tonight. I'm invited to this dinner, and I've never gone to anything black tie before."

"You'll do fine." Matthew's voice was soothing. "It's not the environment fundraiser where the prime minister's speaking, by any chance?"

"I think so. Jessica Dunne invited me to go with her family."

"Some of your classmates may be working it."

"Huh?"

"A friend owns a firm that caters a lot of these events. When she's short on staff, I ask my students. I think it's a great opportunity to get them up close to the politics."

Clare wondered if he was intentionally abetting a killer.

"She asked me for one more server tonight, so I thought of you."

"You did?" Clare scowled at her dress again, and wished she'd had the invitations in reverse. She would have been much more comfortable serving than being served. "Well, if Jessica's family hates me, maybe I'll duck into the kitchen and ask for an extra uniform."

Matthew laughed. "I don't think you need to be this nervous. It's only dinner, and they're only people. How about we hook up later?"

"You mean after the event?" Clare shivered, remembering how his hands had felt on her hips while he was thrusting from behind, pushing her against his desk. "Yeah, I'd like that."

"You want to meet me in my office?"

"Sure." Was there a reason he didn't he want her at his house?

"I have some marking to do, so don't worry about how late it is when you get there."

"I'll call you when the wild times subside." Clare clicked off the phone, and resumed frowning at herself in the mirror.

FORTY-NINE
ANNABEL

Utopia Girl: *Closing in on my conclusion. Well, technically only halfway there, but the hardest work is done.*
Death Reporter: *I guess congratulations?*

The sun was beaming through her panoramic windows. Annabel's slippers were on. She had a glass of Sauvignon Blanc on the table beside her. The world was beginning to look okay again.

Utopia Girl: *Good news for you is I'm ready to say more re: motive. Cryptically, of course. Always liked guessing games.*

Death Reporter: *So I might have guessed.*

Utopia Girl: *You think you're funny.*

Death Reporter: *I settle for my own amusement. What did you want to tell me?*

Utopia Girl: *The dead politicians all have something in common.*

Annabel grabbed her notepad. Was a real clue about to surface?

Death Reporter: *Beyond having policy you hate?*

Utopia Girl: *Duh. You don't kill someone over policy.*

Death Reporter: *I've never killed anyone for any reason, so you'll have to guide me slowly.*

Utopia Girl: *Was on the streetcar with you yesterday. You went to the Beaches to see your boyfriend.*

Had she told anyone she'd taken the streetcar? She couldn't remember telling Matthew.

Utopia Girl: *Followed you halfway down Kenilworth Avenue. You were so cute. The way you turned around to see if anyone was following you. If you actually want to catch someone, you might not want to stop walking and freeze for three seconds before you gather up the courage to turn around. Gave me ample time to slip behind hedge.*

Annabel got up and closed all the blinds in her living room, though it was only five o'clock — still daylight for a couple of hours. Then she moved into her bedroom and did the same.

Death Reporter: *What do you want from me?*

Utopia Girl: *Loyalty.*

Death Reporter: *Through fear?*

Utopia Girl: *I'm fine with whatever works.*

Death Reporter: *Do you threaten your victims before you poison them?*

Utopia Girl: *Stop calling them victims. And don't be ridiculous. I want them dead.*

Death Reporter: *So you're not planning to kill me.*

Utopia Girl: *Not currently. No offense, Annabel, but your corpse would hardly make headlines.*

Death Reporter: *Small mercies, I guess.*

Utopia Girl: *Religious reference?*

Death Reporter: *If so, it's unintentional. I got thrown out of Sunday School for not singing the words God, Lord, or Jesus in any of their stupid songs.*

Back when she'd been confident. When she'd tell someone to fuck off without worrying incessantly about what they'd think about her. When she hadn't been afraid of stupid things, like bees.

Utopia Girl: *You sound bitter.*

Death Reporter: *Maybe slightly.*

Utopia Girl: *Well, glad to see you're lightening up. Seriously, your life is not in danger unless you do something to piss me off.*

Death Reporter: *Have we met in real life?*

Utopia Girl: *Real life. Cute expression. Why would you ask me that, Annabel?*

Death Reporter: *Have we?*

Utopia Girl: *Ha ha. You think I'm your boyfriend?*

Death Reporter: *Maybe. Well, not boyfriend, technically. Well, are you?*

Utopia Girl: *Dr. Easton is one of several people I could be.*

Death Reporter: *God, please just tell me.*

Utopia Girl: *Thought you didn't like to use the word God.*

Death Reporter: *Taking it in vain is fine.*

Utopia Girl: *I'll try to remember not to scream it out in bed.*

Annabel got up, poured the rest of her glass of wine down the sink, and boiled the kettle for tea. *Control,* she reminded herself. As in, don't give it all away.

Death Reporter: *You said you were willing to tell me something new. A clue.*

Utopia Girl: *See, the fact that you call it a clue is alarming. Means you see yourself as a sleuth. Which means you're trying to solve this case.*

Death Reporter: *Wouldn't you be?*

Utopia Girl: *No. I'd be minding my business, so the killer wasn't caught. Because that's where the book is.*

Was that true? Annabel thought the best book was if Utopia Girl *was* caught, admittedly after her mysterious mandate had been completed.

Death Reporter: *So you won't tell me anything?*

Utopia Girl: *Not now. Have to get ready.*

Death Reporter: *Am I supposed to ask, ready for what?*

Utopia Girl: *If you like. Have to get ready to poison a politician. If you open your blinds, you might even see some of the action.*

FIFTY
LAURA

Laura drained the last gulp from the giant, oversweetened coffee she had picked up on the way to the *Star* office tower. She smacked a thin pile of paperwork onto the desk.

"This is every single article I could find in your archives that connects all three politicians. We might actually get some sleep tonight."

"Who's talking sleep? It's not even seven p.m." Penny sipped at her own coffee, made from the automatic espresso machine in her office.

"I've been awake since sometime yesterday."

"Right. Susannah. Have you heard from her yet?"

"No."

"She's young." Penny picked up Laura's stack of articles. "She needs to stew."

"She isn't young. She's thirty-five."

"We're fifty." Penny waved the stack. "Did you find anything interesting in here?"

"Too much, if anything. The article on top is the one I'd look at first."

Penny glanced down. "Health care?"

"Manuel Ruiz and Hayden were on the city's Board of Health together. That was twelve to fourteen years ago."

"What about Leighton?"

Laura shook her head. "I can't connect her yet. But she was a city councilor at the time, so she was on the scene."

Penny frowned. "What else did you find?"

"Ruiz introduced a tough welfare bill a few years later. I liked it. But as you can guess, it was not in keeping with the bleeding heart position my husband and Libby took."

"I thought you were a bleeding heart."

Laura smiled. "I am, usually. But not when it comes to welfare."

"Anything about housing?"

"I found a statement from Hayden, condemning Libby for capitalizing on a photo op for a successful public housing project she'd tried to quash in its development."

"Hayden?" Penny's thin eyebrows shot up. "But he and Leighton were in the same party. Weren't they friends?"

"Not friends, no. But they normally got along. I think he was personally outraged about this project. It was a public co-op in a high-end neighborhood — remember when those were all the rage? None of the residents wanted it built, but Hayden had supported the concept from the beginning." Laura recalled the days when her husband had been willing to take a stand other than the safe, electable viewpoint. They hadn't lasted long. "Libby had been against it, but when the co-op proved to be working well, she rushed in to cash in on the glory. I can see why Utopia Girl chose her."

"Laura!" Penny laughed gleefully. "You can't say things like that."

"Why not?" Laura stuck out her chin. "The police think I'm a suspect; I might as well have the pleasure of behaving like one."

Penny took her head between her hands. "I've created a monster."

"Oh, ha ha. So were you able to find out more about the secret society?"

Penny nodded. "Affirmative. It's a university group, like we suspected." Penny told Laura about the Elise Marchand case, and the other not-so-legal causes the SPU was said to have championed. "One year — supposedly, because although their business card was left, they were never caught — they managed to break into the Humane Society and let out all the dogs. They did it right after Christmas."

"The poor animals must have frozen to death, half of them. What could their motivation have been?"

"You got me." Penny shrugged.

Laura slouched in her chair. Her heart sank to think of Susannah belonging to such an organization. Even if she wasn't guilty of these particular murders, what kind of radical things was she doing with her spare time?

"I also had the chance to phone one of my police sources." Penny leaned closer, as if protecting a secret, though they were the only two people in the room. "They confirmed the card that you found, but couldn't find anything about the one Sam Cray allegedly found in his wife's belongings."

"Why would Susie lie?"

"I have no idea." Penny couldn't seem to care less. "Would you like a glass of wine? I have a white Burgundy chilling in the fridge."

"Sounds delicious," Laura said.

Penny moved to the bar by the window, and pulled the wine from her built-in cooler.

Laura had an idea. "Can we email Utopia Girl?"

"I've tried. Little bitch wants nothing to do with me."

"No response at all?" Laura admired the view behind Penny, of the harbourfront and Toronto Island beyond.

"Worse." Penny set two stemless wine glasses on top of the bar and went to work with the corkscrew. "She says I'm a self-serving whore and she'd rather no one hear her story than I get credit for it."

"She must know you."

"Funny." Penny handed Laura her glass of wine.

"What about the girl on the obituary desk?" Laura sipped her wine and decided she liked it a lot.

"Annabel?" Penny sneered. "She'd only mess things up. Besides, if I allowed her any contact with the killer, she'd think the story should be hers."

"Which I take it would be a bad thing?"

"Terrible," Penny said. "She's aching to get moved off of that obituary desk. She wants to be an investigative journalist."

"So isn't this the perfect test case for her? With Utopia Girl knocking at her door."

"It would be," Penny said. "Except that she gave me her portfolio — you know, to show me that she should be moved up the ladder or into a more journalistic role — and I think she's one of the worst writers I've ever come across."

"Ouch. Did you tell her that?"

"Of course not! Do you think I like to hurt people?"

Laura shrugged. "It might be kinder in the long run."

"At any rate, what I told her was the truth. She has an extremely organized mind, and she is excellent at her current job. I said I needed her to keep plugging away at that for now, and I'd keep my eye out for assignments that might suit her style." Penny paused briefly. "So are you still a lesbian?"

"Pardon?"

"I mean, was Susannah your wild oats because you never experimented in college? Or do you think you'll keep dating women?"

"Uh . . ." Laura supposed it was a good enough question. "I hadn't thought about that. I've always considered it a permanent conversion. But then, in many ways I guess I traded one marriage for another. You fall in love with the person, don't you?"

"Hmm." Penny tapped the desk with her fingers.

"Did you experiment in college?" Laura would not normally ask such a thing, but Penny had opened the floor.

"Extensively." Penny grinned. "But that's top secret intelligence."

"It's in the vault." Laura didn't know where this conversation could be going, so she changed it. "Do you think these old archives of yours hold our answer? Or are we lunatics for trying to make a logical connection where none exists?"

Penny topped up Laura's wine. "How could no connection exist? The murders are real. There must be a motive."

"Maybe the motivation isn't political." Laura took a long sip. "Maybe the pope is going to give all his money to charity."

FIFTY-ONE
CLARE

Jessica nearly took out a waiter in her haste to find her family's table.

"Ach. Finally. I'm sorry we're late. It's totally my fault. This is Clare."

"You didn't miss much." A young man at the table offered Clare a wry grin. "Just some overdressed watercress and a few choice words from the Honorable John Alton. I'm Rory."

Clare hoped she didn't look as awkward as she felt.

"Ha." Jessica snorted. "Mr. Alton is a walking speech. Gramps, thank you so much for getting these tickets."

"My pleasure, sweetie. Happy birthday. Clare, you take that seat beside Rory."

Clare sat, and Harry Dunne introduced himself and his wife. Barbara Dunne looked about as pleased to meet Clare as she would have been to learn that Ragu was on sale at the Superstore. Clare returned the smile, though she hoped hers held more warmth.

"How was your politics class today?" Mr. Dunne asked. The question was directed at both of them.

"Which one?" Jessica said. "It's our major."

"That one you're always talking about. Where you get to change the world."

"Poli Real World," Jessica said.

"Isn't that the prof who, like, dates his students?" Rory asked.

"Do you go to U of T?" Clare wondered how Rory might know this.

"Used to," Rory said. "Until I realized that school isn't for me."

"What do you do instead?"

"I'm a snowboard instructor at Blue Mountain."

"It's summer," Jessica said. "You're unemployed."

"Yeah, but come on. Chicks don't want to go out with some unemployed dude who lives with his grandparents."

"Clare wouldn't date you even if you had a job. Stop hitting on my friends."

Mr. Dunne smiled thinly. "Clare can make up her own mind. I'm interested in your thoughts about the utopia class, Clare."

Clare took a breath, reminded herself of what Matthew had said: they're just people.

"I'm enjoying it. I love the structure of the course. We filled in these questionnaires to determine which party we belong to ideologically, rather than what party we support in real life." Wow, she'd sounded like a moron.

But Mr. Dunne continued as if she'd actually been lucid. "Jessica mentioned that you were surprised with your result."

"Yeah. I mean, I've always considered myself more conservative." Had she? Clare had no idea. "But it's interesting to look at things from the other side. I mean, the point of utopia isn't partisan politics anyway."

"And Jessica, you came out as a Tree-Hugger."

Clare let out her breath as the spotlight moved away from her.

Jessica gave her grandfather a sheepish grin. "I kind of guessed the point of the exercise, so I answered in a way that I knew would lead me to the Tree-Huggers."

Her grandmother eyed her critically. "Sometimes, Jessica, it helps to put some faith in someone else's ideas, rather than try to ram through life on your own."

Jessica exchanged a look with Rory. "Grandma, this is one course where my having opinions is an asset."

"And that's wonderful, dear. But I think you lose out when you refuse to entertain a notion other than your own. That professor had a fabulous idea for party assignment, and he gave you the chance to learn something about yourself in the process. See what your friend Clare learned? You should take a lesson from her."

Jessica rolled her eyes. "This is my education, Grandma. I'm sorry you never had yours."

"All right, that's enough." Mr. Dunne's voice was soft, reasonable. "Jessica probably had a good reason to fix the questionnaire."

"A few reasons." Jessica nodded assent as the same waiter with whom she'd nearly collided offered to fill her wine glass with red. "The Tree-Huggers are as fiscally responsible as the Rednecks, and as into low taxes, but instead of focusing on big business, their primary goal is to keep the world alive."

"Hear hear." A spectacled man clapped Mr. Dunne on the shoulder. "That's a smart kid you raised, Harry." He turned to Jessica. "Although I prefer the term Conservative to Redneck, if it were up to me, we'd be merging with those Greens to soak up what wisdom they can offer us."

Jessica smiled brightly. "Hi, Mr. Alton. Sorry I was late, and missed your speech. Congratulations on your cabinet post."

"Yeah, congratulations," Rory said. "What's your new job, Minister of Forestry and Trees?"

"Finance Minister." He peered at Rory as if checking for signs of drug use. "At least you got one kid right, Harry. Thanks again for your generous campaign contribution. Barbara, lovely to see you."

When John Alton had flitted off to his next contact, Jessica took a sip of wine. "Blegh. Why do they always have to serve

Ontario wines at these dinners?"

"It's about promoting local industry," her grandfather said.

"Which I support. But until we have a consistently decent vineyard in the province, we're embarrassing ourselves by pretending. Is this what we serve to visiting ambassadors?"

"Ontario makes some beautiful wines," Mrs. Dunne said. "Our ice wines are world renowned."

Rory snorted. "We should drink ice wine with our steak."

"Oh, not you, too." Mr. Dunne shook his head. "When I was in university, my definition of fine wine was anything that didn't make you blind."

"You've spoiled us with that cellar of yours." Rory took a gulp from his glass and smiled with obviously fake appreciation. "But you're right. Who am I to knock an open bar?"

"Is that Diane?" Clare pointed out a waitress serving one of the tables across the room.

Jessica turned to look. "Looks like her."

"What would she be doing here?"

"Um, working. Putting herself through school, you know."

Of course. Dr. Easton's band of merry servers. And all the society members had gigs, so Clare couldn't narrow her list of suspects that way.

"Do you have a part-time job, Clare?" Mrs. Dunne asked.

"No." This was an easier question, because she'd rehearsed it. "Just student loans until I'm eighty."

"Have you always been passionate about politics?"

Clare figured she might as well give the Dunnes their money's worth on her dinner ticket. "Not until recently. My dad always called politics the rich person's sport."

"What did he mean by that?" Harry inclined his head toward Clare.

"He meant it was another thing to follow, like hockey or football. He thinks that people get all riled up over loving their candidate and hating the other guy, but it doesn't make too much difference who gets into power."

Rory leaned back in his chair and shoved his salad plate toward a waiter who had come to clear it away. "So what made you choose poli sci? Was it total and utter rebellion?"

Clare laughed. "I started in general arts, but then a bunch of people told me poli sci would help when I applied to law school, so I changed majors, as well as universities, this year. I have some catching up to do, but so far, it's been surprisingly interesting."

The main course arrived. Boneless chicken breast with mashed sweet potatoes and ratatouille. Clare eyed hers with amusement. At least the money from the tickets was going to the cause, instead of being squandered on the food. She picked up her fork once she saw that Mrs. Dunne had taken the lead.

"And what made you choose law?" Mr. Dunne asked. "I assume that's not a common choice in the trailer park."

Clare smiled blandly. Educate a Fool, huh? "It was when I was fifteen. My dad's business partner screwed him over massively. It took everything my dad had to sue the guy — and win — but the guy couldn't pay out, and my dad had to declare bankruptcy and go work for the competition. The only people who gained were the lawyers."

"Fucking typical." Rory poked at his vegetables. "Is that how you ended up in the trailer park?"

"Rory!" His grandmother gasped.

"What? I can't ask an honest question?"

"It's fine," Clare said, though she wanted the attention as far away from her real self as possible. She had to work more on her cover story, so the truth didn't slip out by default. "No, we already lived in the trailer park. It was a nice place — lots of trees, a river with great fishing. It was more like a campground, but almost everyone was a permanent resident."

"So are you gonna be one of those do-gooder lawyers, you know, fighting for the common man? Or are you attracted by the money those fuckers are making?"

"A bit of each." The thought of being stuck in uncomfortable clothes and a law office all day made Clare's heart sink, but she reminded herself that she already had a job; the ambition was a cover. "Do you have a part-time job, Jessica?"

Jessica sipped her wine and made another face. "Yeah. In catering. I was actually on the schedule for this party, but then my wonderful grandfather landed me this role as guest."

"I'm glad he did." Clare was enjoying the meal more than she had planned to. The sweet potatoes were surprisingly flavorful. But she set her fork down quickly when she remembered that somewhere in the room, someone's plate could be laced with something fatal. "So who else from the class works with you?"

"Diane and Jonathan both work a lot of shifts. Susannah does the odd one. And I think Brian took my shift tonight." Jessica sipped her wine one more time, then set it down with a scowl. "We should ask Diane if they're hiding anything imported in the back."

"For the bigwigs." Rory nodded knowingly. "No way the prime minister's drinking this piss."

"The prime minister *only* drinks Canadian wine," Mrs. Dunne said. "He's quite patriotic, you know."

Jessica waved in Diane's direction. "I think she sees us. Let's ask."

"You guys!" Rory pointed toward the podium. "Get a load of Mr. Alton."

The Finance Minister, who had seemed fine when he had been at their table minutes ago, was staggering around on the stage with a handful of papers in his hand.

"Do you think he wants to make another speech?" Jessica's mouth fell open.

"Course he does," Rory said. "A bit of the sauce makes anyone like the sound of their own voice."

Harry pushed his seat back and went over to John Alton, who had dropped all of the papers and was clutching his stomach in pain. Harry knelt beside him, then rose and spoke into the microphone, which screeched. "Damn it. Isn't anyone here a doctor?"

FIFTY-TWO
JONATHAN

Jonathan couldn't breathe. He knew he should be out there, being helpful, doing something, but it was suddenly too much. He sat slumped on the floor of the St. Lawrence Hall kitchen, the tray he'd held moments ago lying with its contents scattered across the tiled floor.

Where was Diane? How could she be so blasé? She was probably enjoying the drama with the rest of them. And Jessica? Was she watching the scene with her family, just another evening's entertainment? And what about Brian, who was supposed to be Jonathan's trainee for the evening? He seemed more interested in positioning himself close to the politicians than in learning the ropes of the job.

And why were politicians so interesting to all these people, anyway? From Jon's observation, they were a bunch of insecure men trying to puff out their chests far enough to convince themselves that they belonged in the job. No one normal would run for office. Anyone with real confidence would know that you don't change the world by debating about it.

But Jonathan wasn't in a position to judge his classmates' or anyone's interests. He would still be a computer science major if

he hadn't met Jessica in frosh week, and had that conversation —
the one she'd probably forgotten about ten minutes after they'd
had it — that had made him want to follow her until she felt the
same way about him. He'd been shy until now, but it was happening . . . she was falling for him . . . but the timing was terrible.

This was too much — way too much — but he had to push
himself forward. Jonathan found his tray and slowly picked up
its fallen contents. Only one mug had broken, which he chucked
into the broken dish bin.

Elly Shore burst through the swinging door from the main
hall. "I can't take this. This fundraiser is the third event I've been
put in charge of where a prominent guest is going home dead.
Someone is out to get me."

"Out to get *you*?" Jonathan wasn't sure how that added up.
She wasn't the one gasping for life in front of two hundred people.

Elly glanced at Jonathan as if they'd never met. "When the
connection gets made, which is only a matter of time, who's going
to want to book Elly's Epicure, the Killing Caterer?"

"Maybe a Hallowe'en party."

"You're lucky I'm understaffed tonight. Otherwise I'd fire you
on the spot."

Jonathan half-wished she would fire him anyway. "You didn't
cater the event where Manuel Ruiz dropped dead."

"So?"

"So you're not the connection." He got to work refilling the
tray he had dropped with tea and coffee service. "Sorry about the
Hallowe'en crack. I really appreciate this opportunity."

"Matthew Easton is a good friend." Elly watched what
Jonathan was doing. "Don't fill the sugars too much. We can't
reuse what they don't consume."

Jonathan removed a third of the sugar from each dish and
replaced it in Elly's plastic bin. "Dr. Easton's a great professor. He
encourages us to act upon what we believe in. And he doesn't treat
us like children, which is a bonus."

"And what do you believe in, that needs acting upon?"

Jonathan could feel Elly's eyes burning a hole in the back of his tuxedo shirt.

"I guess I'm trying to figure that out." Jonathan took some table cream from the huge stainless steel fridge, and began to fill the creamers. "Isn't that what university's supposed to be for?"

"Yes." Elly's tone softened. "That's exactly what university is for."

"So it's a good place to make mistakes, right? Sort out who you are, what you stand for, before going out into the real world."

"It's all the real world. Now stop talking and get those coffee services set up. If we can't keep these politicians alive, at the very least we can keep the show going for the guests who've paid good money to be here."

His tray ready, his arm fighting to stay steady, Jonathan pushed out once more into the main room, where John Alton lay fighting for his life.

FIFTY-THREE
CLARE

Clare watched the action unfold with nothing less than horror. She had never seen a dead body, much less watched a person die. She supposed it should be all in a day's work for a police officer, but she was quickly finding out that she had a lot to learn about her own job.

She couldn't rush to Alton's aid — that would look ridiculous. And she couldn't go poking around the back of the house to see if she could find Diane or Jonathan or some other society member gleefully rubbing their hands together with a vial of poison in their pocket. Clare wondered if Cloutier had passed along her suggestion — or if anyone had thought of it themselves — and had an antidote kit at the ready.

Rory leapt up and flapped around his grandfather. Clare couldn't tell if he was helpful or in the way, but she could sympathize with his need to be doing something.

The crowd knew the score. Some of these guests would have been at the Working Child benefit, and they were all aware of the recent political deaths. Although the *Star* still hadn't printed the obituaries from Utopia Girl, it was obvious to the casual observer that foul play was going on.

But who was the non-casual observer?

No one had turned the microphone off, which may have been a good thing in that it kept the attention of the room focused on the podium, and therefore orderly. A doctor had been found; he pronounced Mr. Alton to be alive and struggling (a diagnosis which Clare found mildly obvious, as it was confirmed by the sound of his moaning and gasping for air). Within several minutes, paramedics arrived, and John Alton was taken out of the hall on a stretcher. On his way out, he turned his head and vomited all over a middle-aged couple. The couple remained stone-faced, continued to hold hands, and stood in place to watch the stretcher leave the room.

Alton's wife followed, sobbing but not uncontrollably. Clare wanted to cry at the sight of her. Within hours at best, her husband would likely be dead.

Left alone at the podium, Harry Dunne seemed at a loss. He asked the event's coordinator if he wanted to say anything to the crowd.

The coordinator looked like he wanted to do anything but. Clare didn't blame the guy. If he broke up the party before dessert and the speech from the prime minister, would he have to refund the guests' thousand dollars per head? If he kept the evening going and Alton died of the same mystery ailment that had killed the others, the organizers would look like they valued donations more than people's lives. Still, the man rose from his seat at one of the front tables and tentatively addressed the room.

"I think I speak for everyone here when I wish John Alton a speedy recovery from tonight's medical emergency."

The crowd murmured its agreement.

"This episode is particularly alarming in light of recent happenings at other events." He paused to wipe sweat from his brow. "We can only hope that if this is a related event, our haste in securing medical attention will ensure Mr. Alton's revival. I would like to thank everyone here for maintaining order. Special thanks to Harry Dunne and his grandson Rory, and to Dr. Alex

Cummins for coming so hastily to John's aid."

A couple of audience members applauded, but they quickly stopped when the mood in the room remained somber.

"Dessert is being passed around by the catering staff. I'd like to propose that we skip the preliminaries and move right to the prime minister's speech. I think it's only right that we end this evening early in honor of our friend and colleague's grave distress."

Murmurs of "of course" and "absolutely" passed through the room.

FIFTY-FOUR
LAURA

"John Alton!" Laura's voice echoed in her empty wine glass. "Well, that throws all bets out the window. He's about as much of a socialist as *you* are."

"Sting." Penny topped her up from their second bottle. "Still, I'm holding out for a connection. If we're lucky, his 'obituary' will be arriving any second."

"I thought those were being sent to your employee. Can you monitor your staff's emails?"

"Of course I can. Troops don't command themselves."

Laura stood by Penny's window and gazed directly down. It felt impossibly late to her, but there were plenty of cars, taxis, and foot traffic five floors below. For the young people out clubbing, the night had barely begun.

"Here!" Penny clapped. She motioned for Laura to join her at her computer screen.

Laura stumbled a bit as she moved around the desk. They read the obituary together in silence.

John Alton: October 2, 1948–September 11, 2010

We are pleased to announce our fourth step toward a political utopia for the real world. The outrageously honorable John Alton, Finance Minister with dreams of saving the planet, made his final speech last night at an environmental fundraiser.

Unlike the other so-called victims, we believe that Alton generally did a good job for the public. He was recently appointed Finance Minister, and his first budget managed to be both balanced and generous — a rare feat by anyone's standards. And he cared — we think he really did — about making the world a greener place. But there is a stain in Alton's past, and it has finally come back to haunt him.

We cannot yet reveal what this stain is, but you can rest assured that John Alton was not the honorable man he was alleged to be.

Our mandate will come together soon.

You're welcome.

This has been a message from the Society for Political Utopia.

Laura reminded herself to breathe deeply. Penny had shown her the other emails, but it was different reading one as it came in. She'd never been this close to evil.

"Well," Penny said. "Out of our three committees in common, Alton was on none of them."

"Was he even a city politician?" Laura heard herself slurring. It sounded more like "shitty politishun."

Penny's mouth crinkled up in amusement. "Not that I recall. I think John went straight from his father's company to federal office. We can find out easily enough on the Internet."

Laura watched as Penny loaded the search engine. "If he wasn't, will we have to throw out all our theories?"

"Not necessarily." Penny went over to the bar and picked up their second wine bottle, which was empty. "Coffee?"

"Coffee would be perfect. What do you mean not necessarily?"

"Sometimes the three levels of government work together, forming a supercommittee, or a think tank of sorts. We can rule out homelessness — that's the city's all the way; neither the province nor the feds want to touch it."

"Figures." A lot of Laura's Brighter Day work dealt with homelessness, an issue that she felt consumed a lot of money without ever being humanely addressed. "Most of the homeless don't vote, so to hell with 'em."

"My my, such public passion." Penny pressed the On button on her coffee machine. "Have you been cleared of these murders, incidentally?"

"You're the one with the police source. Besides, I've been here with you while Alton was being killed." Laura typed John Alton's name into Google.

"Where's Susannah tonight? You two could be in cahoots."

The thought of Susannah, combined with the wine, made Laura feel heavy.

"Kidding," Penny said. "Well, at least we can be each other's alibi."

"Why would you need an alibi?" Laura clicked on a link that promised a mini-biography of Alton.

"The *Star* stands to gain a lot from our involvement with this case. You and I know that I wouldn't kill anyone to get ahead, but let's face it — the police are looking everywhere the smallest link might be."

"I have something." Laura's eyes skimmed the web page about Alton. "About ten years ago, he was on a think tank for health care."

"What was it called?" Penny placed a cup under the spout of her coffee machine and pressed a button.

"Very original. Project Health."

"Cream and sugar?"

"Yes, please." Laura returned to the search engine, squinted at the screen, and after a couple of efforts, succeeded in typing in *Project Health Think Tank*. She clicked on the first result, read for a moment, then said, "The group had six members. Good Lord!"

"What is it?" Penny set Laura's coffee on the desk in front of her. Not that she needed it anymore: she suddenly felt stone cold sober.

"Of course I remember this think tank. Hayden was on it. It was all he could talk about for weeks."

"Honored to be a member?"

"At first it was that innocent." Laura rolled her eyes. "Then he started citing it as proof of his intelligence. Every time we had the smallest argument — like which route to take to my parents' house for Sunday dinner — he would remind me that he was the one who had been asked to join the think tank, and clearly I could benefit from listening to his wisdom."

"Men are insufferable." Penny pressed the button to make her own coffee. "That's why I'm —"

The machine's internal grinder kicked in, truncating Penny's sentence.

"Pardon?" Laura said, once the beans had been ground.

"Nothing. Who were the others in the think tank?"

Laura read from the screen. "Manuel Ruiz, Simon McFarlane, Marisa Jordan, and Sam Cray."

Penny shook her head. "Not Libby Leighton. This can't be the connection."

"Sam Cray is her husband. Might she have swallowed his poison accidentally?"

"Utopia Girl seemed confident she'd nailed the right victim." Penny pulled up Leighton's "obituary" and she and Laura re-read it together.

"This doesn't condemn Leighton's policy," Laura said. "Just her lack of . . . well, anything."

"I don't think the other letters reference the real motive either." Penny moved over to her own desk. "We have to keep looking."

"Tonight?" Laura found the thought exhausting. "I think we should pack up until tomorrow."

"In a minute." Penny was looking at something on her computer screen. "Motherfucker." Penny clapped a hand over her mouth. "Sorry, I forgot you hate swearing."

"I don't hate swearing."

"You never swear yourself."

"I was well brought up." Laura took a sip of coffee. "But I have many friends who weren't, so go right ahead."

"Oh, crack me up. So I guess you don't care what I've found." Penny moved her mouse and clicked.

"Of course I care."

"Marisa Jordan — she's not a politician anymore, so I doubt she's next to die — introduced a housing bill. Ten years ago. It was the brainchild of Carl Haas, a Communist Party member who was also a rogue lobbyist. Hayden was on the committee in charge of assessing the bill's viability."

"I remember that, too," Laura said. "Carl Haas wouldn't leave us alone. At home, at restaurants — he even found us at one of the kids' soccer games."

Penny's eyebrows arched. "Haas stalked you. Why didn't you call the police?"

"We felt sorry for him, I guess." Laura wondered if Penny understood that her reporters did the exact same thing, and worse. "Plus the guy seemed harmless."

"He probably *is* harmless. But someone is killing these men — and woman — and this is exactly the sort of connection I think we're looking for."

"His housing bill was dropped, I guess?"

"Killed in committee. Wasn't even brought to Parliament."

"Who else was on the committee?" Laura asked.

"Why do you think I flagged it? Leighton, Ruiz, and Alton."

Laura wrinkled her brow. "Why would Alton be on a municipal committee?"

"Again, it was one of those supercommittees. They think if they take people from all parties and all levels of government, they'll come out with an unbiased result."

"Or at least it will look unbiased to the scrutinizing public." Laura didn't know why she felt so bitter about the reality of the political system. She put it down to the fading effect of too much wine. "Were there others on the committee?"

"About twenty in total. But they were mainly low-profile civil servants. My guess is only the politicians will be murdered."

"Do you think this is it?" Laura looked at Penny excitedly.

"I think we should sleep on it."

"You don't think we should phone the police? Warn Marisa?"

"Oh, Laura." Penny shook her head. "If we go to the police, they'll take all the credit for our hard work."

"But if we don't, and someone else is killed —"

"No one else is getting killed tonight. We'll sleep on it, and meet again tomorrow to decide how to proceed."

"I don't know . . ." Laura felt like the right choice was obvious. "I thought our goal was to stop more murders."

"Please?" Penny widened her eyes, and appeared oddly vulnerable.

Laura didn't buy the act, but she was too tired to argue. "Fine. Tomorrow."

FIFTY-FIVE
CLARE

Clare pulled out of her parking spot, careful not to let her dress touch the exhaust pipe. At least tonight's events had distracted her from her own self-consciousness. She'd barely remembered she was wearing a dress until she had to get onto her bike.

She drove north through the city. Jessica's family, for all their in-fighting, had welcomed Clare, reminded her of what a functional family was supposed to feel like. Jessica may have lost both of her parents, but her grandparents had stepped in and given her and Rory everything that mattered. Clare hadn't been so lucky. She'd lost both her parents while they were still alive.

Cloutier was going to hate her in the morning, but Clare was unwilling to blame herself for the evening's horror. Yes, another man had been poisoned, and would probably soon be dead if he wasn't already. Yes, it was Clare's job to watch the small group of people that probably contained the murderer(s). But what more could she have done, without compromising her cover?

She arrived at the campus. There was nothing going on at street level, but music pumped loud from the nearby residences, and Clare felt that she might have missed out on something by not having gone to university.

She climbed the large stone staircase to Sidney Smith Hall. She tried the front door, but it was locked. She pulled out her phone.

"Clare?" Matthew's voice was welcoming. "How was the party?"

"Terrible. I'm outside. I'll tell you about it when you let me come in."

He was there in under a minute.

"Hey, great dress."

"You like it?" Clare frowned.

"Don't make that face. You look fantastic. Come on upstairs."

But something wasn't right.

"I need you to level with me." Matthew unlocked his office door and held it open for Clare.

"Sure." Clare took her now-familiar seat on the couch.

"On Friday afternoon, when you were in my office, did you maybe have a look around?"

"Um."

"I'm not angry." Matthew poured two glasses of red wine. "But why didn't you ask me what you wanted to know?"

"Um."

"For example, do you still have any questions about the society?"

Clare was horrified, then she relaxed. He couldn't possibly know that she'd been in his drawer. There were no cameras in the room, and there must be someone other than him with access — a janitor, the department head. "I'm so sorry, but I don't know what you mean."

"No?" Matthew handed her the wine.

Clare eyed the glass — she'd watched him pour it, so it must be fine, right? She'd wait for him to take a sip first. And then maybe she should somehow execute a trade.

Matthew lowered his brow. "Someone's gone through my drawers. You're the only person who's been in my office without me being present."

"Does anyone else have a key?" Clare wondered what she'd

left out of place. Or was he one of those freaks who stuck a hair on his lock to ensure the privacy of his drawer. Shit, he probably was.

"Dr. Rosenblum has one. But there's nothing she would want in here."

"But there's something I *would* want?" Clare widened her eyes. She should never have dropped out of drama class. "Why are you constantly mistrusting me?"

"Constantly?"

"First you thought I weaseled my way into your class." Clare wondered if it was a mistake to remind him of this. "And now you think I searched your things when I was sleeping off a migraine. I'm just —" She pushed her wine away forcefully, but without spilling any. "Look, I'm not sure if I've done something to upset you, or if you have trouble trusting people in general. But I'm obviously causing you more grief than pleasure, which isn't the point, is it?"

Clare stood up, and began to put on her leather jacket.

"Clare — I —"

FIFTY-SIX
MATTHEW

Matthew knew that he should let her leave, that she *was* more trouble than she was worth. He needed to think about the situation away from her. But she seemed so sincere; it was hardly fair to accuse her of this then send her off all alone.

"Clare, I'm sorry. Please stay."

Clare froze. Looked at him. One arm was already inside her jacket, and the other held the sleeve it was about to slip into.

"Why should I?"

"Because you're right. I haven't been fair to you. I was thrown when I was forced to accept you into my class. I guess I haven't gotten over it as quickly as I should have."

Clare perched on the arm of the couch, her coat still half-on, half-off. "So it's better if I leave."

"No."

Clare chewed on her lip.

"I'm sorry, Clare."

She looked tiny. Was she shivering? Why couldn't he go to her? Matthew felt like all motion in the room had been suspended.

"I don't understand your suspicion. What is it you think I

want from you?"

He obviously couldn't answer that. Assuming he was wrong, she'd tell the whole class he was paranoid she was a cop, and he'd be a laughingstock among his students.

"Matthew?"

He swallowed. "There's a club that I head up. It's a secret society. I guess I thought you wanted to get in."

"The SPU?" Clare's eyes widened.

He nodded.

"That club is real? I totally thought that card the cops showed us was a hoax. I even told Brian, when he came around asking if I was a member, that if he hadn't found a way in for three years, there was no way the club could exist."

"Will you keep it a secret?" He was relieved by her reaction.

"Of course." Clare smiled warmly. "Now can we get out of this dark room, and grab a drink somewhere more lively?"

FIFTY-SEVEN
ANNABEL

Utopia Girl: *Guess who.*

Anna switched on her bedside light and rubbed the sleep out from her eyes.

Death Reporter: *That's a hard one, since your name displays automatically.*

Utopia Girl: *Did you watch the show from your living room?*

Annabel opened her blinds, and looked out at the street. Everything seemed intact.

Death Reporter: *What show?*

Utopia Girl: *The one I told you to watch this afternoon. Look south.*

Death Reporter: *I'm looking south.*

Utopia Girl: *Past the park.*

Death Reporter: *There's nothing there. The St. Lawrence Hall seems fine. All the buildings on King Street. The Cathedral. All there. Same as this afternoon.*

Utopia Girl: *Are you drunk? I didn't blow up a building.*

Death Reporter: *So tell me what I should have seen.*

Utopia Girl: *Never mind. Watch the news.*

Annabel grabbed her TV remote and found the 24-hour news

channel. Images of John Alton being carried out of an impressive-looking banquet hall. Words running by at the bottom of the screen. An announcer's even voice: "... speculated to have died in the ambulance ... pronounced dead at the hospital ... fourth in an extremely rapid series of killings ... who might be next? ... how will we protect our politicians?"

Death Reporter: *Were you there when he died?*

Utopia Girl: *I was there when he collapsed. I wasn't in the ambulance.*

Annabel put the kettle on. Okay, so her head was getting clearer. She wasn't sick, she wasn't delusional like she had been at the beginning of all this. How could she turn this exchange around so that she was helping the investigation, instead of adding fuel to a murderer's fire?

Death Reporter: *Why do you message me? What's in this for you?*

Utopia Girl: *You don't remember the book we're collaborating on?*

Death Reporter: *That's what's in it for me.*

Utopia Girl: *I'm sure Penny wouldn't give me this third degree. But she's a real reporter.*

Death Reporter: *When were you talking with Penny?*

Utopia Girl: *After you showed her my email, she suggested I send further correspondence directly to her. Her words: "Once the publicity ban has been lifted, I will be writing an article about you and your case. Annabel Davis, while competent at the obituary desk, will never be a star reporter, and she should have no further access to you. She poses a security risk that could compromise our exclusive, and therefore compromise the quality publicity that you are clearly seeking."*

Death Reporter: *You're lying.*

Utopia Girl: *You wish I was.*

SUNDAY / SEPTEMBER 12

FIFTY-EIGHT
CLARE

Clare looked up at Cloutier. "This is pretty bad, right?"

"Pretty bad." Cloutier started eating his second donut. "No matter how well you think you played it, your professor's suspicion alone should be enough for me to yank you off this case."

"No!" Clare pleaded with her eyes. "I'm getting valuable information. Matthew believed what I said, and I have an in with virtually every suspect."

"Virtually?"

"Jonathan's tricky. We have no points in common, and when I try to talk to him, he responds briefly and then turns away."

"And you're too polite to follow."

"Jessica Dunne is his girlfriend. I'm hoping to make headway through her."

"You've gotten somewhere with Mateo?"

"I haven't learned much, but we're talking."

Clare had phoned Diane and apologized for the morning they'd met up on the subway. Diane had laughed it off — it seemed that to her, the course was a game of strategy, so she wasn't offended that Clare might be playing a different game than hers.

"I like the bill she brought to class. She thinks politicians should earn exactly the national average salary, plus expenses."

"Who'd do that job for forty grand a year?"

"Someone who cared more about the job than the rewards. And it would give them some incentive to improve the quality of life for the rest of us."

Cloutier looked bored. "The inspector's going to let the paper run the story."

"The obituaries? You can't be serious."

"Four people are dead, and no one's in custody."

Clare looked into her coffee. It was murky and unappealing. "Can we ask for editorial approval of the story before they run it?"

"There's no 'we' here, Vengel."

"Simpson."

"Not for much longer."

"What does that mean?"

"Jessica Dunne — she's the rich kid who invited you to last night's party?"

Clare nodded.

"Did you arrive together? She leave your sight at all?"

"We met outside on King Street, and went into the hall together. Jessica was a few minutes late, but waiting beat going in alone and trying to guess which family was hers." Clare opened her bag of donut holes and looked inside. "We were together all night — until Alton collapsed — except for a couple of washroom breaks each."

"Long ones?"

"Excuse me?"

"Long washroom breaks. Like the sort Matthew Easton took the other night."

Damn. As in, did Jessica have time to head toward the washroom, then veer off in the direction of John Alton, slip something into his drink, and come back to the happy family dinner table?

"I don't remember." Clare chose a sour cream donut hole from the bag. "I wasn't counting the minutes she was gone."

"You weren't suspicious of her?" Cloutier's voice contained a weary scorn. "We already know that Jessica is in the society. People are being murdered at events just like last night's, and an invitation is delivered to your clueless little lap. How can you even for an instant forget what you're there for?"

Clare had been star-struck, pure and simple. A month ago, she wouldn't have known a cabinet minister from a cabinet maker. Now that she was learning about them and discussing them every day in class, politicians had taken on a celebrity status for her.

"I'm sorry."

"Why don't you say you're sorry to John Alton's wife of forty-three years?"

"It's not my fault he's dead!" Clare exploded. "I lost focus for a couple of hours; that's hardly criminal negligence."

"God, you frustrate me." Cloutier crumpled his donut bag into a ball and tossed it into the nearby garbage can. "And you can keep your voice down. If you haven't already blown your cover to smithereens, we might be wise not to let the rest of the world in on it."

"Good shot."

Cloutier raised his eyebrows. "I insulted you. What are you complimenting me for?"

"I meant the toss was a good shot, not the insult." Clare glowered. "Do you still want me to get in touch if I find anything useful? Or should I crawl into a hole and shut up forever as far as you're concerned?"

"You're still being paid — you don't get a free ride."

"Heaven forbid. If I waste any tax dollars I might end up as Utopia Girl's next victim."

"That's right." A smile tugged at Cloutier's lips, but he quickly stifled it.

"Did you pass on my suggestion about the antidote kit?"

"The paramedics had an injection ready, in case it was cyanide."

"Let me guess. It's wasn't."

"Aren't you clever?" Cloutier rolled his eyes. "But you have nothing to feel good about. I've never seen someone cock up an investigation like this in my life. Except once, and that guy's never gonna see another undercover gig again."

"I'm going to smoke. I'll be right outside if you think of anything else encouraging to say."

Clare grabbed her helmet and her cigarettes, and left the table.

She stood outside the donut shop trembling. It took her three tries to get her cigarette lit. She thought she'd been doing a good job, despite the odd fuck-up. Was she supposed to be perfect at everything her first time through?

Cloutier came outside after a few minutes. He stood a few feet away, and smoked his own cigarette without speaking.

It was Clare who broke the silence. "Both Diane and Jonathan were on staff last night. I think I saw Brian there, too."

"You talk to them?"

"I spoke with Diane. Matthew Easton has been getting his students these gigs."

"Hmmph." Clare would have preferred *Good work, kid.* "You think you can get a job passing pastries around too?"

"Yep." Clare told him about Matthew's job offer the previous afternoon.

"It's not a secret society invite. But I suppose it's a start."

Clare was about tell Cloutier not to be too overwhelming with his praise when she saw Kevin approaching along Dundas Street.

"Shit! There's this guy I've been seeing. He can't see me with you. Quick. Hide."

"Where should I hide?" Cloutier smirked. "Should I duck behind a car? That's not obvious."

"I don't care. Just go somewhere. Away."

Cloutier stayed put. "What's wrong with our cover story?"

"I don't want to lie to him. We've barely started dating and I've had to lie so much already."

"Like about the fact that you're fucking your professor?"

"Can't you, like, go back inside the donut shop until I give you the all-clear?"

"Forget it, Vengel. Sorry — *Simpson*, at least for a couple of hours. As your handler, I'd like to see how well you can handle yourself. Besides, he already sees us talking, and he's headed this way."

"Kevin!" Clare turned and tried like mad to act natural. "How's it going? Day off?"

"Yeah, I like to take Sundays off." Was he being ironic? It would be cute if Clare wasn't so stressed by the meeting.

"You must be Clare's new flame," Cloutier said. "I'm her uncle Steve. Glad to finally meet you."

Great. Now Kevin would think Clare was some over-eager freak, telling her family about him after a couple of dates.

"Great to meet you." Kevin shook Cloutier's hand. "Do you two have time for a coffee?"

Clare shook her head. "I have to get going. I'm meeting some friends to work on a school project. And there's no way I'm leaving you alone with Uncle Steve. Who knows what embarrassing baby stories he'd pull out of the woodwork?"

"I'd love to hear those sometime." Kevin grinned.

"Maybe if we're still dating in a thousand years."

Clare kissed Kevin lightly and then zoomed off on her bike, first making sure that Cloutier was well on the way to his car.

FIFTY-NINE
JONATHAN

"Let me help you with that, Mom." Jonathan watched his mother strain to reach the top shelf.

"Got it." Anita showed her son the honey bear she'd retrieved. "You could put this on the floor for me, though. That horrible businessman is out there, so I'd prefer to stay back in the kitchen."

Jonathan took the honey and put it at the coffee station, scowling at the man in the cheap suit who flirted too heavily with his mother. Did the guy think that because he tipped her a quarter each morning on his lousy cup of coffee, Anita should be grateful enough to go on a date with him? His mother was too good for the assholes who patronized this place.

Jon smiled at Wendy, the woman with Down Syndrome who'd been working the cash since his mother had opened the café. He was sad that this would end soon. In the last several years, in addition to the smoking by-law that had cut business by half overnight, property taxes had risen to such a level that the small coffee shop would have to triple its numbers in order to keep its doors open, never mind run a profit. At least he liked to blame the property taxes. It was easier than questioning his mother's business acumen.

Wendy smiled back. "Is that girl Jessica your girlfriend?"

"Not yet. But I'm hoping." Jonathan ducked back into the kitchen.

"A boy called Brian phoned," Anita said when Jon returned. "He said thanks for last night, and could you give him a call before today's meeting?"

Why did his mother insist on calling friends his age "boys"?

"What did you tell him?"

"I said you'd phone back. Is that a problem?"

"It's perfect."

Jonathan pulled his iPhone from his pocket and went out into the back alley for privacy.

"Brian. Hi."

"Jonathan? Thank you so much for getting me that catering job last night. It was amazing. I know it sucks that John Alton collapsed — you heard he died in the ambulance, right? But wow — to be that close to so many cabinet ministers. It was amazing."

"I would have thought politicians would be old hat to you. What with your dad so involved."

Jonathan fished his marijuana pipe from his pocket and lit it. It looked like a cigarette, in case anyone wandered by.

"The Communist Party has never won any seats."

Jon held his breath a moment longer, then exhaled. "Well, you're welcome. Now are you sure you want to crash this meeting?"

"More sure than I've ever been about anything."

"Okay." Jonathan looked around. Of course no one was listening. "Here's what to do."

SIXTY
LAURA

"I think we can narrow our field down to three main probabilities." Penny passed Laura the cappuccino she had just finished making.

"Great," said Laura. "Then we're ready to go to the police."

"Not just yet." Penny pursed her lips thoughtfully. "We have all this information at our fingertips. Wouldn't it be great if we could narrow it down and hand them only the theory that's right?"

"It would be fantastic." Laura sipped her coffee, and thought it would taste better if she hadn't had so much to drink the night before. "But don't you think, with all their detectives and resources, they might come to that conclusion faster than we can?"

Penny shook her head. "Just hear me out. First, there's Project Health — although we're still missing the explanation for Libby Leighton in that case. This would make Marisa Jordan, Sam Cray, and Simon McFarlane the next likely deaths."

Laura decided to humor Penny, at least for the moment. "Do we know the result of the Big Think?"

"Nothing of significance. Mostly shuffling around resources. Deciding which hospitals got MRI machines, that kind of thing."

"Why would McFarlane be on that committee? Isn't his

specialty business management?"

"I think that was the point," Penny said. "The left-wing city council wants to show that it can think like a businessman, too."

Laura rolled her eyes. "If our politicians spent half as much time on substantive concerns as they do on their image, we'd have the best-run country in the world."

Penny grinned. "Some might argue that we do have the best-run country in the world. Barring those perfect places like Denmark who just do everything right."

"What else did this think tank do?" Laura asked. "Allocated MRI machines, anything else?"

"They decided which hospitals would close their emergency rooms and become mainly research or specialty centers."

"I remember that. It caused a bunch of havoc — when my son broke his ankle playing football, we had to drive him around to three hospitals before we found one with an ER."

Penny sipped her coffee. "Next we have the integrated public housing bill, making Marisa Jordan the only remaining victim. Unless the killer goes after the civil servants on the committee as well. But something tells me he or she will stop with politicians."

"Poor Marisa. She's on both lists. So in this second scenario, is Carl Haas our culprit?"

Penny's eyes twinkled. "Possibly. But his son goes to U of T. Maybe Susannah knows him?"

"How could I possibly find that out? She's gone, remember?"

"You don't have her cell number?"

Laura shook her head. "I'm not calling."

"Right. We'll look into that later. And our third possibility is homelessness."

Susannah's pet project at the Brighter Day. "Why homelessness?" Laura said. "I thought we'd ruled that out."

"This one's complicated. Hayden increased business taxes every year he was mayor."

"Okay." Laura breathed easier. Susannah would definitely not care about that.

"One of the reasons he cited year after year was the home-lessness budget."

Again, this should make Susannah pleased, not displeased.

"And then a committee was formed."

"How familiar that sounds."

"Doesn't it?" Penny smiled. "Its job was to assess the costs — administrative, shelter, food, et cetera — that the city was paying, per homeless person, to offset the homelessness issue."

"Offset the issue?" Laura laughed bitterly. "They threw money at the problem, but nothing ever changed. Maybe some bureau-crats got fatter salaries, but any real change happened at ground level, from volunteer efforts." An opinion Laura knew Susannah shared. It was what had brought them together in the first place.

"Right. Except that the committee assessed the costs at $40,000 per year per homeless person. Someone said at the time that it would have been cheaper to send all the homeless to Cuba to an all-expenses-paid resort."

"So who would the victims be?" Laura asked. "The committee who assessed the cost, or the politicians who spent the money?"

"I think the politicians." Penny consulted a piece of paper in front of her. "Hayden is clear enough. He was mayor. Leighton makes sense, too. She didn't care what she spent, if she could get her picture in the news. I'm having trouble connecting John Alton into this. Manuel Ruiz did introduce a homelessness bill, and gen-erally supported large spending — so again, he makes sense, even if obliquely."

"Who would the next victims be?"

This theory was the murkiest, and the one Laura feared the most.

"That's just it." Penny shook her head. "It could be almost anyone in city politics."

"We have to go to the cops," Laura said.

"No! Laura, you promised. Give it until the end of the day. We're so close to solving this thing."

"I promised until the end of yesterday. But all right. One more day. Then we go to them together."

"Sure." Why didn't Penny sound convincing? "Tomorrow. Absolutely."

SIXTY-ONE
CLARE

Clare revved her engine and sped out from the parking spot behind her apartment. A small stone flew up and smacked her helmet. She knew she should be more careful on the gravel, but at the moment, road safety was the last thing that concerned her.

Cloutier was an ass. Who the fuck was he to criticize her work? If Clare had taken her cues from him since the beginning, she would have been back on her beat and doing paperwork by now.

She glared at the lines on the road. She didn't have a destination in mind, but she soon found herself heading north on Highway 400, toward Orillia and the trailer park where she'd grown up. She hadn't been home in ages, and of course while on assignment she wasn't supposed to go now. But Clare was in a mood for breaking rules. She was clearly going to lose her job anyway; it might as well be on her terms as theirs.

She had loved the trailer growing up. It wasn't thrilling — she spent the average summer evening sitting on the porch with her parents, drinking iced tea while they guzzled a two-four, chatting with whatever neighbors wandered by. But it had been companionable, a pleasant place to be. Not like now.

Her father's good days were numbered. He had been diagnosed with emphysema two years before, and Clare knew that he was still smoking. So far — she had no idea how — he'd managed to fool his doctors into thinking he'd quit, so he remained a lung transplant candidate, but if they saw the signs of smoking, he'd be off the list immediately. Clare couldn't figure out if the addiction was too powerful (she knew her own was, though she always told herself she'd stop on her twenty-fourth birthday, which was still two years away). Or was it worse than that? Did her father, the town's official arm wrestling champion for twelve years running, simply not feel that he had anything to live for?

When she arrived in Orillia, she stopped downtown first. Her mother loved flowers, and her father never bought them anymore. Clare parked her bike, but she kept the helmet with her. The bulky half sphere served as a constant reminder that she'd moved beyond this place; that she'd packed up after high school, zoomed away, and created a life of her own.

She saw Shauna Bartlett in some stupid yellow skirt. Even half a block away, there was desperation in Shauna's walk; it was too bouncy, too obvious in its attempt to look purposeful. How could Lance begin to find her attractive? Clare smiled broadly as they passed on the sidewalk.

She hugged the helmet tight against her body. There was Ricky with a shopping bag from the butcher's, dancing to some tune inside his head. Had he really left Lorraine, like Roberta had said? Clare had always been attracted to Ricky, quietly offbeat, comically self-deprecating. She unzipped her leather jacket and let the straps jangle with the movement of her body. She nodded a greeting, told him maybe she'd see him later that evening at bingo.

Bingo was her mother's preferred way to pass a Sunday evening. If Clare stayed until evening. She went into the florist and picked out some sunflowers — her mother's all-time favorite, and her own. But on the way back to her bike, she dumped the flowers in the trash. What was she thinking, going home while undercover?

As she sped back toward the city, Clare told herself it was job devotion that had kept her from continuing on to see her parents. She told herself again, but she didn't believe it. She couldn't bear to hear her father's wheezing, then listen to his half-baked excuse about going to the store for some milk, or popping by the garage to check on someone's car, when Clare knew all he wanted was to go and be alone and smoke a cigarette.

When Clare pulled back into her parking spot at home, she was lost. So much for taking a ride to clear her head. She felt worse than when she'd started out.

She needed to blow off some steam. Not through drinking — she'd tried that once this week already, and besides, it wasn't obliteration she craved. She wanted to skydive or mountain climb or do something big, that could use up some of her wild energy.

Like spy on a society meeting.

SIXTY-TWO
ANNABEL

Annabel was in Starbucks ordering a half-caf, half-soy, half-skim vanilla latté, when her BlackBerry buzzed in her back pocket.

Utopia Girl: *You still think we're writing this book together, don't you?*

She paid for the drink, then leaned against the wall to wait.

Death Reporter: *Have you changed your mind?*

Utopia Girl: *No. Made up my mind not to let you long ago.*

Death Reporter: *Why?*

Utopia Girl: *Don't like you.*

Death Reporter: *But this is about mutual benefit.*

Utopia Girl: *What will I gain if you publish this book? Can't collect royalties whether I'm caught or not.*

Annabel glanced around her. No one was close enough to watch her type.

Death Reporter: *I told you that I'll find a way of getting them to you. An anonymous bank account — even I won't have to know who you are.*

Utopia Girl: *No, you tell the cops the number of the account and they find me withdrawing from it. Think again, Death Whore.*

Death Reporter: *So why have you been talking to me?*

She grabbed her latté from the shelf, and stuck a lid on it, before heading for the door.

Utopia Girl: *Sanity. You think it's easy to kill a bunch of people and keep all that emotion bottled up. It would be enough to give the fittest person ulcers.*

Death Reporter: *So you don't want your story told to the world?*

Utopia Girl: *Screw telling the story to a bunch of ignorant assholes. The world will read it with amusement then go on their merry way.*

Death Reporter: *So why do you trust me with this stuff?*

Utopia Girl: *I haven't told you anything that matters. Besides, it's easy to trust someone when you know they'll be dead soon.*

Death Reporter: *Are you threatening me?*

Utopia Girl: *Do you think you're hard to find, in your downtown starter condo, as you walk to work along Adelaide and down Yonge Street and then home again by the same route? Sometimes you meet your sister for drinks, and more occasionally you see the man you wish was your boyfriend. On Friday you wore pink. It didn't suit you.*

Starter condo? Where did Utopia Girl live, some glamorous student dormitory?

Death Reporter: *You need to stop this. I've put up with your abuse, for the sake of a good story, but I won't stick around to hear threats.*

Utopia Girl: *Then turn off your BlackBerry. I'm calling the shots. This is the story of your life.*

Annabel had arrived back at her building. Something had to change. This was not going according to plan.

Death Reporter: *I'm not willing to pay with my life.*

SIXTY-THREE
MATTHEW

"Are we all here?"

Matthew glanced around the small room, lined with boxes of restaurant supplies. He was proud of this group. Once the pudgy little kid who was last picked for sports teams and forgotten on schoolmates' party invite lists, Matthew had created a society with so much mystique that he could hand-pick his members from each year's academic elite.

But now someone was threatening all that — from within or without, Matthew didn't know. He had to decide whether to disband the society — at least temporarily — or to keep it together and fight.

"We're all here, sir." Brian's voice was higher-pitched than usual. Poor kid was clearly nervous. He'd found out about the meeting somehow, and shown up at the beginning, forcing an impromptu membership vote.

Diane shook her head. "You've been a member for five minutes, Haas. You'd think you could start out by listening."

Ah, Diane. She was a sexy little thing, even if she came across as a tight-assed bitch. Matthew had enjoyed his time with her. She'd been a surprisingly good lover for her then eighteen years.

Shame she hated him now.

"Brian didn't join this group to listen." Jonathan shot Diane a glare. "Just like you didn't come into our lives to make them any more pleasant."

Nice kid, Jonathan. Bit of a one-issue wonder. Matthew's goal with him was to bring him out of his angry anti-small-business-tax phase and help him look at society as a whole.

"Dr. Easton, can you make him be quiet?" Diane's quirky silent dig — she called him Dr. Easton as often as possible and even when they were alone, though he had told her several times to continue to use his first name after they stopped sleeping together.

"No." Matthew smiled.

"I can make you be quiet." Jonathan shook a fist at Diane.

"Really? With violence?" Diane looked around the room for some support, but found none.

"Anyway," Jessica said, "I'm interested in hearing this new order of business Brian wants to propose."

Jessica was odd. Although she was one of the most naturally attractive women he had ever taught, Matthew had not once been tempted to make a pass at her. She seemed open, she acted laid-back, and yet he actually felt depressed at the thought of getting her in bed.

"I'm not suggesting we do anything all at once." Brian reached into his knapsack and pulled out an expensively bound notebook that looked about five hundred pages thick. "This is my family's manifesto."

Susannah toyed with her ceramic coffee mug — refreshments courtesy of Jonathan's mother, who had loaned them her store room for the meeting. "You say that like you're proud to have a family manifesto. Like you don't think it's weird at all."

"I recognize that it's not the norm." Brian's voice lowered slightly in pitch. "And I certainly don't mean to gloat about it."

"Gloat?" Susannah's eyebrows lifted.

"I've been sent here for a purpose. There are goals that I would like to see accomplished."

"Sent here?" Diane hooted. "You mean, like, to Earth? Does anyone want to take a re-vote on Brian's acceptance?"

Jessica leaned forward in her chair. "What goals, Brian? Forget what these negative ions have to say. I'm interested."

"Spare me." Diane rolled her eyes at Jessica.

"Why should I?" Jessica rolled her eyes back.

"Guys, this is nuts," Matthew said, in the most authoritative voice he could muster. "Brian, we'll get to your manifesto in a bit. First we have to cut some of this tension."

Jonathan spoke. "It's the Utopia Killer. We want to believe that someone's framing us — or misdirecting the cops toward us — but when it comes down to it, we're scared. What if the killer is one of us?"

"What if?" Susannah said. "How could it not be one of us? Who else has access to the business cards?"

"They're left at rallies and protests all the time. Anyone could grab one and make copies."

"Did anyone else receive the card? Or only Libby Leighton?" Jessica asked.

"How would we know?" Susannah looked at her like she was simple. "Do you think the police come to us with every new clue they find?"

"It could be someone from another year," Jessica said. "Is that Elise girl still in jail? Maybe she's out and back in business."

"She's still in jail," Matthew said softly.

"It's kind of too much," Jonathan said. "If it's all the same to you, Dr. Easton, I'd prefer not to be given any more catering gigs until the killer is caught."

"I think it's best if no one does any more catering until the killer is caught." Matthew studied his students. "I'm sorry if you've come to depend on it as a source of income, but it isn't worth being implicated in these murders."

"Who was working the events?" Diane clicked her pen.

"Let's not go there." Matthew was firm.

SIXTY-FOUR
CLARE

No. Heaven forbid they "go there." Why would Matthew want to help narrow the field of suspects? Clare desperately wanted to smoke, but the store-room window was open, and she didn't want to draw attention to the bin where she was crouching in the alley.

Susannah's voice was strong and clear. "Look, we all had access. If we weren't working a given event, we could have stopped by and made up any lame excuse if we were seen by the others."

"I told you I thought I left my bow tie in Elly's van." Diane's nasal tone pierced Clare's ears even at a distance.

"So how come you needed to crash Libby Leighton's house party to get the tie when you weren't working?" Susannah said. "Some freaky sex ritual with your accountant boyfriend?"

Clare could picture Diane glowering, and the room filled up with laughter.

"Let's leave the alibi checking to the police," Matthew said. "What's the point of mistrusting each other and saying things that will damage friendships going forward?"

"What's the point of an action-based society if we run away from solving our own problems?" Susannah said. "If it *is* one of us, we have more information than the police do to solve this thing."

A car turned into the alley. Clare was well enough hidden to avoid being seen by the driver, but the noise muffled the meeting for a couple of minutes while the car crunched the gravel and settled into its parking spot a few buildings over.

"Dr. Robertson," she heard Susannah saying as the noise abated. "Maybe one or two others in the Poli Sci Department. They hate this class, Dr. Easton, everything it stands for."

"Why?" said Jessica. "Who would —" Her voice was softer than the others', and Clare lost the rest of her statement.

Susannah's voice was not so soft. "Because they represent the status quo. They're teaching the old system they know and love. Dr. Easton challenges all that. He makes politics positive. He empowers us to ask the questions they don't want us to think about. The questions that will truly lead to change."

"The fuddy-duddies wouldn't be behind the calling cards or murders, though." Good old Brian. Clare was glad he'd found a way into the club. He would likely be disappointed soon. Even if the club stayed intact, Clare doubted that his belonging to the SPU would bring him any closer to seeing his father's manifesto realized. But it would be better than feeling forever shut out. "If they hate change, they wouldn't create it, not even to discredit Dr. Easton."

"I might resign from the society," said Jonathan. "I see Susannah's point, about sticking it out and solving this together, but I don't think we can change the world by devouring ourselves from within."

"I agree with you." Matthew's response surprised Clare. "I'm thinking of disbanding the society."

It obviously made sense to disband the club, but Clare hoped like hell it didn't happen. How was she supposed to crack this case if her one major source of clues was eliminated?

"Disbanding it?" Susannah sounded stunned. "Isn't that extreme?"

"Isn't murder?"

Jessica spoke again. Clare couldn't hear her words, but she sounded sad.

"Yes," Matthew said, apparently in response to Jessica. "I'm afraid I do."

"Who do you think it is?" Diane asked.

"I honestly have no idea."

Frustratingly for Clare, the overall voice level subsided after this. From the clips she could gather, the fate of the society was left tentative. No meetings, and no activities — legal or otherwise — would be organized until the Utopia Killer was caught. Which at the rate the investigation was going, Clare estimated would be sometime the following decade.

SIXTY-FIVE
ANNABEL

Annabel's gaze darted around the busy restaurant. Normally she loved the city. Crowds of people buoyed her up and gave her energy. But tonight, everywhere she looked she thought she saw someone listening in on her conversation.

Her eyes stopped moving when they came to Katherine. "Do you think she's misleading me? Maybe she's not really a student, has heard about that secret society some other way? Knows I'm dating Matthew?"

"No," Katherine said. "In fact, I'd put money on most of what Utopia Girl says being true."

"Why?"

"She's arrogant. Thinks they'll never catch her. So she throws out some clues. Adds to the adrenaline."

"Like murder doesn't give her enough adrenaline. Why am I doing this again?"

"Reach for the stars, right?" Katherine picked up her wine glass.

"Yeah. Like Mom used to say."

"Yeah, but, *Oh Honey, I didn't mean that star. It's the brightest one in the sky, for heaven's sake."*

"So why shouldn't I reach for it?" Annabel impersonated her younger self, or her sister's.

"Yeah." Katherine laughed. "And then she'd say, *Why don't you try this star, right here? It's a bit lower, it may be easier for you to reach.*"

"But Mom, that's a planet."

"There's nothing wrong with planets. Planets can be wonderful."

"So I shouldn't reach for the stars?"

"I'd hate to see you disappointed."

"Good Lord." Annabel drained her glass of wine. "And I wonder why I have no confidence. How'd you get so strong?"

"Me?" Katherine raised her eyebrows. "I might hide behind my law degree, but any confidence I have is skin deep."

"Can I sleep at your place tonight?"

Katherine looked at her sister with concern. "Of course you can. Mike's out of town, so it'll be you and me and Lucy. Should we rent some '80s movies and pig out on sundaes and popcorn?"

"Really?" Annabel felt her anxiety begin to lessen. "Can we get the low-fat Cool Whip?"

"Have you tried that stuff recently?" Katherine made a puking gesture.

"Pretty gross?" Annabel motioned for the bill and gave the waiter her credit card.

"The worst. But I bet it tastes fabulous with *Footloose* and *Sixteen Candles.*"

"You'd let your six-year-old watch *Sixteen Candles*?"

"Sure." Katherine shrugged.

They went to an all-night grocery store, and loaded up on the comfort food of their adolescence. By the time they arrived at Katherine's Gloucester Street townhouse, Annabel had all but forgotten the stress that had motivated the sleepover to begin with. So it was with not much trepidation that she pulled her BlackBerry from her pocket in response to the familiar beep.

Utopia Girl: *Having fun with your sister?*

Katherine was in the kitchen blending margaritas. Annabel was supposed to be figuring out the DVD player, which couldn't possibly be as confusing as it seemed.

Death Reporter: *Come on, that's not funny.*

Utopia Girl: *Cute kid. She your niece?*

Annabel shut off her BlackBerry and collapsed on the sofa trembling. Katherine came in shortly with the oversized cocktails. She set them down on the coffee table and hurried to Annabel's side.

"Close the blinds," Annabel said.

"You're worrying way too much." But Katherine closed them.

"Utopia Girl just asked about you."

"Come on. She isn't watching through the window." Katherine pried open a slat and peered through. "She probably saw me pick you up at work, or saw us walking to the restaurant."

Annabel looked at the drink tray, but the last thing she wanted was alcohol. She needed to stay lucid; she needed to win this war.

"She mentioned Lucy."

Katherine froze. "Maybe it's time to go to the police."

"I don't think I *can* go to the police anymore. I'm pretty sure that I'm already an accessory."

"An accessory helps commit the murder, or cover it up. You've done neither." Katherine took a sip from a margarita, then pushed her drink away. "I'll make some tea."

Annabel followed her sister into the kitchen. "Obstructing justice, then? Aren't I obliged to give them what evidence I have?"

"Evidence, yes. But this is speculation." Katherine filled the kettle from the sink. "You don't know this is the real killer. You don't know that what she's saying is true. You're not hiding anyone out in a basement or lying about something you've seen."

Annabel pulled three mugs down from the shelf. "Do you think there's a possibility I'm not really talking to the killer?"

"Let's hope you're not. Where's Lucy?"

"Putting on her pajamas. I asked her if she wanted help but she looked at me like I had green cheese for brains."

"She never wants help with anything." Katherine smiled grimly. "Like her lunatic aunt."

"Please. Like her mother." Annabel pulled down the blind on the kitchen window. "We have to get Lucy out of here."

"Where would we take her?"

"You're right," Annabel said. "I'm being stupid. I'll leave. Then the danger leaves with me."

"No! Don't go anywhere." Katherine followed her sister back into the living room.

Annabel put on her jacket, grabbed her purse. "I have to. I can't believe I was selfish enough to come here in the first place."

"Stay! It's not selfish. We'll block the doors, make a fort, and watch our movies. It'll be like an adventure."

"Make a fort?" Lucy came stomping down the stairs in railroad train pajamas. "Really? Can we?"

Annabel put on her brightest smile for the kid. "You and your mom can. But I have to get going."

SIXTY-SIX
CLARE

"Not into this tonight?"

"Sorry. It's nothing you're doing. Or not doing. I'm just stressed."

"What's wrong?" Kevin shifted away a couple of inches, but still lay facing her. "Is it something to do with your uncle?"

"My uncle? Oh, the one you met this afternoon."

"He isn't your uncle, is he?"

"Of course he is."

"What was his name again?"

"Are you testing me?" Clare tried to act annoyed while she was panicking inside.

Kevin laughed. "Wow, you really are stressed. I just forgot your uncle's name."

She relaxed a bit. "His name is Glen."

"Wrong!" Clare could feel Kevin trying to meet her eyes. "It isn't Glen. It isn't Steve — which, incidentally, is the name he used to introduce himself."

Clare decided on the hostile approach. "Jesus, Kevin. Why do you think you can interrogate me like this?"

"I like you. A lot." Kevin shrugged the shoulder he wasn't lying on. "But you're afraid to talk to me. You act like you're protecting some great important secret, but I have no idea what that might be. Since we're not in an alternate universe, I'm thinking it's not the location of the Philosopher's Stone."

"I've known you less than a week. I don't expect to know all your secrets by now. Why should you know mine?"

"The difference," Kevin said, "is that I haven't lied to you."

"Yet."

"Forget it, then." Kevin was out of bed and into his jeans within seconds. "I was worried for you. I thought that you might be in something over your head. Call me an idiot, but I thought I could possibly help you."

Clare felt wretched. She wanted to pull him back into bed and tell him everything. But what kind of cop would that make her?

"Over my head?" Fine, her anger reaction was a few seconds delayed. But she made up for that with passion. "The guy's my fucking drug dealer. He sells me marijuana. Sometimes blow if I'm in the mood, which isn't often. I'm sorry he didn't introduce himself more candidly, but his job is illegal and he prefers to stay out of jail."

Kevin rolled his eyes. "So show me your weed supply."

"What?"

"This is our fourth night together, and I've never seen you smoke anything stronger than cigarettes."

This guy would make a better detective than Clare. It was breaking her heart to get rid of him.

"You don't get it, do you? I don't care if you think I'm a government spy or riddled with biker gang debt, or whatever it is you think I'm 'into.' I am so not cool with being the object of your scrutiny."

"Fine." Kevin took his watch from Clare's dresser and put it on. "I get it. I'm out of here."

Clare locked the door behind him, and trembled with frustration. She grabbed a beer from the fridge, and sat on her couch with the lights out. She dialed Lance, but got a stupid voice message where his floozy said that "we" were not in. Clare hung up, not wanting to leave "us" a message. Roberta was out — on a date, of all things. She couldn't call Matthew — she'd been with him the night before, and besides, she needed someone she could be real with.

The smallest tear fell down her cheek as she realized that only left herself. She lit a cigarette, and sat smoking in the light that came in from the street.

The country music in the background was probably not helpful to her mood. She remembered the old joke, and was tempted to play it backwards so she'd get her dog back, her truck back, her man back. She couldn't shake it; she was pining for the old days, when she and Lance would run around being stupid, when she wasn't over her head in an impossible job, when her parents were healthy enough to be present in a conversation.

MONDAY / SEPTEMBER 13

SIXTY-SEVEN
ANNABEL

"I need to speak with Detective Inspector Morton. It's concerning the dead politicians." Annabel was working to keep her voice from warbling. Despite her sister's assurances, she fully expected to be arrested for something. Still, that was better than dying.

After ages on hold, a man's voice came on the line. "David Morton here."

"I'm Annabel Davis. You interviewed me after Hayden Pritchard was killed."

"I know who you are."

"I, um. I think I might have done something stupid."

"You contacted the killer." His voice was even.

"How did you know?"

"You had access. You're a reporter. It would have been nice if your concern for our investigation had prevented you from exploiting the opportunity, but I won't pretend that I'm surprised you took the low road."

Ouch. "I'm coming to you now."

"Why?" Morton's voice dripped with scorn. "Did you receive a death threat?"

"Um."

"Surprised I knew that, too?"

"Yes." Annabel didn't think her voice could get any smaller.

"You're dealing with a killer. The threat is real. And now — let me guess — you want protection."

"Um." Annabel clenched the telephone handset tightly.

"You're a criminal yourself, for impeding this investigation."

"I accept that," Annabel said weakly. "I'll take full responsibility. And obviously I'll share everything I've learned, all the transcripts of our conversations."

"Obviously," Morton said. "Okay. Come in with what you have."

"Um."

Morton groaned. "You think she's watching you."

"I know she is."

There was a long pause, and Morton finally said, "I'll send a car for you now, and we'll find you someplace safe to sleep. I'm not promising red carpet protection, but if you can live with a limited social life, we'll get you to and from work safely."

"Thank you." This was more than Annabel had hoped for.

SIXTY-EIGHT
CLARE

Clare squished out her cigarette with her sneaker and entered the campus café.

"Jessica!" Clare was pleased to see a friendly face.

Jessica's eyes lifted briefly from the newspaper, and returned to her reading. "Hey."

"Can I join you? I'm going to grab a coffee."

"Sure. You can have a section of the paper."

"You're reading the obituaries." Clare pulled up a chair when she returned with an oversized dark roast.

"I find death comforting," Jessica said with a wry smile.

"Anyone you know in there?"

"Not today."

Thankfully, Morton hadn't given the *Star* the go-ahead yet to publish the politicians' fake obituaries. Clare wondered if Cloutier had been bluffing for some stupid reason, or if Morton was waiting out the right time.

"Why do you find death comforting?" Clare blew on her coffee.

"I'm weird I guess." Jessica shrugged. "It should make me sad. But reading the obituaries — you know, the loving ones, written by the families — makes me feel closer to my parents, however briefly."

"I'm so sorry. At least your grandparents are nice." Clare realized how dumb that sounded once it was out.

"They *are* nice. But old. They never understood me the same way."

"How did your mom die?"

"She killed herself."

Clare was stunned. "I'm so sorry."

"Don't be," Jessica said. "If anything, my parents' tragedy gives me more reason to make a difference."

"Because your parents never got to fulfill their own destinies?" Clare wished she could get to that place with her own father, instead of resenting the emotional havoc he wreaked on her mother and her.

"Maybe. But I don't like to play the sympathy card. I appreciate that you cared to ask. But I'd rather people just think I'm an overprivileged tree-hugger." Jessica grinned.

"You got it. I can actually understand where you're coming from."

"You think?" Jessica looked at Clare dubiously.

"Not about the tree-hugging." Clare told Jessica about her own father, killing himself with tobacco.

"My god." Jessica looked pointedly at the pack of smokes on the table between them. "Wait. Wasn't yours the smoking bill? As in, you wanted to make cigarette sales illegal?"

"I know." Clare eyed her pack on the table and gave Jessica a lopsided grin. "We are creatures of contradiction, aren't we?"

"Well, certainly you are."

TUESDAY / SEPTEMBER 14

SIXTY-NINE
JONATHAN

Jonathan's bill passed easily through Utopian Parliament. Churches would no longer be exempt from paying property taxes, and small businesses would no longer be forced to contribute the lion's share.

Jon felt almost as elated as if the bill had passed in real life. It was too late to save his mother's café, but maybe, if his classmates were remotely representative of the politicians of the future, stories like hers would one day be nothing but news from the past.

When the class was dismissed, Diane approached him.

"I respect your viewpoint," she said. "I thought your bill was intelligently drafted. You made taxes make sense, which isn't easy."

Jonathan looked at her. "What's the catch?"

"I have an amendment I'm going to propose."

Ugh. Why did Diane insist on being such a thorn in his side? "The bill's already been passed. You should have proposed the amendment when it was on the table."

"Don't you want to hear my side?" Diane looked hurt, which was obviously an act.

But Jessica was engaged in what looked like an intense

conversation with Dr. Easton, and Jon would only be waiting around in the hall.

"Fine."

Diane's cross sparkled in the sunlight coming through the window. "I agree that churches and mosques and other places of worship should contribute. But they should get credit for any good works they do in the community."

"What good works? Taking little children's minds and brainwashing them with scary tales about floods and Satan?" Jonathan felt his nostrils flare, and reminded himself that this wasn't worth losing his temper over. He made an effort to speak evenly. "The Catholic church has got to be the most hypocritical organization in the universe. They take money from the suckers in their congregations, preach the virtues of poverty so no one minds paying more than they can afford, then they funnel the cash away so the pope and cardinals can live in gay luxury in Italy."

"Vatican City isn't technically in Italy."

"So you agree the rest is true?"

Diane smiled benignly. "You can't win an argument with an ignorant man."

"My point," Jonathan said, "is that religious organizations look out for their own interests. I'm not willing to offer a tax credit for that."

Diane put a finger to her chin. "What about credit for good works outside of religion? Like employment projects in the community? Habitat for Humanity is a faith-based organization — don't tell me you think they're hypocrites."

"Okay. I'll agree to your amendment *if* businesses can get a tax break when they're adversely affected by a new law, like a smoking ban."

"I think it's great that people can't smoke in bars and restaurants," Diane said. "I, for one, go out way more often since that ban has been put in place."

"I'm sure the herbal tea you order more than makes up for the dozens of people who now drink beer at home."

"I don't think those two laws should go together," Diane said. "It makes for a convoluted American-style bill."

"We have all year to debate it." Jonathan tossed his knapsack over his shoulder. "You prepare your amendment, I'll prepare mine."

Jonathan headed toward the door, but the exit was congested. There were only six or seven people in front of him, but the line was moving surprisingly slowly. When he came to the door, he saw a uniformed officer standing with Inspector Morton. A table was set up with a bunch of bags on it, and two more uniformed cops were going through them. A woman in baggy khakis had her own small desk set up, where she appeared to be examining a cell phone.

"We'll need your bag, please." The officer at the door spoke abruptly.

Jonathan faced him. "Can I see a warrant?"

Inspector Morton produced a piece of paper from his breast pocket.

"Fine." Jonathan handed over his knapsack without reading the warrant. "What's this about?"

"You can wait over there." The officer pointed toward the opposite side of the hallway, where a group of his classmates was gathered.

"What's going on?" he asked Clare, who was standing among the other students.

"I'm not sure." Clare shook her head. "They seem interested in anything electronic."

"They —" Shit. "What do you mean?"

"They're going through the bags, and when they find a phone or a laptop or anything, that lady turns it on and does something."

Jonathan relaxed. His iPhone was in his jacket pocket, and his laptop was at home.

"I'm gonna need your jackets, too." Could that asshole read his mind?

Jonathan and a couple of others who had jackets took them

off and placed them onto the pile of bags. "This is like airport security, but without the social graces."

"Tell me about it." Clare grimaced.

"You can clear out of here once you have all your things back."

Four or five people had had their bags returned, but no one was leaving.

"Come on. Move. This hallway isn't a frat party." The uniformed officer looked pointedly at Brian, Susannah, and some others.

"The coffee house," Susannah said loudly to the group as she began to walk away. "I look forward to seeing any and all of you there. Well, maybe not you cops."

The collective laugh was louder than Jonathan thought was respectful, so he joined in.

Jessica came out of the classroom and joined Jon and Clare in the hallway. "This is so weird. They have no leads, so they decide to hassle us."

"They must have a lead," Clare said. "Or they wouldn't have a warrant."

Jonathan snorted. "I think suspicious breathing would be enough to get a warrant. This case is so high-profile, they have to be seen to be doing something."

Clare said goodbye as her bag was returned, and said she'd see them in the campus café. Dr. Easton and Diane came out of the classroom — which was odd, because didn't they hate each other? — and Dr. Easton locked the door behind them.

The searchers were looking through Jonathan's things now. One gave his knapsack the all-clear while the other pulled his handheld from his inner jacket pocket.

"Wish me luck," he told Jessica.

Her eyes widened. "Do you need it?"

Jonathan watched as the woman turned on his phone and attached a cord to his dock connector.

"What's she doing?" Jessica asked.

"I think she's recording the logs. Emails sent, websites visited, that kind of thing."

Jonathan didn't take his eyes from the woman. While the data was being transferred, she was looking at his phone, pressing buttons, pressing more buttons.

"So why do you look so worried?"

The woman stopped what she was doing and held Jon's phone in the air. "Whose is this?"

How could she have found what she was looking for so fast? Jonathan shrugged. He could run, but what was the point?

"It's mine."

SEVENTY
CLARE

C lare felt like her veins were made of coffee. She shouldn't
be drinking another one, but what else was there to do?
It was eleven a.m., and if anyone had a class, they were
not inclined to go. The entire Poli Real World class, with the excep-
tion of those not yet released by the cops, was gathered in this café.

When Matthew, Diane, and Jessica approached the group
together, it was clear from their posture that they were bearing
what they thought was bad news.

"Jonathan was arrested," Diane said, when they got close
enough. "They think he's the Utopia Killer."

Clare set her coffee down slowly. This was the end. She could
pack up her things and go back to her uniform job. She had made
exactly zero contributions to the case — at least none that
Cloutier or Morton deemed relevant. She wanted to stand up, to
pound the table, to scream obscenities in everyone's direction.
She breathed deeply, folded her hands on the table in front of her,
and settled in to listen to what her classmates had to say.

Susannah spoke first. "Sorry, Diane. I thought it was you."

Of course it wasn't Diane. That first letter, the rant about small
businesses closing up shop because of municipal tax hikes — and

then in the third one he mentioned the smoking by-law's effect on cafés and restaurants — Clare should have put it together long ago.

"I think the important question here," said Matthew, "is what is our collective responsibility to Jonathan?"

Diane spoke quietly. "He went willingly. He didn't seem surprised to be arrested."

"But a killer?" Brian said. "We've known the guy for three years."

"Let's think generally if we can," Matthew said. "When someone we know is arrested, do we assume he's guilty because the police do? Do we assume he's innocent because we know him and like him? Or do we try to figure out how to act like his friend regardless of what he may or may not have done?"

Although no one spoke up right away, Clare could see glimmers of comprehension flicker through the students' eyes.

Finally Diane said, "I think we have to consider the probability that he's guilty. I'm sure that if we looked at statistics, we'd see more accurate arrests than false ones."

"Why are you sure about that?" Susannah asked. "Faith in the system? I guess when the system has treated you well, blind faith is a logical response."

"Come on, Susannah." Diane's tone, for once, was conciliatory. "I know that the system can fail us. I just think that it's a safe bet that there are more true arrests than false ones. So our *a priori* assumption would be that Jonathan is guilty."

Jessica shook her head. "That seems too detached when it's our classmate. If we determine that he *is* guilty, do we consider his motives before deciding if we should help him, or do we write him off as a bad seed and go on with our lives?"

"If he's a killer?" Diane stared at Jessica. "That would be the end for me. I couldn't help him get out of jail time no matter what his motive was."

"I wouldn't help him get out of the jail time," Susannah said. "But there are other ways to be there. We can help him figure out how to make the most of his time inside, sort out what he wants to do once he's out of jail."

"Are you insane?" Diane exploded. "The guy's a killer. Killers kill. There's only one wise course of action, and that is to distance ourselves as far from him as possible."

"Sure," Susannah said. "If you live your life based on fear."

"Fear has nothing to do with it." Diane's face colored to almost precisely match her pink headband. "It's survival. The most basic human instinct, which you all seem to be lacking."

Matthew laughed. "Diane has a point. And so do the rest of you. Listen, let's leave this discussion open. Think about your positions, put them into writing, and we'll reconvene next class."

"Into writing?" Brian looked horrified. "Are we throwing the curriculum out the window and turning this into a social studies class?"

"No." Matthew looked at him. "We're turning it into Political Utopia for the *Real* World."

Clare stood up. She needed nourishment, or the coffee would erode her guts. She went to the counter and picked out a yogurt cup and a bottle of juice. As she was paying, she saw a sign beside the cash register. *Now Hiring.*

"Can I get an application?" she asked the woman working the cash.

"Be my guest." The woman reached below the counter and pulled out a sheet of paper. "The hours are long, but at least the pay is crappy."

Clare smirked. "It's still a job, right?"

SEVENTY-ONE
LAURA

"An arrest? That's wonderful news." Laura clenched her teeth together as she waited to hear the name.

"A kid called Jonathan Whyte." Penny spoke quickly. She clearly had a thousand places to be. "He's a poli sci major at U of T."

"Wow." Laura sat down at the kitchen table. "Were we anywhere close with our motive?"

"Don't know yet. The police have a confession, but they haven't granted me that interview yet."

"You must be so excited."

"Excited?" Penny seemed not to have heard of the word. "Certainly gratified."

"Well, congratulations. I won't keep you. Thanks for letting me know."

"You're welcome." Penny paused. "It's been a pleasure reconnecting with you. We should go for drinks. Or dinner."

"Sounds great." Laura knew Penny was only being polite.

"Maybe one night this week. I'll be in touch once I have a better grasp on my schedule."

Laura clicked off the handset and stared out the window into her backyard. It was less than a week since she'd watched Susannah muck around with the tomatoes. What she wouldn't give to have that week to live differently.

SEVENTY-TWO
ANNABEL

"What can I do?" Annabel sat glumly with her sister in the dingy Tex-Mex restaurant. "I've messed this up so badly.'

"You still have your job," Katherine said.

"For now. I don't know what the inspector plans to tell Penny in her precious exclusive interview."

"You're alive. No psycho killer came through the window or sliced you up in the shower."

"That's something."

"So what's eating you up? You got out of this unscathed."

"The guilt. I could explode from all the guilt. How many people might still be alive if I'd called the police as soon as I'd established contact with Jonathan?"

"You're kidding, right? I read those letters. There was nothing in there to give any clues to Whyte's identity. He was leading you to someone else. He was making the women look guilty, the professor. Not himself."

"But the police used my correspondence to identify Jonathan's computer. The letters he sent to the *Star* weren't traceable in the same way."

"So you've done them a favor." Katherine poked at her burrito, with which she didn't look enthralled. "Without you, he'd still be out there killing people."

"Maybe."

"Pick it up, Annabel. You're alive, you're healthy. You're in your twenties, unlike some of us."

"For one more year. Besides, it's okay for you. You turned thirty with a husband, a daughter, and a job you love. What do I have to show for my years except a string of bad boyfriends and a boss who keeps me chained to my dead-end desk job?"

"Oh my god, where's the waiter with more caffeine?" Katherine twirled her empty mug by its stem. "First off, I don't love my job. It takes me three drinks to unwind after a day at work. Second, life doesn't come around and happen to you. You have to take control of it yourself."

"That's what got me into this mess." Annabel sipped at her virgin margarita. Too sweet, and not nearly slushy enough. "Look where it got me last time I decided to take control."

"You have to keep the control." Katherine gratefully accepted the coffee refill from the waiter. "You can't throw in the reins when they become hard to hold onto. Have you thought about going down to the jail and visiting Jonathan in person?"

"Why would he talk to me? Our last correspondence was a threatening message from him, followed by me going to the cops. I think he might blame me for the fact that he was arrested shortly thereafter."

"Maybe he still has something to say. It's a much safer research scenario when the kid's behind a layer of tamper-proof glass."

"Isn't that stuff plastic?" Annabel asked.

"Whatever. Maybe they'll let you sit together in a room."

"Are you kidding? The police hate me. They think I'm a selfish little bloodhound who hampered their investigation."

Katherine shrugged. "So give up. Wallow in self-pity and do nothing with the rest of your life."

Unfortunately, that sounded quite appealing.

WEDNESDAY / SEPTEMBER 15

SEVENTY-THREE
CLARE

"You can clean our your locker. Your assignment is finished." Cloutier munched his chocolate-glazed donut.

"You don't have lockers at university."

"A week of education and already you're dumber. You never heard of a metaphor?"

"Well, did I manage to get you anything useful?"

Cloutier grunted. "Not this time, kid."

"Okay." Clare didn't know what was worse: to stay in a job she was obviously no good at, or to leave a failure and be forced to find another dream for her future. "I think I need a leave of absence."

"Yeah?" Cloutier hooted. "What for?"

"I was hoping I could stay in school. I know I'm not enrolled through the official channels, but maybe I can talk to someone in administration . . ."

Cloutier shook his head. "You don't get a leave of absence in your rookie year. You want to stay in school and go have a bright future somewhere? I can applaud that. I'd want it for my own kid. But you can't hem and haw about whether you want to stay on the force. You're either a cop or you're not."

"Um . . . and do you think . . . that I . . . I mean . . ."

"Do I think that you have what it takes? Put bluntly, no."

Clare didn't know how she felt. "Well, congratulations on solving the case."

"Thanks, but it wasn't my fine efforts that nabbed the kid either. I'm your handler, remember. You fail, I fail."

"Stop saying that." Clare stroked her helmet. "I feel bad enough for all those deaths we could have prevented."

"At least two murders were stopped."

Clare raised her eyebrows. "How do you know?"

"We found these in Jonathan's home computer." Cloutier passed one final sheet of paper across the table. "Unsent."

Simon McFarlane: October 3, 1949–September 14, 2010

We are pleased to announce our fifth step toward a political utopia for the real world. Simon McFarlane, dubbed Snazzy McJazzy because he was always so impeccably turned out on the taxpayer's dime, will no longer be sermonizing about why he is so wonderful.

McFarlane was a key profiteer from the TransCanada Highway Redevelopment scandal — you remember the one, when $1.5 billion got funneled away from the project for several politicians' home renovations. But that's not why he died — we'll stop pretending now. McFarlane was killed for a reason that will soon be revealed.

This has been both a public service announcement, and a clue. As in, get one. There will be one more death, and then our mandate will be complete. Can you save this next life? Do you want to?

You're welcome.

This has been a message from the Society for Political Utopia.

"September 14 was yesterday." Clare looked up at Cloutier. "And McFarlane is alive and well. Read the second one."

Marisa Jordan: July 17, 1946–September 15, 2010

We are pleased to announce our sixth and final step toward a political utopia for the real world. Marisa Jordan has been retired from public life for three years now, but her role in a decision made ten years ago has sealed her fate today.

Our killing spree is over. Although our reasons will be addressed in one final letter, perhaps tomorrow, perhaps next year, and perhaps even in an exclusive book interview, the remaining politicians can sleep safely in their beds. From here on in, it's up to voters to seriously examine the people you elect to represent your interests.

You're welcome.

This has been a message from the Society for Political Utopia.

Clare set the printouts on the counter. "I guess there's no doubt it's Jonathan."

"Not in my mind. The courts will decide if he did it."

"I think I've decided to quit the force." Clare felt lighter for the decision, and she knew it was the right one. "After our meeting, I'm going to the Registrar's office to see if I can stay on as a student."

"Yeah? Well, the job isn't for everyone."

"Were you ever in the field?" Clare fingered her pack of smokes. "Undercover, I mean."

"Once." Cloutier nodded.

"Did you like it?"

"At first, I was having the time of my life. But I managed to cock up the investigation so badly that three wanted gang members walked free after trial. I was given the choice of a desk job or this one."

"You could have left the force," Clare said. "You have a college degree, right?"

"No," he said. "I mean yes, I have a general arts degree. But I'm a cop — I don't want to be anything else. I have to take what they give me."

That didn't sound nice to Clare at all. "I need a smoke. Are we all good here?"

"We're good," he said. "Good luck, kid."

SEVENTY-FOUR
MATTHEW

Matthew was beginning to consider himself something of an expert on prison visitation. After taking his leave of the guard who signed him in, he strode confidently down the corridor to where Jonathan was waiting to see him.

"Was that Jessica I saw leaving out front?" Matthew asked.

Jonathan shrugged. "She wasn't here to see me. I doubt she has another friend awaiting trial."

Matthew knew only too well what this felt like from Jessica's position. "She'll be here. It might take her some time, but she'll come."

"So why are *you* here?" Jonathan slouched in his chair, and managed to look relaxed despite the uncomfortable metal design.

Matthew took the chair opposite, and sat down. He studied Jon, knowing that the bright mind and good looks would inevitably follow the same pattern as Elise's. Probably faster — men's prisons weren't nearly as hospitable as women's.

"I'm here to help you."

Jonathan's eyes were wild. "What on earth could you do to help me?"

"I feel responsible, to a certain extent, for encouraging you to take radical action. The society and the class are behind you, too. I — we — are not going to sit back and watch you hang for this."

"There's no death penalty in Canada."

"You know what I mean."

"Do I? I mean, thank you. But really. I committed a crime. Several crimes, and I was caught. I'm not going to lie about my guilt."

Matthew admired the kid's integrity, though it might be stupid in the long run. "Have you considered that a lighter sentence through plea bargaining might give you a better chance at a future?"

Jonathan smiled wearily. "What future?"

"Have you been assigned a lawyer?"

Jonathan nodded. "He came by this morning."

"Do you like him? Do you feel that he'll adequately represent your interests?"

"He's a legal aid lawyer," Jonathan said. "No, I don't want to hang out with the guy. But I'm sure he'll get the job done."

"You had Annabel terrified."

"Good." Jonathan sneered, which Matthew had never seen him do. "She should have gone to the police at the beginning. Instead she wanted to write her damn book."

"You think she should have turned you in?"

"I was leading her right to the trough."

That didn't make sense. "Why? I'd understand at the end, when you've finished killing whoever you've set out to. But why would you want to be caught before you were done?"

"Because what difference did I make? No one's standing up, taking notice, and changing policy as a result."

"What was your objective?" Matthew said.

"I'm trying to remember." Jonathan slouched further in his chair, then suddenly shifted himself upright. "Can you get in touch with your girlfriend for me?"

"Annabel?"

"Yeah." Jon smiled wryly. "I don't mean your flavor of frosh week."

"Of course I can contact Annabel. What do you want me to say?"

"Tell her I'm willing to talk. If she's still, you know, interested."

"I'm sure she'd be interested," Matthew said. "Look, Jonathan, I have to get back to campus, but I'll be back within the next day or two. You're not alone."

SEVENTY-FIVE
CLARE

"Where did you take this thing?" Roberta picked a large dead bug off Clare's windshield.

Clare cracked a can of Bud, and passed Roberta one from her workshop fridge.

"I drove to Orillia on the weekend."

"Yeah?" Roberta's eyes lit up. "Your parents must have been ecstatic."

"I didn't make it home."

"You just went to Orillia for the hell of it."

"I meant to stay. Or at least say hello. Instead I drove back to the city."

"I don't get it." Roberta heaved Clare's bike up onto its center stand. "You're stronger than this."

"I know."

"So what are you afraid of?"

Clare sipped her beer. She liked the way the cold bubbles felt as they moved down her throat. "I don't want to remember them like this."

Roberta put her hand on the motorcycle's gas tank. "Tell me again what was wrong when you were driving."

"Backfiring. I've checked the spark plugs, obviously. And I tried adjusting the air/fuel mixture, but no luck. I don't know what else to look for."

"It's your state of mind. Here, hand me that plug wrench. Some days, if my head's not in it, I can do more harm than good to an engine."

Clare passed said wrench. "I told you I already checked the plugs."

"I'm checking again. Do you miss being a cop?"

Here was better ground. "No."

"You left the force on good terms, right?"

Clare shrugged. "I didn't tell anyone to go fuck themselves."

"And the university let you stay on, like a regular student."

"Pretty much. If I do well enough this year, I can enroll like a regular student next year."

"That's great." Roberta held up a plug — clean, like Clare had told her — and checked the gap. "Are you going to stay in political science?"

"For now. I think I want to study law. Be a lawyer, not a law enforcer."

"You'd be a powerful opponent." Roberta cracked a grin as she replaced the spark plug, then went on to check the next one. "You really want to spend your days in offices and courtrooms?"

"I'm sure I can find a way to make it work for me." Take that, Lance, and your stupid bimbo wife. Clare hoped she would one day have the privilege of defending Slutty Shauna for some petty misdemeanor. Like whoring herself out for beer money. Clare would do that job *pro bono*. "So how's Lance?"

"He's good. Not that you care." Roberta let out a heartfelt belch.

"I care that he's happy."

"It's not the plugs."

"No kidding."

"Have you drained the gas?"

Clare shook her head. "I didn't think of that."

Roberta found an old container that she set under the bike. "You care if I drain this, or did you want to ride tonight?"

"Go ahead." Clare's apartment was just up the street, and she could take the subway to school in the morning.

Roberta opened a valve, and gas came pouring out of the engine. "You need to go home, Clare. Avoiding the place doesn't change what it's doing to you."

"What's it doing to me?" Clare thought she was fine, overall.

"It's taking away your empathy."

"I have plenty of empathy."

"Sure, for the rest of the world. But for your parents you have judgment. They're polar opposites."

Clare was quiet.

"It's the fuel." Roberta looked pleased with herself. "There was water in it. Your little bike's gonna be fine."

"Cool." Clare smiled.

"Which bodes well for you being fine, as well."

"Why?" Clare said. "Are you going to fix me, too?"

"Nope. You are."

SEVENTY-SIX
LAURA

Susannah stretched her legs underneath the kitchen table. "I guess I know where you were coming from."

Laura scrubbed absently at the counter. "You told me the truth. I should have believed you."

Susannah shrugged. "We're all human, right?"

"Does that mean you're home to stay?"

"It means I'm not taking any grudges away when I go. I can't stay. Trust is too big a thing for me."

Laura set down her scouring pad and looked at Susannah's long, muscled body. Would she never feel it pressed against her again? "But I do trust you."

"Now. When it's not being tested."

"Susie, that's not fair."

"Isn't it? If all the signs were pointing to you sleeping with Penny Craig, and you said no, you were being faithful, that would be enough for me."

"You'd still have doubt." Laura thought Penny was a strange example.

"No." Susannah laughed bitterly. "That's just it. I wouldn't have doubt. Because I trust you."

Laura tossed the pad in the sink, and sat opposite Susannah. "So you'll never —"

"I don't think so."

"This is sad."

"You'll be fine." Susannah reached across the breakfast table and took Laura's hand. "You need to get out in the world and date more, anyway. Between Hayden and me, you've never had those free-wheeling single years that every thinking woman deserves to have. But maybe," she said with a smirk, "when you get another girlfriend, try not to accuse her of murder unless she's guilty."

Laura couldn't find a smile.

Susannah took her hand away. "I'm going upstairs, to figure out what else I need to pack. Come if you want."

"No." Laura was on the verge of tears, and knew she wouldn't be able hold them back if she watched Susannah put her things away for good. "I'll stay down here."

"Okay. Well. If you need me . . ."

Laura watched her go.

The phone rang. Penny Craig, calling from her desk.

"Laura! Did I catch you at a bad time?"

"Kind of. Susannah's here, taking the last of her things."

"I'm sorry," Penny said. "Is it awkward?"

"Sad, but not awkward."

"Of course. I'll let you go. But I was wondering if . . . later on, I mean, tonight . . . you wanted to go get a drink somewhere?"

Laura was caught off guard. "Sure. Is there something more about the case?"

"Nooo." Penny dragged the word out. "Well . . . god, this is hard to say."

Penny didn't sound like herself.

"What's hard to say?"

Laura heard Susannah walking around upstairs. She decided she did want to be with her when she packed, tears or not. She wished Penny would get to the point.

"I meant that, well, maybe tonight could be . . . more like . . .

a date?"

"What?!" Laura didn't know what she felt. "You? Perfect Penny Craig? My world is upside down enough at the moment."

"I thought you might say no, but that's a strong rejection."

"It's not a rejection. It's a yes to the drink and a who-the-hell-knows to the rest. I'm shocked to find out you're a lesbian."

"I thought you knew all along. Why do you think I've never been married?"

"For starters, there's your acerbic personality."

Penny laughed. "I love it when you talk dirty."

Laura ended the call and clicked off the handset. She had no idea if she liked Penny romantically or not. She definitely hadn't considered it, but at the same time, the idea wasn't repulsive.

Susannah clomped down the stairs and tossed her large duffel bag down at the front door. "I think that's everything."

"You're done? I was headed up to join you."

"It's better this way. Thanks again for the coffee."

"My god, Susie. Don't get polite on me."

"Sorry." Susannah grimaced. "I'm a bit lost. I'm going to miss you."

"Well, let's stay friends." Laura meant it.

"Yeah." Susannah picked up her bag. "I'll see you at the Brighter Day."

SEVENTY-SEVEN
JONATHAN

Jonathan sat alone in his cell. He didn't have a roommate, which was lucky. But that was for now. Soon he would be some guy's bitch, and there wasn't fuck-all he was going to be able to do about it.

He was terrified of prison. This holding jail was bad enough. They had taken away his computer and iPhone, and he couldn't talk to anyone without the fear of being overheard or recorded.

What had he been thinking, talking to Annabel fucking Davis without any encryption? Was he so capable of leaving the real world that he believed Annabel wouldn't go to the cops in the end? And if he had believed her, why had he antagonized her, made her fear for her safety? Of course Annabel's life had never been in jeopardy. The politicians were the only victims, real or imagined.

But she had been as deluded as he was. The two of them, with their *folie à deux*. "I'm killing politicians." "Really? I'm writing a bestseller." How was that healthy in anyone's world? Maybe if Jon was lucky he'd convince a judge to send him to a psych prison. Crazy people didn't rape each other in jail, did they?

Who had he been trying to save? His mother's business was

still closing, and his relationship with Jessica wasn't going anywhere good as long as he was locked away. Is this how Elise Marchand had felt, when the adrenaline was gone and the consequences had loomed massively in front of her?

He picked up his paperback, and was about to attempt to get lost in a world of fantasy fiction, when a guard tapped on the door of his cell.

"You have a visitor."

Had Jessica finally come? Jonathan moved slowly from his bunk and walked with the guard to the visiting area.

"Here she is."

Not Jessica. Annabel.

"We finally meet." Jonathan wouldn't have bothered to hide his disappointment, but he was trying to hide it from himself as well. "That was fast."

The guard moved away, and Jonathan took the seat across from her.

"I'm sorry for getting you arrested," Annabel said.

"You are? Oh, no problem then." Jonathan stared at her. "Don't be sorry for all the lives you could have saved by going to the police sooner."

"Excuse me?" Annabel looked stunned.

Jonathan studied her face. "You're ugly in person."

"What?"

"I thought you were pretty, when I looked up your picture online."

"But in person you're not so sure." Annabel didn't pull off the amused look she seemed to be going for.

"No, I'm sure."

"Why did you ask Matthew to send me?"

"For the book. I've figured out how you can pay me."

"So you'll work with me?" Annabel leaned forward into the table. Hungry little bitch.

"You can donate my share — I think fifty percent is fair — to Habitat for Humanity. You'll be donating it in your own name, so you'll get some of it back as a tax credit."

"Sounds fine. Is there a reason you've chosen that charity in particular?"

"Someone I hate brought it up in an argument we were having."

"Isn't there a cause that's more connected to your motive?"

"My motive is to make the world a better place."

"Killing the politicians wasn't enough?"

"I wish I could explain."

"You can. That's why I'm here."

"I'm sorry. I know I called you here. I thought I'd be ready to talk to you today. But I'm still too angry. Why didn't you turn me in sooner?"

"I didn't turn you in. I went to the cops when you terrorized my family." Annabel looked like she was losing patience with him, and Jonathan didn't blame her.

"Can you come back tomorrow? I want to do this. I want to tell you everything, so you can write your book and maybe get the message out."

"But not today?"

He shook his head.

Annabel stood up. She was trembling so much that it took her almost a full minute to put her things away and do up her slim leather briefcase.

When she left, Jonathan stood up to be led back to his cell.

"You can stay," the guard said. "You're popular today."

Please let this be Jessica. His mother had already been in, and Dr. Easton wouldn't come until later. Jonathan stared at the door where the visitors were shown in and out. His heart leapt a thousand feet high when he saw her. He got up to run over, to give her a hug. He was confused when the hug she returned held no warmth.

"I'm going to confess." Jessica slung her shoulder bag over the chair where Annabel had been sitting.

"Don't be insane. I already have." Jonathan took her hand,

but she wrestled it gently away. Jessica sat in the visitor's chair, and Jonathan had no choice but to sit back down, too. "What's wrong?"

Jessica met his eye. "What do you think is wrong? You've confessed to a series of murders you haven't committed."

"What are you talking about?" Jonathan's eyes skimmed the room for microphones. But they'd be well hidden. And the guard was probably listening in anyway. "Of course I'm guilty."

"Right. Well, even if you were, why would you confess? That makes it so much easier for them to prosecute. All the evidence they have is circumstantial."

"They have my iPhone. And my mom said they came by for both my computers at home."

"Why would you . . . ?"

"I don't know." Jonathan held his hands in the air. "I have no idea why I did any of it."

Her eyes met his with so much sudden kindness that suddenly everything had been worth it. "I'm sorry, Jon. I know you did it for me."

"Do you care if I tell the story?"

"The real story?" Jessica frowned. "About my dad, and my mom's suicide, and everything?"

Jonathan nodded. "The obituary writer is willing to work on it. I told her I want my side of the proceeds going to Habitat for Humanity. But if you can think of a better cause — maybe something environmental, 'cause your dad was so into saving the planet — let me know."

"Something environmental would be wonderful. But I can't believe . . . screw it, I'm going to confess."

"Confess to what? Go live your life. Do something great with it, like you're meant to."

"I'll try," Jessica said. "By the way, confessing was Brian's idea first."

"What?" Why would Brian confess to the murders?

"I think he was really, really grateful for how you got him into the society. He figures that if we all confess, we can create enough confusion to get you into minimum security, if they don't end up throwing out the entire case. My point is that Brian's not as dumb as he seems."

"No," Jonathan said. "He's even dumber. Come on. I appreciate all the support. But I was stupid. Let me see this through to the end."

"I can't." Jessica took his hand.

"You can," he said. "You've got the power."

THURSDAY / SEPTEMBER 16

SEVENTY-EIGHT
CLARE

Clare topped a mochaccino off with whipped cream and placed it on the counter. When she looked up she was surprised to see Jessica.

Jessica smiled at her as she took the coffee from the shelf. "God, this looks delicious. I've been up since five this morning and I haven't had a thing to eat. Are you going to be in class this morning?"

"Of course." Clare looked at the clock on the wall. "I'm off in half an hour, if all goes well."

"Do you work here every day?"

"Starting today. I, too, have been up since it was dark out. Though I'm not sure why I'm bothering. My student loans are so massive that the wages here will barely put a dent in them." If that wasn't true already, it would be soon. Clare had somehow been approved for a bank loan the previous morning.

"I don't see why higher education isn't free," Jessica said. "It seems so random to educate people right up to the point where they qualify for a minimum wage job, and then leave them on their own to sort the rest out."

"Thanks for the theoretical support." Clare laughed.

"Anytime. Well, I'm off to finish that ridiculous assignment about how to help a friend if he's a killer."

Clare hadn't finished the assignment either. She hadn't known where to begin. She had more information than the rest of the class, and it all but incriminated Jonathan conclusively. She obviously couldn't bring the letters and the correspondence with Annabel Davis to light — she was hoping for a seamless transition into being a student, not a "Hello. Good to meet you. I've been an undercover cop, basically spying on you all, but I screwed up the investigation and I'd really like to stay on as your friend." So she was forced to put herself into the hypothetical assumption of Jonathan's innocence.

Jessica came back to the counter after sprinkling cinnamon onto her coffee at the self-serve station. "Hey, by the way, did you hear the news this morning? I'm sure it's totally unrelated to those other deaths. I mean, Jonathan's in custody and she's not even a politician anymore — but Marisa Jordan died yesterday afternoon. She was speaking to a school group in the west end."

And then Clare twigged. Jonathan wasn't the killer. He was guilty of something that Clare found a million times scarier.

She made up an excuse about menstrual cramps, and asked the shift supervisor if she could cut out early. When she'd been approved, Clare raced out of the campus café to phone Cloutier.

"You see it, right?" she said, once she had explained her new theory to her ex-handler.

"Hmmph." Cloutier was typically gruff. "The problem with this theory is that we have a confession, evidence, and a closed case on Jonathan Whyte."

"So how do you explain Marisa Jordan's death? Her obituary was found in Jon's computer."

"Whyte was in custody when Jordan died. And she wasn't a politician anymore. It doesn't fit."

"Doesn't fit?" Why was he stonewalling her? "What's her cause of death?"

Cloutier cracked a piece of gum. "Since we're not treating it as suspicious, her autopsy isn't being hastened in the morgue."

"You can't be serious." Clare stopped walking and sat down on a bench. "Even the press is tying it together. She vomited, she collapsed, she died. You know it's the same."

"You're off the force. And because of that, I'm off the case. Why would I share information with you, even if I had it?"

"I thought you said things were good between us."

"The main reason for that is we don't work together anymore."

"My god. Watch the scorn."

Cloutier was quiet for a moment. "All right, kid. So how can we get this confession?"

"Have Morton and those uniforms who arrested Jonathan come back. There's a class in twenty minutes."

"And your guilty party will spill?"

"I don't know," Clare said. "But I think there's a chance."

SEVENTY-NINE

MATTHEW

Matthew set his mug of coffee onto the heavy oak desk. He surveyed the room, and its now-familiar faces. They'd hated this assignment on impact, but this was politics in real life. If he turned his back on Jonathan, Matthew would be no better than the rest of the poli sci faculty, hiding behind textbooks and hoping their theories stayed passably current as the world carried on. He'd be worse than the others, because Matthew would be masquerading as someone who cared.

He faced the class. "Who's first?"

Susannah, as usual, seemed interested in opening, but a knock on the door interrupted them.

Matthew opened the door to the two officers who had conducted the electronics search, accompanied once more by Detective Inspector Morton.

"Are they here as guest speakers?" Matthew heard Jessica ask.

"Maybe they're going to tell us more about Jonathan," said Clare.

"Did you ride into school on the pumpkin truck today?" Susannah turned around to look at Clare. "Police don't gratuitously share information."

Inspector Morton put an end to the suspense. "Can you tell me which one of your students is Jessica Dunne?"

Matthew was stunned. He looked at Jessica, willing her to stand so that he didn't have to point her out.

"Well . . ." Morton tapped a foot impatiently.

"Um. Jessica?" Matthew said.

She wasn't moving.

Susannah jumped up. "I'm Jessica."

"No, you're not. You're Susannah Steinberg. I interviewed you with Laura Pritchard, if you've forgotten," Detective Inspector Morton said calmly.

"Right." Susannah sat down.

"I'm Jessica." Diane stood up, feigning reluctance. "Should I pack up my things?"

"Yes, please."

The two uniformed cops headed down the aisle toward Diane, nodded at her to give up her hands, and placed them in cuffs.

Clare stood up. "Leave her alone. I'm Jessica."

Morton scowled. "Cuff her too, then."

Matthew didn't understand what he was seeing.

"This isn't funny," Morton said. "We've interviewed you all before. I'm sure I can find a physical description in my notes, and barring that, we can look at your ID."

"What about me?" Jessica stood up. "I could be Jessica."

Morton rolled his eyes. "I don't think we have enough handcuffs. Would you like to tell me what's going on?"

Susannah stood back up. "We want to be in the loop. The other day, you came along and snatched one of our classmates, telling us nothing. Now you come back and want to take another one? We'll give you Jessica, as soon as you tell us why you want her."

"And why you wanted Jonathan, too," Brian said.

"All right, kids. I'm sure your loyalty is admirable." Morton looked at Matthew as if he expected him to impose some kind of order. "But this isn't how justice works. Anything I tell you now can mess up the prosecution, which I'm sure is not your real objective. Kindly identify your friend Jessica for me, or we'll lock down the room and inspect everyone's identification."

"Can I tell them, then?" Jessica looked tired. "I get it. You know I'm the killer; I'm going to jail."

"You?" Brian's eyes widened. "But — how come — when Jonathan was arrested . . . ?"

Jessica's gaze made it clear she thought the half-formed question was a stupid one.

"Is this the real Jessica?" Morton asked the class.

Most people shrugged. Clare nodded, and Matthew confirmed her identity verbally.

"Was it because you weren't finished?" Clare asked, still in handcuffs.

"What do you mean?" Jessica seemed more interested in this question.

"Killing politicians," Clare said. "Did you not confess because you still had more to go?"

Jessica rolled her eyes. "Sorry. For a moment I thought you had an intelligent question."

"Don't be rotten," Susannah said. "Clare wants to know — we all do — what your motivation was."

Matthew nodded. "We were prepared to come up with a plan to help Jonathan, beginning with understanding his motive. The same applies to you, if you'll allow us."

"My god, you're all so naive. I'm a murderer. I've killed five people. My mandate was for six, but I'm going to call it a successful outing. What does it matter to any of you why I did it?"

"Of course it matters." Clare's face was dark, and she was scowling. "These were specific victims that you sacrificed your future for. And you put us all under scrutiny while you were doing it. It's only fair that you tell us what was going on in your mind."

"You feel betrayed, Clare? Because you thought I was your friend?" Dripping with sarcasm.

"Don't give me that shit," Clare said. "You're more than this. You know you are. Just let us fucking help you."

To Matthew's surprise, this seemed to pacify Jessica. When she spoke again, she was more the soft-spoken hippie he'd grown accustomed to.

"Okay," she said. "If you guys really want to know, I'll tell you."

Detective Inspector Morton cleared his throat. "First we read you your rights. Then I can give you five minutes to speak to your classmates."

When Clare and Diane were taken out of handcuffs, and Jessica had been read her rights, she stood before the room and addressed her peers.

"Sorry for losing my cool a few minutes ago. It's been stressful, and I guess I needed some release."

Matthew nodded. "I think we all understand that."

"Thanks. I wouldn't be talking if it weren't for this week's assignment. I think it's really decent the way everyone's rallied around Jonathan. Brian, your idea for us all to confess was sweet. You can see now why I jumped on that."

The nervous energy in the class started to bubble into laughter, which stopped as soon as Jessica spoke again.

"When I was eleven, I lost my father," she said. "He didn't die right away. But I remember the day in slow motion, when we found him passed out in front of his favorite TV nature show. We rushed him to our local hospital, but the emergency room had been closed down. We showed them my dad — there were three of us carrying him, and my brother and I were so young I don't know how we could have supported much of the weight. But rather than help us or call an ambulance to transport him, the hospital gave us half-assed directions to the closest ER that was still in operation.

"After fighting through rush hour, we got him to the ER at Sunnybrook. The waiting room was overflowing. Between getting him triaged, being seen by one resident and another until they could settle on a diagnosis — a total of twelve hours after he lost consciousness — they operated on my father's ruptured aneurysm.

"I'm not going to go into boring medical details, but those twelve hours were the difference between my father possibly retaining his cerebral functioning and the reality, which was that he lived the remaining year of his life as an idiot, before my mother poisoned him with Spanish Fly."

Jessica paused, looked around the silent room.

"So I guess the logical question is: What does this have to do with the dead politicians?" She explained to the class about the hospital cuts, and the think tank, and the careless way in which the new policy was implemented and communicated to the public.

"I got one wrong, though." Jessica grinned sheepishly. "Libby Leighton wasn't on that think tank. It was her husband's wine I poisoned. But the bitch took his drink and made him come to the bar for another one."

Even less nervous laughter than before.

"So why was Jonathan arrested?" Susannah asked.

"He was an idiot," Jessica said without emotion. "I guess he saw what I was doing at one of the events, and couldn't bring himself to turn me in. So he started writing letters to the paper."

"Are you in love with him?" This was from Clare.

Jessica shook her head. "Of course I'm not."

"You said all but one," Diane said. "Did you mean Sam Cray, Leighton's husband?"

"No, taking his wife was enough. Although some might argue that I did him a favor getting rid of her. I was talking about Simon McFarlane. He was the sixth person on the think tank that killed my father. He was supposed to have been victim number five, but Dr. Easton pulled us all off that party."

"Snazzy McJazzy?" Brian used McFarlane's press nickname. "Why wasn't he first on your list?"

Jessica smiled wearily. "I went in order of availability."

"So you're the one who sent the spu cards to your victims?" Brian asked.

"I only sent the one. To Hayden Pritchard, incidentally — I guess the cops told us it was Libby Leighton to try to throw us.

Then I realized it was dumb. I would have loved to have sat each politician down and told them why I planned to kill them. Shown them a picture of my father both before and after he got sick. But then I realized I should just kill them, maybe find a way to tell the story if I got caught."

Matthew watched Jessica's face as she was talking. It seemed to be losing color, becoming paler by the minute. Her voice, too, was growing more and more dispassionate.

"Except Jonathan did it for you," Brian said. "Told your story to the world."

"Please. He told *his* story."

"How did you . . ." Susannah, for once, was grasping for words. "What did you use, to . . . you know . . . kill them?"

"Spanish Fly, like my mom used to poison my dad." Jessica said. "She told my brother and me what she was thinking of doing, and asked us if we had any objections. I know it's technically illegal, but my father had lost it — he couldn't function at all. His speech was impaired, he couldn't be left home alone in case he burned the house down, and he couldn't go out on his own in case he never found his way back." Jessica smiled again, this time far away. "He was so nice, though. He would sit there and smile, for hours on end."

"Wasn't it cruel of your mom to consult you?" Susannah asked.

"No." Jessica shook her head. "She didn't want to take him away from us if we got something out of him being alive. But she was right. It was no life for him. And it was less of a life for her."

"But to make the two of you accomplices . . ."

"We weren't accomplices. We were in Muskoka with our grandparents when she killed him."

"Did she go to jail?" Clare asked.

"Only the prison she created for herself. My dad's death was put down to natural causes. Organ failure. But my mom never got over the whole thing, and she killed herself a year later."

"Okay, I'll be the idiot," Susannah said. "Isn't Spanish Fly an aphrodisiac?"

"Farmers use it to get their bulls erect for mating. And yes, a super tiny dose would have the same effect on the human penis, though the guy would be severely nauseous and probably not have too much fun. But any more than a microdose, and it's certain death. Your internal organs are literally corroded. You vomit, you collapse . . . well, we all know what happened to the victims."

Brian raised his hand, and Jessica nodded at him to speak. "If your mom loved your dad so much, why would she have chosen such a painful death?"

"Because there's no antidote. Once swallowed, the effects are irreversible. My mom was terrified that she would chicken out after poisoning him, that she'd rush my dad to the hospital and try to save him, even if it meant confessing. By using Spanish Fly, she took away that option. Just like I did, for the politicians."

"Do you regret killing the politicians?" This was from Clare. "Now that you know you're caught? Or would you do it again? Do you still consider it justice?"

"I'd do it again in a second." Jessica's eyes were wide; Matthew thought she looked like a madwoman. "I've avenged my father's death. He's not a victim anymore."

"Like Hamlet," Susannah said.

"Precisely," Jessica said. "And if Hamlet was all right with his gory fate, I think I can handle a cushy stint at Kingston Women's Prison. Are there any more questions?"

Matthew had one. "Will you accept the help and support of the class through your trial?"

"Yes." Jessica's voice shrank, and for the first time, her perfect composure seemed like it might give way. "I plan to plead guilty, but I'd love it if you guys would visit."

EIGHTY

JONATHAN

Jonathan wanted Annabel to stay forever, to take down his story in one long, gushing tale.

"What was the question again?"

"It was why." Annabel spoke softly.

He liked her better today. She seemed less like a whore reporter, more like a person who cared.

"Why the letters? Why was I in love with her? Or why didn't I go the normal route, and turn Jessica in when I saw her poison Pritchard's dessert at the Working Child benefit?"

"I'm interested in all of that. Start with Jessica."

Jon's hair was in his face. He'd only been in custody for two days, but it had been ages since he'd even had a trim. He wondered when someone would think to cut it.

"I'd known her — wanted to date her — for two years. I'd been having this relationship with her in my head — have you ever done that? Songs would come on the radio, and I'd imagine her listening to them, thinking about me. And when we started spending time together for real, she was more amazing. She had all the qualities I'd given her, but spicier. More three-dimensional. I won't call it love, because I know I was delusional. But there was no way I could turn her in."

"So why write the letters?"

"What else could I do?" Jonathan felt like he was exploding, in a good way. It felt incredible to talk finally, out loud, to a real person. "I couldn't do nothing. She had to be caught."

"Were you hoping I'd tell the police about our correspondence earlier?"

"At first, yes." Jonathan nodded slowly. "I never even tried to encrypt what I sent you, like I did with the letters to the *Star*. I was trying to give you clues, and then I'd wish I hadn't said anything. I think I had no idea what was going through my own head."

"Utopia Girl sounded arrogant, almost like she was having fun. Were you having fun with this, at any point?"

"Um." This was a hard one. "I wasn't glad that anyone died, so I wasn't having fun with the murders. But I was on this constant high because of Jessica. I thought there was nothing I couldn't do. Does that explain things?"

"Maybe." Annabel gave a slight grin. "As you so eloquently said one time, I'd make a terrible psych student. Did you ever tell Jessica you knew?"

"I dropped hints here and there, and who knows what she thought I meant by them? But no, I never said anything to her directly."

"How did you know I was frustrated with my job?"

"Lucky guess," Jonathan said. "Obituaries aren't exactly a winning destination out of journalism school. Plus you wanted the story, so clearly you weren't moving up on your own."

"And in the end, when you tried to make me fear for my niece's life . . . ?"

Jonathan looked at the gray walls surrounding him. Would it be this drab when he finally got to prison, or a psychiatric institution, or wherever he was going to spend the time he needed to learn how to live in the real world?

"I needed it to be over. I needed you to pack it in, tell the cops everything you knew, and catch Jessica once and for all."

"Did you ever think you'd be arrested instead of her?"

"I didn't care."

The metal from his chair was becoming uncomfortable.

"And now?"

"Now?" Jonathan felt his face contort into a painful expression. "I'm just petrified of being raped in prison."

"Do you feel bad for your mother?"

"Don't you mention my mother!" Jonathan was out of his chair and about to attack Annabel's throat when two guards intervened. He worried that they would take him back to his cell and end the meeting early, so he forced himself to act calm. "I'm sorry. My mother is a sore spot. She's alone now, and I would prefer not to talk about her."

To Jon's relief, the guards released him.

"I'm sorry I upset you. Would you like to continue the interview later?"

"Yes." Jonathan didn't have any life left. "You'll come back, right? I'll sign a contract and everything. I promise I won't back out on you."

Annabel nodded. She put her pen and notebook into her briefcase, and stood up. "Of course I'll come back."

EIGHTY-ONE
CLARE

Cloutier handed Clare a black coffee and took a seat on the park bench beside her. "Still wanna resign, hot shot?"

"I already have. The force doesn't want someone who bails at the first sign of failure."

"On the contrary." Cloutier took a cigarette for himself, then offered his pack to Clare. "You kept working when you weren't technically employed."

Clare accepted the cigarette and a light.

"I wouldn't make quitting a regular thing. But if you're interested in being a cop, I think that we can convince the powers that be that it would be in everyone's interest to disregard your resignation."

"You'd help me?"

"You did good work."

Clare glanced slowly around Queen's Park Circle, the lush green space that separated the eastern and central St. George campus. The parliament buildings provided a majestic backdrop. In not even two weeks, she had come to love her life here, as a student.

"I would love my job back."

"Good. So are you gonna tell me how you figured Jessica for the killer?"

"I opened my mind." Clare took a drag and held it in a moment before exhaling. "Jonathan didn't sit right with me, but it was Brian I was looking at, not Jessica."

"Why Brian?"

"He was obvious. He was the one with the frustrated mandate. And I was willing to part with him."

"You were what?" Cloutier looked blank.

"Jessica was my friend — she made me feel good about myself." Clare had been horrified when she'd realized that this had prevented her from looking at Jessica as suspect. "And then I considered her, for the first time with an open mind, and I realized it couldn't be anyone else." Clare was quiet for a moment. "I'm going to miss those people."

"You're just going to miss your sexy professor."

"Nah, I can live without a dirty old man in my life. I'm gonna try to hook up with Kevin again."

Cloutier looked doubtful. "You still like that guy? He struck me as a bit thick."

"Oh, fuck off," Clare said good-naturedly. "He's twice the man you'll ever be."

"You know how to play poker?"

"I can hold my own at Texas Hold'em. I haven't played much stud or draw. Why?" She grinned. "Am I one of the guys now? Are you inviting me to a poker game?"

"Not quite. Feeling you out for another potential case."

"Playing poker? I'll take it."

"It's not mine to offer. There have been a couple of deaths on the pro poker circuit. All the regular undercovers are as good as made by the players, so the feelers are out for someone new. Someone who doesn't fit the same old cop stereotype."

"I'd love to." Clare would have clapped her hands, but she held a cigarette in one and a coffee in the other.

"Hold your excitement back for the meantime. You still don't technically have your job back."

"Okay." Clare tried to be cool. "But if I get it back, then will you give me this assignment?"

"It isn't up to me. And while I would recommend you based on how I've seen you work — as well as on the mistakes I know you won't make again — I'm not sure I'd feel comfortable sending you into such a tricky situation."

"Why? Would you miss me too much?" Clare felt a drop of rain hit the top of her head, and then another.

"That's not it. You'd have to travel — the Canadian Classic Poker Tour has events all over the country."

"I can travel." Clare had never been outside the province. "How hard is it to get on an airplane?"

"The gambling scene is dangerous. There are lots of people willing to do horrible things to each other in the name of a couple of bucks."

"You could come with me." Clare tossed her cigarette onto the cement pathway. More raindrops fell, dousing the lit end in seconds. "You're big and strong. You could be, like, my handler-slash-bodyguard."

"I have a family here. A wife and son. I can't take off on a whim."

"It's not a whim. It's an assignment. Tell me you wouldn't want to go, if they'd let you."

"Nothing's going to be decided this morning." Cloutier stood up. "Take the weekend off, stay out of trouble, and keep an eye on your phone messages."

EIGHTY-TWO
MATTHEW

Rain was pouring down. The roof of Matthew's car was leaking in two places; drips of rusty water were falling onto the seat cushions.

"Matthew? It's Clare."

He shifted the phone to his left ear so he could drink his coffee and drive. "It's great to hear your voice."

"I . . . um . . . I'm dropping out of school. I won't be able to see you for a while."

"What? Clare, that's crazy. You're more than halfway through your degree."

Matthew hoped she wasn't leaving because of him. Maybe the murders had been too much for her. He should make sure he offered support to the rest of the class, not only Jonathan and Jessica.

"It's nothing to do with what's been happening," Clare said. "My dad's sick — I think I told you that — and it's eating me up not being with him and my mom through it all. Somehow listening to Jessica's story made me see that. I need to take this year off — he could be dead by this time next year."

"But that's —" What kind of parents would let their daughter drop out of university to look after them? "How can they — ?"

"It's my choice," Clare said. "They don't know yet."

Matthew wished he cared so much about his own family. "Where do your parents live?"

"Up north. I thought of commuting — it's not even a two-hour drive — but I'd be spread too thin. There's no point."

"Can I visit you there?"

"I don't know. Maybe."

She was breaking up with him. And then Matthew knew. Of course she was leaving school, cutting ties. She was an undercover cop — the arrests had been made, and it was time for her to move on.

"I'm here if you change your mind," he said, on the off-chance he was wrong, and there really was a crisis. "Or if you want to talk."

"Thanks, Matthew. And thanks again for, well, those nights we spent. They were pretty fucking awesome."

Matthew smiled. "The feeling was mutual."

"Bye."

The news on the radio was all about the murders. Jessica had been labeled the Utopia Killer, and rumors were beginning to surface about the letters Jonathan had sent the *Star*. Matthew's name was mentioned often, mostly in reference to the society, which was being demonized beyond proportion.

This was not the road to fame Matthew had dreamt about. When he moved to change to a music station, Matthew's sleeve caught the edge of his coffee lid, and the steaming, full cup was thrown all over the passenger seat.

What was it with him and coffee? Were other people this unlucky? Annabel would tell him it was his bad karma. He grabbed some napkins from the center console and mopped it up as best he could.

He dreaded what awaited at the courthouse.

His phone rang again. Annabel.

He answered the phone as warmly as he could. "Hi there. Are

you calling for a nooner?"

"No. I'm actually planning to break up with you."

He looked forlornly at the remains of his coffee. "That's probably smart of you."

"It's nothing personal. It's not even why I called. It's just, I've been reading this book, and I think I understand you now."

"What do you mean? Is the book about politics?"

"No," she said. "You're just not that into me."

"Annabel!" Why today, of all days?

"I'm not angry. There's no law that says you have to be."

"Of course I'm into you." Matthew turned down the radio so it wouldn't distract him. "These past two years haven't been nothing."

"I want to be with someone whose world is wrapped up in mine. That isn't you. So I think we should break things off."

Matthew sighed. Of course she was right.

"I'll still consider you my friend," Annabel said. "I was actually wondering what you're doing now. I'm kind of fired."

"I'm so sorry. What happened?"

"It's kind of amazing." Annabel was gushing. "I mean, I'll have to figure out my finances — maybe get another job soon — but I have a book deal, kind of all of a sudden, and it involves an in-depth interview with you."

"Is it about your correspondence with Jonathan?"

"Yup. And Jessica's agreed to take part, have her real story told. I don't need to do the interview now. But I'm rushing with all this nervous energy. I thought maybe we could grab some lunch. You could come over to my apartment and we can go from here."

"Are you propositioning me in the middle of the morning?"

Annabel laughed. "I already told you I'm not. I just happen to be working from home, effective today."

"Well . . ."

Jonathan and Jessica would have to wait for Matthew to come to their side. He would be there for them through their separate trials — he was clear on that — but Annabel first.

"Hey, don't change any plans for me," she said when he hadn't responded for several moments. "Whenever works for you is fine. I have tons I can do in the meantime to keep myself busy."

Matthew changed lanes somewhat precariously to make a left turn onto Bay Street.

"Are you kidding? I wouldn't miss this chance for the world. I'm going to stop and grab a coffee first. What should I get for you? That half-caf, half-soy thing you're always torturing those poor baristas with?"

"Sounds great," Annabel said. "But today give me full soy. I'm burning calories way too fast to bother counting them."

FRIDAY / SEPTEMBER 17

EIGHTY-THREE
CLARE

Clare threw a leg over her Triumph and kicked it into gear. The sun was shining, a bunch of people were dead, and Cloutier had actually told her she'd done a good job.

She was heading north, to the trailer park near Orillia. She wasn't moving in, like she'd implied to Matthew. But she did plan to stop and say hello.

ACKNOWLEDGMENTS

So many people helped bring this book to life. Chronologically:

My husband, Keith Whybrow, helped me create a writing space and told me to follow my dream.

A few Toronto politicians got under my skin and inspired the plot.

Kim Moritsugu and the Humber School for Writers killed several atrocious writing habits and gave me new skills to replace those.

Lyn Hamilton at the U of T School of Continuing Studies gave such fantastic plotting and pacing advice that it almost feels like cheating.

Family and friends gave amazing early feedback: my sister, Erin Kawalecki; my aunt, Shelley Peterson; my mom, Dona Matthews; my friend Scott Hicks. They helped me gut this story and make it stronger. My dad, Robert Spano, plucked the title from his head after I'd been pulling my hair out for a while.

Jack David at ECW not only decided he liked this book, but he thoughtfully answered any random question I had, and he made me feel involved throughout the publishing process.

Sally Harding and her colleagues at The Cooke Agency gave genius editorial advice and insightful tips for navigating the industry. They've also helped me shape the series into something I'm excited to keep writing.

Emily Schultz kicked ass as an editor. She is astute at sniffing out where more detail is needed and where characters aren't quite true to themselves.

The people at ECW — Simon, Erin, Sarah, Crissy, Jen, and no doubt more behind the scenes — are smart, positive, and professional. I also love following their tweets.

Scott Barrie at Cyanotype designed this eye-catching cover.

Alex Gross, my creative techie stepbrother, turned the cover into a cool flash graphic for my website.

Finally, my friends and family are amazing. From sharing cover design feedback to pre-ordering copies to leaving funny notes on Clare's Facebook fan page, they make me feel enthusiastically supported.